PRAISE FOR JENNIFER GOLD'S *UNDISCOVERED COUNTRY*:

"Gold captures the poignancy of a mother's death with authenticity, alternating it with an adventure story."

—*Booklist*

"A sensitive portrayal of the different aspects of grief that will strike a chord with readers."

—*Kirkus Reviews*

"A thoughtful coming-of-age tale about finding purpose even in the midst of despair."

—*ForeWord Reviews*

PRAISE FOR JENNIFER GOLD'S *SOLDIER DOLL*:

"A memorable debut. Both timely and universal in themes."

—*Kirkus Reviews*

"Well researched…virtually cinematic. Superb writing."

—*CM Magazine*

On the Spectrum

ON THE SPECTRUM

JENNIFER GOLD

Second Story Pres

Library and Archives Canada Cataloguing in Publication

Gold, Jennifer, author
On the spectrum / by Jennifer Gold.

ISBN 978-1-77260-042-1 (softcover)

I. Title.

PS8613.O4317O5 2017   jC813'.6   C2017-902650-X

Illustration © Talya Baldwin, i2iart.com

Editor: Carolyn Jackson
Copyeditor: Patricia Kennedy
Design: Melissa Kaita

Printed and bound in Canada

*Second Story Press gratefully acknowledges the support of the
Ontario Arts Council and the Canada Council for the Arts for our
publishing program. We acknowledge the financial support of the
Government of Canada through the Canada Book Fund.*

ONTARIO ARTS COUNCIL
CONSEIL DES ARTS DE L'ONTARIO
an Ontario government agency
un organisme du gouvernement de l'Ontario

Canada Council   Conseil des Arts
for the Arts   du Canada

Funded by the Government of Canada
Financé par le gouvernement du Canada

Canadä

Published by
SECOND STORY PRESS
20 Maud Street, Suite 401
Toronto, ON M5V 2M5
www.secondstorypress.ca

For my dad

CHAPTER 1

When I was four, my mother dressed me up for Halloween in a miniature tutu and pinned my still-fine baby hair on top of my head in a tight knot that matched her own. The tutu had been a gift from Alice in the wardrobe department—dear old Alice, who hid me behind the curtains during *The Nutcracker* so I could see my namesake, Clara, on stage while my mother danced the part of the Sugar Plum Fairy. That pink tutu was among my most cherished possessions. Dressed in one of her own exquisite costumes and a pair of delicate warm-up slippers, my mother led me down the halls of our New York apartment building for my first trick-or-treating. I trotted proudly behind her, half hidden by her impossibly long legs.

"Don't slouch, Clara." She grasped me by the shoulders, pulling them firmly back. Her hazel eyes wandered downward, her mouth twisting ever so slightly. "And suck in your stomach."

If my smile faltered, it was only for a moment. Confused, I stared at my protruding belly, poking out of the top of the tulle skirt. I took a deep breath in, watching my abdomen contract.

"Good girl." Mom patted me gently on the head as my eyes watered. *Was I allowed to breathe?* I waited until she turned away, and exhaled, gasping. Quickly, I moved my Disney Princess Halloween bucket so that it covered my midsection.

"Go ahead, Sweetheart. Knock on the door." Mom motioned towards the Ancasters' apartment. Julie Ancaster sometimes babysat me, when we were between au pairs. She let me stay up past my bedtime and bought me Mallomar cookies.

I banged my tiny fist on the door, hopping from foot to foot in anticipation. Mrs. Ancaster opened the door and beamed at us, her hands full of bite-sized Baby Ruths and Butterfingers.

"Trick-or-treat!" I squealed, staring hungrily at the candy. "Trick-or-treat!"

Mrs. Ancaster dropped some sweets into my bucket and smiled at me fondly. "Aren't you a pretty ballerina, just like your Mama," she said. She exchanged pleasantries with Mom, who showered her with compliments on a new short haircut.

"Oh, do you like it?" Mrs. Ancaster fluffed at her ginger bob self-consciously. "I'm worried it's a bit short."

"Oh, no." Mom shook her head vigorously. "It absolutely suits you, with those cheekbones of yours."

Mrs. Ancaster flushed and tittered, thanking her repeatedly as she tossed another couple of Baby Ruths my way. I eyed them greedily as my mother led me away from the door.

"Good lord, did you see her hair?" Mom shuddered. "Never cut your hair, Clara. Women should have long hair."

I stared up at her, puzzled. "But you said you liked it."

Mom smiled. "You tell people what they want to hear. But that doesn't mean it's the truth."

"Oh," I said, because I didn't know what else to say. I remembered the Baby Ruths and brightened, holding up my bucket. "Can I have one of these now?" I reached in to retrieve one of the little candy bars, tearing eagerly at the foil.

"Absolutely not!" My mother reached over and snatched the chocolate from my hands. Holding it by the corner as if it were radioactive, she tossed it down the nearby garbage chute. "We don't put garbage into our bodies." She wrinkled her nose, as if she had had a whiff of something rotting.

I peered longingly at the chute, then back into my bucket, where three little bars remained.

"But why?" I asked, timidly. "That's why we're trick-or-treating. To get candy. You said it's a special night."

Mom squatted in a deep plié to meet me at eye level. "Clara, at the end of the night, you can have one piece of candy. One. But the rest is going in the trash. Candy is like poison for your body. It's full of sugar."

"It doesn't taste like poison." I clutched my bucket tightly, feeling defiant. "Everyone else gets to eat it."

"I don't care what other children are allowed to do." Her voice was hard now, and she was hovering in front of the Chans' door, as if she was reconsidering letting me knock. "I haven't had chocolate in nearly five years."

She said this with pride, as if it was an achievement to be respected. I blinked at her, confused and unsure how to respond. I like chocolate. I didn't know why we got dressed up to trick-or-treat if we were going to throw it all out.

"Mrs. Cooper says it's wrong to throw out food," I said, feeling bold. "She says there are poor children who are hungry."

"Poor children don't need sugar and high-fructose corn syrup any more than rich ones," Mom snapped. She placed her hands on her narrow waist. "No one needs to be overweight. It's unhealthy. And I especially don't want that for you."

My lower lip trembling, I nodded my head. I knocked on the rest of the doors, but my heart was no longer in it. I watched as grinning neighbors plunked Smarties and Junior Mints and Hershey Kisses into my bucket, knowing that at the end of the evening it would all disappear. At the end of the night, I fished out a KitKat, my favorite candy bar, and held it tightly.

"Throw the rest of it out," Mom commanded, pointing at the trash bin. "Go on, dump it."

I watched, pained, as the colorful confections tumbled from my pretty bucket into the filth of the garbage can, mixing with banana peels and coffee grinds. When she wasn't looking, I swiped a Butterfinger and two lollipops, tucking them into my leotard sleeve.

I polished off the KitKat, but it didn't taste as sweet as usual. When I was done, I noticed my stomach peeking over the top of the tutu waistband. I tapped at it, willing it to deflate, but it remained, soft and round, bulging like an inflated balloon.

"Suck in your stomach," I whispered to myself, inhaling again.

Still holding my breath, I rushed back to the garbage disposal and threw in the remaining treats. My hand frozen momentarily in midair, I almost reached to retrieve them. I turned away, the regret mingled with pride.

The high-school counselor called it orthorexia. We had a special conference, me, her, and Mom, after I was spotted surreptitiously using one of the chem-lab scales to weigh apple slices. Mrs. Cartwright, or "Call-me-Jane" as we referred to her behind her back, sat at her desk, which was cluttered with textbooks and education journals, and stared at my mother, gesturing at her computer screen. It was just past the lunch hour, and on the corner of the desk were dirty plastic containers, still smelling faintly of reheated spaghetti Bolognese. There was also an open can of Fanta. Regular Fanta, not diet. My mother nodded politely at Call-me-Jane, but her eyes kept straying towards the soda.

"Clara eats, but she's unhealthily preoccupied with what she's eating, and the amount." Call-me-Jane leaned across the desk, shuffling papers in an effort to clear some space. "Orthorexics typically obsess over whether what they're eating is healthy and pure. They overexercise. Clara exhibits all these behaviors."

It felt weird, being referred to in the third person while

sitting right there. I cleared my throat, trying to signal my displeasure.

"Clara?" Call-me-Jane looked over at me, and I noticed she had a small smudge of Bolognese sauce on her left cheek. "Would you like to say something?"

I played with a strand of my hair, twisting it around my index finger. "It's just...I don't think it's fair to single me out for trying to be healthy." I released the hair, which immediately drooped, refusing to be anything other than straight. "Why is it okay for people to have, like, chips and a chocolate bar for lunch, but I'm in trouble because I want to eat quinoa and work out after school?"

I noticed my mother's bobbing head out of the corner of my eye, and felt a surge of resentment, even though she was agreeing with me.

"But, Clara," Call-me-Jane put on her best Concerned Counselor face and pointed again to the laptop screen, which was open to the Wikipedia entry on orthorexia. "Some healthy eating and exercise is good. But taken to extremes, it's dangerous. For example, how much time do you spend exercising per week?"

I shifted uncomfortably in my chair. It was exceptionally hot, even for June, and I had worn a skirt that day. My thighs brushed against one another as I crossed and uncrossed my legs, and I felt a wave of nausea at the sensation of sweaty flesh rubbing against itself.

"Twenty hours?" I said vaguely. "I don't really keep track." I glanced involuntarily at the clock on the wall. *How long was she going to keep us here?*

"See, twenty hours is unreasonable!" Call-me-Jane looked immensely pleased with herself as she sat back in her chair. It had one of those padded thingees on it for people with back problems. I wondered if she ever exercised. She wasn't fat, exactly, but she certainly wasn't sporting a flat stomach.

"Now, just a minute." Next to me, my mother perked up, looking indignant. Her long fingers clutched at the edge of the desk, and she sat up straighter, if that was even possible for a dancer with perfect posture. I stared enviously at her jutting collarbones and wondered why I hadn't been equally blessed in the genetic lottery.

"Who are you to say that twenty hours is too much? Do you have a reference for that, Mrs. Cartwright? A source?" Mom crossed her arms across her almost-flat chest. Her cheeks were flushed pink. Strands of hair escaped from her ponytail as she shook her head, waiting for a response.

"Please, call me Jane." I coughed into my arm, trying not to laugh as the confused-looking guidance counselor continued. "I don't have a source, as you say, but given how much time children should spend doing other things, like homework, or extracurriculars, or—"

"I'm afraid I don't see that trying to maintain a healthy lifestyle is dangerous somehow." Mom's eyes flickered again towards the soda can, silently judging. "I myself spend many more hours than that in the studio, and I've never given it a second thought."

I watched as Call-me-Jane's expression changed. I could almost see the light bulb go off over her head as the realization set in. *Like mother, like daughter.*

"I understand, Ms. Malcolm, that as a ballet dancer you would need to spend quite a fair bit of your time…rehearsing. But Clara is a sixteen-year-old high-school student. She should be able to enjoy a slice of pizza or join the yearbook committee without worrying about her weight."

I pictured a large pizza, the greasy cheese sliding off and curdling in corners of the cardboard box. It's exactly what I imagined the inside of my thighs to look like. I shuddered.

My mother turned to me. "Clara, do you want to be on the yearbook committee?"

I blinked. "Um…I don't know." I picked at a hangnail, still not looking at either my mother or Call-me-Jane. "I've never thought about it."

"You see?" Call-me-Jane said triumphantly. "She hasn't had time to think about it. She's been so focused on exercise she hasn't had the opportunity to pursue other interests."

"I do like photography," I said lamely. "I bought an SLR camera with my Christmas money."

"There you go." My mother stood up. "She has her photography, and last time I checked, she was doing well academically." She picked up her vintage Chanel purse, which had been a gift from the ballet-company director for her thirty-fifth birthday.

"But, wait." Call-me-Jane stood, looking somewhat desperate. I don't think she was used to parents dismissing her in such a manner. "I really don't think—"

"I think we're finished here," Mom cut in. "Clara is a healthy, happy girl. And look at her." She waved her manicured hand in my direction. "It's not like she's wasting away."

I shrank in my seat at her words, feeling my belt tight around my waist, strangling me. I had a fleeting mental image of a hippo dancing in a ruffled pink skirt. *Suck in your stomach, Clara.*

I gave Call-me-Jane an apologetic look as I gathered my messenger bag and slunk out behind my mother, leaving the poor woman open-mouthed.

"Did I overdo it in there?" my mother leaned over, her voice low and obscured by the sound of her high heels clacking loudly on the tile floor. "She's sitting there with her can of soda, telling us we're unhealthy! I bet she hasn't exercised in a decade. And Wikipedia? I mean, come on."

I didn't respond. Nearby, a group of freshman girls whispered and pointed at my mother. The famous Catherine Malcolm, always attracting an audience. I prayed she would leave before anyone worked up the nerve to ask for an autograph.

"I'll see you later." She leaned in, pecking me on the cheek. Awkwardly, I patted her on the shoulder, feeling the bones poking through her fair skin. "Maybe we could go to a movie. Or an art show. I'll ask Jacques if there are any photography exhibits on." She beamed, glowing at what she clearly believed to be superior parenting, thoughtfully attending to my extracurricular interests.

"Sure," I said automatically, though I knew it would never happen. She wouldn't get home until late, and she'd make some sorry excuse about shin splints or a headache before disappearing into her room.

I watched her glide down the hall. My mother's legs were ballerina-perfect, the gap between her thighs evident even with her feet together. As I trudged to fourth-period American history, I felt the chafe of my own legs, the sensation a burning reminder of my imperfection. *It's not like she's wasting away.* The voice echoed in my head, repeating itself as I settled into my seat.

CHAPTER 2

"What did Call-me-Jane want?" Bree eyed me in the mirror, carefully reapplying her lipstick. "I thought your grades were decent."

I ran a brush through my hair. "She thinks I have orthorexia."

Bree frowned. "You don't even have braces."

"That's orthodontia," I said patiently. Bree was one of those people who came across as sort of dim-witted but then pulled off a report card of straight A's. She was also beautiful and thin, and her father owned a bank or something. She was practically a walking stereotype, as far as high school goes, except she was genuinely nice and free of malice. "Orthorexia is some kind of thing where you're obsessed with exercise and healthy eating."

"Ah." Bree nodded and slung her bag over her shoulder as we exited the girls' room. "Well, you are kind of obsessed with those."

I watched as Bree fished a Milky Way out of her purse. She unwrapped it in one swift movement and devoured it in a series of large, quick bites. I stared, recoiling. Once upon a time, I had occasionally treated myself to a candy bar, but I took tiny bites, savoring it slowly. Bree, however, had a fast metabolism, or whatever mysterious force enabled girls like her to effortlessly maintain their weight. A couple of hip-hop classes a week were enough to keep her in size-zero skinny jeans.

"Not all of us can live on junk food and stay thin." I tried not to smell the chocolate, consciously breathing through my mouth. Mentally it repulsed me, but my body still responded in unpredictable ways. Watering mouth, grumbling stomach. I fumbled in my bag for some spearmint gum, my go-to for curbing cravings. Bree shrugged. She's never understood what it's like for those of us who have to work at thinness, at beauty.

"Are you going to Avril's on Friday?"

"I guess," I said unenthusiastically. Avril was a year ahead of us. Her mother traveled at least once a month, and Avril threw a party each time. It might have seemed desperate, if she were the sort of girl who could seem desperate. Avril was so mean, so ruthless, that no one ever dared even to whisper a bad word about her. Her wrath was notorious. She had tormented three different girls into new schools in less than three years, which had to be some kind of record.

"Good. We can go together." Bree looked around and lowered her voice. "Did you hear she's dating that Japanese exchange student?"

"Hiro Sato?" I asked, shocked. "But he seemed like such

a nice guy." The words slipped out of my mouth involuntarily, and Bree and I exchanged a worried glance.

"Yes, perfect for her, right?" Bree raised her voice and looked around furtively, but no one had heard us. I exhaled, relieved. The last thing I needed was to be unceremoniously renounced by Avril. Not after the years I'd spent carefully climbing the social ladder.

The warning bell rang shrilly, and I swore. "I'm going to be late for AP Calculus," I said. "See you later?"

Bree nodded, and I rushed up three flights of stairs. The school has an elevator, but old habits die hard—stair climbing burns calories.

"Can anyone explain the solution to number five?" Mr. McCormick looked up hopefully, chalk in hand. I knew the answer was eighteen—I was a quick study at calculus—but I didn't raise my hand, waiting instead for some brown-nose in the front row to tackle it. I took the time to doodle little figure eights in my notebook, giving them each faces.

I was about to jot down an answer to problem number six when there was a knock at the door and Call-me-Jane popped her head in.

"Excuse me, Mr. McCormick," she said pleasantly, and I rolled my eyes. Couldn't she just call him Jason? Who cared? She was always telling us to call her Jane.

"Not at all." He put down his chalk and wiped his hands

on the back of his pants, leaving dusty handprints behind. It looked vaguely like someone had tried to grab his butt.

"I need to borrow Clara Singerman."

Sixteen pairs of eyes swiveled and stared in my direction. I felt my cheeks flush at the attention. I stood up.

"Bring your things, dear." Call-me-Jane gave me what was no doubt supposed to be a friendly smile. "We might not be back before the end of class."

Someone—I didn't catch who—gave a loud, dramatic, "uh-oh," and everyone laughed. A classroom visit by Call-me-Jane was widely perceived as signaling bad news. Failing grades, bullying accusations, that sort of thing.

There was another woman waiting in the hall. Her black hair was long and curly, tied into a ponytail, with strands es-caping everywhere. She was wearing a gray pantsuit and bright red ballet flats.

"Clara?" She put out her hand. "I'm Melisa Martinez."

"Melisa?" I repeated. It rhymed with Lisa.

"Yes," she said cheerfully. "Like Melissa, only with one 's,' so it's pronounced Meleesa."

I didn't reply. I wondered if she'd been given that name, or whether she chose it for herself to be different.

"I'm from the City," she said breezely. "Mrs. Cartwright called me."

"Call me Jane," piped up the guidance counselor, and I blinked, realizing suddenly what was going on.

"The City," I said, slowly. "You mean like social services?"

Call-me-Jane and Melisa exchanged a nervous look.

"The Office of Administration of Child Services," Melisa elaborated. She paused. "Why don't we all go someplace where we can talk?"

I breathed deeply, my instinct to tell her to go to hell battling with my desire to keep this quiet, out of the halls of St. Andrew's. It was a brief struggle: pride and fear of social ostracism won out. "Fine," I said, trying to keep my voice level.

I followed Melisa and Call-me-Jane back to the office. In three years here, I'd never visited the counselor's office once, and, now, twice in one day. I sat down hard in one of the spare chairs. "What's going on?"

Call-me-Jane cleared her throat. "Given our earlier meeting, I thought it best to get some...professional help." She nodded at Melisa. "Melisa is here to help you and your mother, Clara."

Inwardly, I cursed my mother. Couldn't she just have said the right things? Promised to feed me macaroni and chastise me for my close relationship with the StairMaster? I wondered if I would be placed in foster care. Would Mom go to jail? I imagined her doing pliés in an orange jumpsuit.

Melisa sat next to me, scooting her chair over so we were elbow-to-elbow. She gave me her best Friendly Adult smile and put a hand on my arm. "Don't worry, Clara," she said. "Everything is going to be okay."

I jerked away. "Why wouldn't it be?" I refused to make eye contact. "I haven't done anything wrong."

"No," Melisa agreed. "But Mrs. Cartwright—Jane—is concerned about your eating and exercise habits. And we want to work with you and your mother to establish healthier patterns for diet and fitness."

"This is bullshit." I slammed my fist down on the desk. Call-me-Jane looked affronted, but Melisa intervened before she could chew me out for swearing at school.

"Clara," she said calmly, reaching into her pocket for something. "I want you to eat this." She dropped a Hershey Kiss in front of me. I stared at the silver foil sparkling in the light of the desk lamp. The little white paper stuck out at the top like a white flag of surrender.

I sat back in my chair. "No," I said quietly.

Melisa kept her calm tone. "Why not?"

"I'm not hungry." I crossed my arms protectively over my middle. "I just had lunch."

"It's just a Hershey Kiss." She nudged it closer to me. "You don't have to be hungry to eat it. It's candy." She smiled cheerfully, pulling a second Kiss from her pocket. I watched her unwrap it and pop it into her mouth. "See?" she said, swallowing. "No big deal."

Eat it, I told myself. *Eat it, and they'll let you go.* But I didn't move.

"Maybe you don't like chocolate?" Melisa fished something else out of her pocket and placed it next to the Kiss. It was pink and wrapped in wax paper. Saltwater taffy, I realized, and took a deep breath. I used to love saltwater taffy. I wondered for a paranoid moment who had told her.

"What are you thinking?" Melisa was watching me carefully.

"I can't eat that," I blurted out. I shrank back in my chair. "It's…it's poison. Chemicals. High-fructose corn syrup."

"What did you eat for lunch?" Melisa asked, ignoring my outburst.

"A roasted chicken breast," I answered promptly. "Boneless and skinless. Some wild rice. And broccoli. All decent portions," I added defensively. "You can ask Brianna Harper. She ate with me."

"I believe you." Melissa collected the candy from the desk, sweeping it back into her pocket. "I agree with Mrs.—Jane. You're not anorexic, but I do think you're orthorexic. Tell me," she paused, "when I ate the chocolate, how did you feel? Disgusted?"

"Yes," I said in a small voice. I felt my cheeks flush.

"Can you elaborate?"

I shuffled my feet on the faded carpet squares, searching for the right words. "Like, how could you eat something so unhealthy without even thinking about it, I guess," I answered finally. "My friend Bree, she does that. Eats whole candy bars without even a second thought. She has a fast metabolism, fine, but it's still putting crap in your body."

Melisa nodded slowly, looking thoughtful. She crossed and uncrossed her legs. Had I blown it somehow, sounded my own death knell. Next stop, foster care? A group home?

"Clean living, right?" she said casually, and I flinched, startled. Had she seen my Instagram account? I cursed inwardly at my failure to set it to private. I didn't post much, but I liked to follow others. Girls like me, ordinary girls who embraced healthy eating and exercise, but had done a better job achieving their goals. Selfies of flat stomachs and thigh gaps abounded. I looked away, trying to appear impassive and confused.

"You live with your mother?" Changing tactics, Melisa opened a folder with the St. Andrew's crest emblazoned on the front.

"Yes." I fiddled with the cuff of my shirt.

"No brothers or sisters?"

"No." Then I frowned, remembering. "Actually, I have a brother. A half-brother. But I don't live with him. He's like six or something. He lives in France, with my father and his wife."

"How often do you see your father?" Melisa peered at me over the top of the folder, her nose and mouth obscured.

I shrugged. I rarely saw my dad, though not for lack of trying on his part. He was forever inviting me to visit, and I was forever coming up with excuses not to. I'd been a couple of times when they'd lived in London, but not at all since they'd moved to Paris. "Not that often. He's really far away."

"Do you speak with him? And your brother?"

I shifted in my seat, feeling irritable. "Not often. How is this relevant, exactly?"

"Sorry." Melisa put the folder down, looking apologetic. "I'm a social worker. I have to take a history, when we open a file."

"So we're opening a file?" The panic set back in. "You're not going to send me away, are you?"

"Goodness, no." Melisa's seemed surprised at my question, and Call-me-Jane clucked dismissively. I glared at her. First she calls Child Services, then has the nerve to mock me? What was she doing in here, anyway? Wasn't this confidential?

"Is this confidential?" I said loudly, looking pointedly at the school counselor. "Because I'd prefer if it were."

"Of course!" Melisa shot an apologetic look at Call-me-Jane. "Jane, I'm sorry. If you'll excuse us?"

"But this is my office!" Clearly flustered, Call-me-Jane began moving papers around on her desk.

"It will only be for a few minutes." Melisa's voice was polite but firm.

"I guess I'll go get a coffee." Looking affronted, Call-me-Jane grabbed her purse and stalked out of the office. I stuck out my tongue at the door as it slammed behind her.

"So." Melisa swiveled towards me. "You have a difficult relationship with your dad?"

I blinked. A difficult relationship? Could you have a difficult relationship with someone you hardly ever saw? I stared at the screensaver on Call-me-Jane's computer, a photograph of her, her husband, and their twin teenaged sons. They were all wearing matching white shirts and jeans, smiling and All-American, looking like a detergent commercial or something. I wondered if they really were like that, or whether they fought and yelled and ate takeout, and the kids smoked pot and got trashed when mom and dad weren't watching.

"No," I replied, glaring. "I didn't say that. My dad is perfectly nice. I just don't have all that much to say to him. I don't remember us ever living together. I wasn't even three when they split up."

"And your brother?"

My brother. Alastair. I'd met him exactly once, when Dad and Mag had come to New York for a conference, when I was in sixth grade. He'd been close to two then, and largely silent. We'd gone to a diner, and Alastair had spent the entire time carefully building an elaborate tower of creamers, not saying a word. When it had finally toppled, he had pitched a fit so loud I was sure they could hear him in New Jersey. Dad and Mag explained that Alastair was "on the spectrum," and at the time I just kept picturing the rainbow. Now, I knew better. Alastair wasn't autistic, not technically, but he wasn't exactly normal, either.

"I met him once. He's on the spectrum."

"Ah." She looked sympathetic. I shrugged again. I didn't really know the kid.

"I don't know why we're talking about this," I snapped. "What do my dad and brother have to do with Hershey Kisses?"

"I'm just doing some basic history here. Intake," she said. "It's important, with eating disorders."

Eating disorder. I groaned. I was now a Girl with an Eating Disorder. Word was bound to get out. I'd spend the last month of my junior year getting misguided looks of pity and all kinds of judgment and potential tattletaling if I didn't feel like going for frozen yogurt.

"Now, we will be working closely with your mother, as your guardian and custodial parent." Melisa smoothed the legs of her pantsuit. I wondered what Mom would think of this woman. She wasn't fat, but she wasn't exactly thin, either. At the very least, she wouldn't approve of the pantsuit—Mom shunned pants as if they were radioactive, opting for skirts and dresses to show off her perfect legs.

"Good luck to you," I said. I sat back and crossed my arms. "She's a dancer with the New England Ballet Company. Diet and exercise are like oxygen and water to her."

"So I've heard." Melisa leaned forward, her expression earnest. "How does that make you feel?"

I rolled my eyes. "What do you want me to say? That I have Mommy issues? Who doesn't?" Then I thought of something else. "Would you come after me if I were at the New York Ballet School? I think orthorexia is a prerequisite for admission."

Melisa didn't answer. She brushed the stray curls back from her forehead and took a deep breath. I wondered if she was stressed. "You think this is unfair," she said finally.

Now it was my turn to be silent. I raised my eyebrows pointedly, and stared at her. She wasn't wearing a wedding ring. I wondered if she had a boyfriend. I wondered if he cared that her thighs looked bigger when she sat down.

Melisa was talking again. I had tuned out, staring at her legs. I heard the words "next week."

"Sorry?" I said, trying to sound polite.

"Next week," she repeated. "We're meeting with your mother next Tuesday."

"You've already spoken with her?" I asked, interested. "How'd that go? She take it well?"

Melisa ignored my tone. "Once we've met with your mother, we'll decide how best to proceed."

I felt my heart rate pick up again. "You said you weren't going to send me away. To an orphanage, or whatever." I had a vision of myself shivering, wrapped in a thin cotton blanket.

"No one's sending anyone anywhere. It will likely be a matter of meetings, classes on nutrition. Observations. That sort of thing."

"Right," I said, though I had no idea what she was talking about. I tapped a foot against the bottom of the chair.

"Here's my card." She pressed a business card into my hand. I stared at it dubiously, then brightened, realizing the meeting was done. I stood, gathering my things.

"My phone and email are on there. You can get in touch with me anytime."

"Thanks," I said automatically. I had no intention of ever initiating contact with her.

I walked past her and out the door, where Call-me-Jane was standing with a Dunkin' Donuts paper cup in one hand and a cookie in the other. Our eyes met, and I gave her my best ice-princess stare, the one I usually reserved for perverts on the subway. She had the good grace to look away, and in doing so, accidentally stumbled and dropped her cookie. We both watched it fall, and I felt a small victory as it hit the tiled floor and crumbled.

CHAPTER 3

My mother's meeting with Melisa went about as well as I had imagined it would. When I arrived home from school the following Tuesday, I was shocked to find my mother actually in our apartment, albeit flopped tragically on the sofa, a gin and tonic in one hand and a cigarette in the other.

I gave her a dirty look. "You can't smoke in here," I said. "I can't breathe." I went over and grabbed the cigarette, furiously stubbing it out in the sink. The asthma that had plagued my early years had abated when I was twelve or so, but second-hand smoke still made me feel as if my lungs were filling with water. I tossed the damp, filthy thing in the trash, silently fuming. Funny how her penchant for smoking was exempt from her general world view about health and the sanctity of the body.

"I'm sorry, Clara." She sat up, her cheeks a faint pink. "I don't know what came over me. That was stupid."

"Give your mother a break." I stiffened. Jacques, the company director, and my mother's surrogate husband, emerged from the bathroom. "She had a terrible time with that absolute beast from social services."

"What are you doing here?" I asked bluntly. I opened the fridge and rummaged for a Perrier.

"Clara!" Mom's voice was reproachful. "Don't be rude."

I popped open the can. I didn't say anything, staring hard at the kitchen counter. I hated Jacques. A miser and a miserable alcoholic, he had been my mother's mentor since she was my age, and his hold on her was—in my opinion—unnatural. It was Jacques who had first encouraged my mother to smoke; who had taught her that eating was for lesser beings; and who discouraged her from dating or trying to engage in meaningful relationships with anyone other than him. When I was little, Jacques' personality had been tempered somewhat by Tim, his live-in boyfriend, who'd kept him grounded and reminded him about things like other people's feelings. When Tim had finally grown weary of being treated like a Nerf football, he'd moved in with a classics professor at NYU. This had done nothing to improve Jacques' moods and personality, and he hadn't been in a serious relationship since. Instead, he moped about our apartment and the dance studio, entangled with my mother in an unhealthy platonic existence that bore more than just a passing resemblance to an emotionally abusive marriage.

"You didn't like Melisa?" I ventured into the living room and perched on the edge of an armchair, a safe distance from Jacques, who stood leaning against the piano with a glass of wine. His jacket was tossed on the piano bench, along with his Hermes tie and set of silver cufflinks in the shape of toe shoes. I resented the comfort he so clearly felt in our home.

My mother made a small noise from the sofa, settling her drink down carefully before hoisting herself into a sitting position.

"She made me feel awful." Mom's cheeks flushed with indignation and gin. "Nutrition classes and support groups. Am I that incompetent?"

"Really." Jacques shook his head, his professionally styled hair flopping down into his eyes. "So awful for you, Kitty Cat."

I suppressed the urge to gag at this pet name. "I don't know," I said. I tugged at a stray thread on the armchair. "I liked her." I hadn't, really, but I felt defiant and combative. Jacques had that effect on me.

Jacques snorted. "You *liked* her?" He brushed the salt-and-pepper hair out of his eyes. "She was such a bureaucrat. And Meleeeeesa?" He made a face, dragging out the second syllable of her name. "How affected is that?"

At this, I nearly choked on my water. Jacques' own real name was Jonathan. He had changed it upon arriving in New York from Montreal, where he'd grown up—in an English-speaking family.

Before I could accuse him of hypocrisy, my mother jumped back in. Her voice quavered, but I couldn't tell if it was from hurt or outrage. "They're actually making me go to parenting classes. At the children's hospital. Like I'm some kind of monster mother."

"It's ridiculous," interjected Jacques. "Clara is sixteen. She's practically an adult. I'm telling you, Catherine, you should get a lawyer. Help Clara become an emancipated minor, like we do with the dancers."

"Emancipated what?" I stared at Jacques. He was now pacing in front of a large painting of two women and a horse. Some famous artist had painted it especially for my mother— why, I never understood, because she had never even been on a horse, but such is art.

"Emancipated minor," he said matter-of-factly. "Then you would be considered an adult, and the government would have to leave both of you alone. There's nothing wrong with either of you. Why should you have to deal with this nonsense?"

I glanced quickly at my mother, to see her reaction, but her face was impassive. Unlike me, she was good at concealing her feelings. I suppose she had to be. A ballerina is not only a dancer, but an actress. Did she want me to be emancipated? On my own? More importantly, did she want to be rid of me?

"We've discussed this, Jacques." Her voice was firm. "That isn't an option. I am not giving up custody of my only child!"

"It's just a formality," he muttered. He took a swig of his drink. "Nothing would change, other than the fact that you wouldn't have to go to silly classes you have no time for."

I said nothing, my hands tight around my Perrier. My heart thudded heavily with relief. My mother, whatever her faults, did not want to emancipate me. *Emancipate*. What an awful word. All I could think about was slavery and Lincoln getting shot, neither of which was particularly cheerful.

My mother yawned. "Jacques," she said. "I'm feeling a bit tired." She settled back against the sofa cushions, her hair fanning out as if she were underwater.

He looked at her anxiously. "Can I get you something, *Chérie?* Another drink? Aspirin?"

I cringed involuntarily at his offer to load my mother up with a mix of pills and alcohol. Staring at her hair, I had a fleeting and frightening image of her unconscious and floating in our soaker tub.

"No, no." She shook her head. "I think maybe it would be best if we spoke again tomorrow."

I emptied my Perrier, crushing the can in my grip. "The *mademoiselle* wants you to *quittez* the apartment, Jacques," I said, drawing on my limited high-school French. "*Tout de suite.*"

He swept past, ignoring me entirely. "I'll see you in the morning," he said to my mother, patting her gently on the head like a pet. "Get some rest." He shot me a final withering glance before exiting. I shut the door behind him with more force than was necessary.

"Really, Honey." My mom stood up and gathered the empty glasses. "Do you have to bait him? He was just trying to help."

"Help." I snorted, shaking my head as I doubled back to the kitchen and opened the recycling drawer. "Help himself, maybe. He's a first-class jerk." I threw the empty can inside with force.

"I think he really was trying to be nice." Mom yawned. She dropped the dirty crystal glasses in the sink, and I cringed as they hit the stainless steel.

"Careful, Mom. They can break." I grabbed the glasses and placed them in the dishwasher.

"They never do, though." She opened a drawer and pulled out a sheaf of takeout menus. "Sushi?" She held up the one for Fukui Sushi, which in good moods we jokingly referred to as F-you Sushi. We both loved sushi. Guilt-free takeout.

"Sure." I grabbed a pen and hovered over the menu. "California roll?"

"You know what?" Mom reached over and snatched the menu, stuffing it back in the drawer. "Let's go out."

I stared at her. "To a restaurant?" We didn't go to restaurants very often. Neither of us liked the temptations. The bowl of edamame. The basket of bread. Fortune cookies. All the hidden treats and perks of dining outside the home, paid for in calories and self-loathing.

"Yes," she said bravely. "I'm sure Melisa would think it's a good idea."

"No doubt," I agreed. "I thought you didn't like her?"

She shrugged and hunched over the marble breakfast bar, balancing on her elbows. "I didn't like her because she made me feel like a bad mother."

I didn't say anything. I knew this was my cue to jump in with "you're not a bad mother" or some similar soothing verbal mush, but I didn't feel like it. I was still angry over Jacques being here, invading our private home and private lives.

"The truth is, when I had that X-ray last year on my hip, the doctor said I had the bones of a sixty-five-year-old." She said it quickly, her gaze fixated on the gray veins of the countertop.

"What?" I was staggered. Mom had had a fall last year, during a rehearsal for *Les Sylphides*. A pas de deux gone horribly wrong. A *pas de don't*, I'd joked at the time, trying to bolster my mother's spirits in the emergency room. Nothing had been broken, but apparently there had been some bone analysis I'd been oblivious to.

She shrugged. "He said it was the dancing and my being underweight. Nutritional deficiencies."

"How could you not tell me?" I stared at her, horrified.

She avoided looking at me. "I don't know. Denial, I guess. But today, when the social worker came…all I could think of was you."

"You hardly acted like it with Call-me-Jane."

She continued to stare at the marble. "What was I supposed to do? Admit I'm a bad mother? A terrible role model?"

I didn't answer that part. "Well, you really pissed her off. If you had been nicer, she might not have called the authorities."

"I know." She looked at me. "Being criticized makes me defensive. Also, that woman is awful."

That much we could agree on. "But…the X-rays. What does it mean for you?"

"It means I'm going to get osteoporosis," she said calmly. "I'm taking calcium supplements, but it's almost certainly too little too late. One day I'll fall, and that will be it." She made a sweeping gesture with her hand. "*Finis.*"

"I can't believe you never said anything." I took a deep breath. "Does Jacques know?"

She gave a hollow laugh. "Are you kidding? How would I

even explain it? You think Jacques understands bone density? You think he cares?"

I blinked at this open criticism of Jacques. Mom rarely said a bad word about him.

"The thing is, Clara," she looked up now, staring me straight in the eye. "I don't know any other way to be."

I stared at the menu in front of me, distrustful of the choices presented. Donatello's was around the corner from our apartment, but my mom and I had never been there together. My dad had taken me a couple of times on his infrequent visits, but Italian food had always been anathema to my mother. Tons of carbs. Loads of cheese. What was my mother thinking? You couldn't fix a lifetime of disordered eating in an evening, but this was classic Catherine Malcolm. A tepid review from a third-rate critic would have her in the studio practicing twice as long and twice as hard.

"They won't write that about me next time," she'd say, hunched over the barre. "You'll see." And she was usually right.

I drummed my fingers on the red-and-white checkered tablecloth. I hadn't had pasta in years. Once upon a time, I'd loved it. I tried to imagine it now, to conjure up the satisfaction of twirling spaghetti onto a fork or loading on the Parmesan. I closed my eyes and inhaled deeply, coaxing my body to respond to the heady scent of garlic and basil in the air. No luck. I opened my eyes and watched as a nearby patron tucked into a plate of ravioli. I stared at the plump little pasta pockets and imagined my stomach similarly puffed and pasty and looked away.

"Well!" Mom smiled brightly. "What are you having?"

"I don't know," I admitted. I picked the menu up, as if holding it would provide some additional insight. My eyes strayed to the salads. Arugula and mushroom salad, maybe? No dressing? I put the menu down, narrowly missing the candle in the center of the table.

"Careful," said Mom. "You don't want to burn the place down before we even order."

"Would it be okay after we eat, then?" I raised my eyebrows.

"Only if the food is lousy."

We both tittered half-heartedly and fell back into silence over our menus.

A waiter appeared. He was unusually hot, and I wondered if he was, like so many in New York, an unemployed actor. "Have you ladies decided?" he asked.

Mom and I exchanged a glance. Neither of us responded. Finally, she cleared her throat. "What do you recommend?"

"The *rigatoni alla vodka* is pretty good," he said, pointing to the menu. "Or the manicotti."

"Great, we'll take one of each and split them." My mother flipped her menu shut and handed it to him. "And some San Pellegrino."

"Sure." He took my menu and grinned at me with a mouthful of perfect white teeth. "I'll bring some bread."

I stared at her as he walked towards the bar. "I can't eat

that," I whispered, panicked. "It's full of fat. Not to mention like a thousand calories. There is *cream* in the rigatoni!"

"You know, in the old days, people had cream every day. In their coffee and whatever." She crossed her hands in front of her on the table. "And no one was fat. Not like today, anyway."

"They also spent the day plowing the fields," I retorted. I resented her ordering for me. Now I would have to go hungry, and then the cravings would set in. "I sat on my butt most of the day."

Mom sighed and spread her hands out in a helpless gesture. "Look. I'm doing my best here. Melisa said I have to model good behavior. Get the message across that food is not the enemy."

I gazed at her skeptically. The waiter returned and placed a bread basket between us. The bread was fresh; I could tell. The white insides were soft and pillowy and the outside had an appealing crust.

Look away, I told myself. *You eat that, you may as well glue it straight onto your butt. Not to mention that the bleach in the white flour has been linked to colon cancer.*

Across the table, I could see my mother struggling. Eventually, she reached over and placed the smallest piece on her plate. I wondered when she had last eaten bread. Real bread, not the fake, whole-grain, gluten-free, low-carb hardtack that they pass off as bread at the health-food store. I watched and waited as she raised the slice to her lips. What could Melisa possibly have said to her?

"My God," she said, taking a bite. "It's even better than I remember."

My eyes grew round. "You did it," I breathed. "You're eating bread."

"I know!" She beamed at me. "Now you try."

I took a deep breath and looked around. Everywhere, diners happily gnawed at heels of bread, chomped on salads, chowed down on plates of lasagna. Skinny ones and not-so-skinny ones and outright fat ones. How could they do it so easily?

"Go on," said my mother, encouraging. "Try it."

"I can't."

"Please, Clara. Just a little."

Reluctantly, I took a piece of bread and tore it in two. I nibbled delicately on the crust.

"Isn't it good?"

"I—I don't know," I said honestly. I felt the crumbs stick to my teeth and tongue and reached for my water. "I can't do this."

"You can. I did it." She beamed at me. "Go on."

I wondered if she had some kind of superpower that made it easy to undo the years of behavioral conditioning and rigid self-control. Or was the issue with me? I couldn't eat the bread. I couldn't abide the texture.

I dropped the bread and grabbed my glass of sparkling water, drinking in gulps. My mother stared at me with sorrowful eyes as she quietly removed the bread from where I'd dropped it next to my plate.

"Why are you looking at me like that?" I snapped. "It's not like we've had bread around the house in, oh, I don't know… ten years?"

"I know. I'm sorry." Her voice was barely a whisper. "It's all my fault."

"Yes, it is!" I put my glass down hard on the table. The Pellegrino bottle and the olive oil rattled in response. The couple next to us glanced briefly in our direction, but then turned back to their salads, pretending they weren't eavesdropping.

I lowered my voice. "Why are we here, Mom?"

She slumped forward, cradling her beautiful head in her hands. Her eyes filled with tears, making them look luminous and even lovelier in the dim light of the restaurant.

"I didn't know how else to be," she said softly again, ignoring my question. "In my world, thin was everything. And I was worried you'd look like…" her voice trailed off.

"My father's family." My voice was dull. I pictured my paternal grandmother. Squat and round, she looked like a postmodern version of Humpty Dumpty.

"And now I've made you crazy, and I've got osteoporosis, and the authorities are involved." She gave a shrill laugh that was devoid of humor. The couple next to us stole another look. I felt like tossing the bread basket at them.

"I'm not crazy," I said stiffly. "I just want to be healthy. You said yourself…I don't look like I'm wasting away." My voice betrayed my bitterness.

"What?" Mom gave me a blank look.

"In Call-me-Jane's office. Mrs. Cartwright," I explained. "You told her I couldn't possibly have an eating disorder because I don't look like I'm wasting away."

Her eyebrows furrowed in confusion. "Was that bad? I was trying to show you aren't sick. Trying to get them off our backs. Now I know it was a mistake, because—"

"You think I'm fat!" It came out as a half-shriek, half-sob. I didn't bother to look at the salad-eating pair—I knew they'd be listening with frank interest now. "You think I'm like Bubbe Singerman!"

"Oh, no. No! Clara—you're beautiful!" She looked shocked. "That's not what I meant at all. You're so slim, Clara. You're perfect. I just meant that you don't have that awful anorexic look to you, like—"

"Like a ballet dancer?" I finished her sentence, my tone cutting. "Is that what you meant?"

She took a deep breath. "I deserved that, I guess. Look—"

"It's not fair!" I burst out. "I've been doing those goddamned thigh presses for three months and my thighs are still touching."

My mother looked guarded now. She poured herself some water but didn't take a sip. "Clara," she said carefully, "I'm a dancer. My legs—"

"You don't have to say it." I stared miserably at the scattered crumbs on the plate in front of me. "I know. I'm never going to look like you."

"Some might say that's a good thing," she pointed out. She took a sip of water. "Seeing as how I have the bone density of an old crone."

"Hmmph," I said. I didn't feel like joining her pity party over the osteoporosis. Why did it always have to be about her?

For a moment, neither of us said anything. I stared at the red walls and wondered if they'd painted them that color to put patrons in the mood for marinara sauce. It made the restaurant feel small and somewhat claustrophobic. It didn't match the red in the tablecloths, either.

"One rigatoni and one manicotti." Innocent of the family drama unfolding at our table, the waiter hovered cheerfully, bearing a plate of steaming pasta in each hand. "Who ordered the rigatoni?"

I didn't answer, glowering. I stared straight across to where the kitchen was, avoiding eye contact with both my mother and the server.

"That's for me," my mother said, breaking the awkward silence. "You can put the manicotti in front of my daughter."

If he thought that was a weird thing to say, he didn't show it, politely placing the tubes of stuffed pasta in front of me. On top was a layer of baked sauce and a sprinkling of Parmesan. I picked up my fork and poked at it warily.

"*Buon appetito!*" he said with a flourish in Queens-accented American-Italian. I tried not to roll my eyes and turned my attention back to the manicotti. Gingerly, I lifted a corner of the pasta shell to get a glimpse of what was inside.

"Eugh!" I sat back, making a face.

"What?" Mom looked at me with a resigned expression. She was holding her fork, but I noticed it was clean. She hadn't tasted her pasta yet either.

"There is cheese in this," I informed her. "Ricotta. Tons of it."

"Ricotta is relatively low-fat," she answered, but she was looking at her plate instead of at me.

"Like Antarctica is relatively cold?" I pulled back the pasta layer for her to see. "Go ahead, then. You eat that."

I stared at her defiantly, waiting. Her fork floated over my plate. Finally, she cut herself a piece.

"Eat it," I said. "Go on, then."

We both stared at the blob of cheese and pasta on her plate.

Taking a deep breath, she cut it into an even smaller forkful and put it into her mouth. I watched as her cheeks went red with the effort of chewing and swallowing, her eyes betraying her inner instinct to recoil.

"How was that?" I asked pleasantly.

"I can't do this." Her voice was a whisper again.

"Well, neither can I." I pushed the plate away, snagging the tablecloth and knocking over the salt.

"I think that's bad luck," my mother regained her voice, nodding at the salt shaker. She seemed relieved at the distraction. "You're supposed to throw some over your left shoulder now. Or maybe it's your right."

"If I pick the wrong one, will I have seven years of bad luck?" I righted the fallen shaker and tapped it lightly against the table.

"No, pretty sure that's just for broken mirrors."

We looked at each other, neither of us touching our food or acknowledging our inability to eat it. I took the salt shaker and shook it aggressively over each shoulder.

"I think you're just supposed to put a bit in your hand. It's all in your hair."

"Now you tell me."

"There's salt all over the floor."

I looked behind me. Tiny salt crystals were scattered across the dark floor in sufficient quantities to, theoretically, cause people to lose their footing. I wondered if anyone had witnessed my behavior with the shaker. "Let's get out of here."

Her eyes traveled to the uneaten plates of pasta before us. "We should eat this. We have to eat this."

I put my hand on hers and squeezed it, probably harder than I had to. "We can't," I said simply. "Ask for the check."

She shook her head and reached into her purse for a wad of cash. "I can't face the waiter."

"He doesn't care, Mom."

"I care."

She dropped a stack of twenties on the sauce-and-cheese-stained tablecloth and stood, her eyes downcast. I followed suit. The waiter called after us, but we didn't turn back.

CHAPTER 4

"We really could have taken the subway." I rummaged through my purse for some lipstick, while Bree repeatedly ran a comb through her already-perfect bangs. "It's only maybe fifteen blocks."

The traffic was moving slowly. Three cars ahead, an ex-asperated-looking woman jumped out of a cab right into the middle of the road, deciding to chance it on foot in her three-inch heels rather than spend another minute in the back of a stationary taxi.

"Don't be silly," sniffed Bree. "The subway is full of germs. We could get syphilis."

"I don't think you can get syphilis from a subway," I said doubtfully. "How would that work, exactly?"

"The poles are covered in bacteria," she informed me. "I saw it on one of those shows. *Dateline* or something."

"Syphilis is…well, let's just say you can't catch it from a subway pole." I raised my eyebrows meaningfully.

"Huh? Ohhh." She dropped the comb back into her pink purse and snapped it shut. "Okay, well, like Ebola, then."

I sighed. I was pretty sure the subway wasn't spreading the Ebola virus, either, but microbiology clearly wasn't one of Bree's strengths.

"Anyway, it would hurt Albert's feelings if we took the subway. Right, Albert?"

Her family's long-time driver peered at us in the rear-view mirror. "What was that?"

"Clara was saying we should have taken the subway."

Albert bristled. "The subway is a festering trash can full of rats and bacteria." He clutched hard at the steering wheel, an offended expression on his bearded face.

Bree nodded and saluted the driver. "Thank you, Albert. Right as always." She sat back, satisfied. "See, Clara?"

"Um, yes. Thank you, Albert. That was…vivid." Discreetly, I checked my teeth for lipstick stains in my phone's mirror app. I cringed at the size of my nose.

"Why do noses look so big in selfies?" I asked, shuddering at the screen. "I look like an anteater."

"It has to do with the focal length of the lens on the camera," answered Bree.

I blinked. "Excuse me?"

She shrugged. "The lens. Really long and short focal lengths distort the face." She narrowed her eyebrows. "Why are you looking at me like that?"

"Like what?"

"Like you're shocked that I know something."

I reddened and stared at the leather upholstery. "I am not!"

"We said we were going to get into photography," she said. "Remember? We both asked for SLRs for Christmas."

"I remember." My SLR was still in the box.

"Well, I've been practicing," she said. "And reading. It's very interesting."

"That's great, Bree," I said sincerely. "Seriously."

"I might apply to work on the yearbook," she added, and I had a brief flashback of Call-me-Jane shaking a finger at me over forsaking the yearbook for exercise. I had never wanted to work on the yearbook, so why did I feel badly now?

"That's great!" I said again, trying to sound enthusiastic.

"I had thought it was something we would both do," she said quietly, "but you're always at the gym."

My phone buzzed then, indicating a text. Relieved, I grabbed it and tapped the screen. The telltale bubble popped up, and I groaned, reading the message aloud to Bree. "Hi Clara. Can we schedule a time to talk? Love, Dad."

Bree snorted, breaking the tension between us. "Does he always sign his texts?"

"Yes. Even though I've told him not to. He doesn't get it at all. He has a flip phone. Or he did, last I saw him."

"Which was when? You *never* see him. Probably everyone still had a flip phone back then."

"Not true," I said defensively. "I saw him maybe a year and a half ago. He was giving a talk at NYU and we met for brunch. He asked about school and showed me pictures of his kid."

"Also known as your brother."

"Whatever." I shrugged. "They live in France. Might as well be another planet."

Bree was about to respond when Albert poked his head around the headrest. "Just pulling up," he said.

The car slowed to a stop outside Avril's brownstone, imposing and tall like Avril herself. We thanked Albert, who made us promise not to take the subway back. He looked at me specifically, his eyes narrowed as if my suggestion to ride public transportation was akin to hitting the streets to score some drugs.

Avril was at the door, which surprised me. She wore a short, tight white dress that on anyone else would have looked like a gym towel. We fake-hugged and she waved her hand at the assorted partygoers, looking disgusted.

"I have to man the door," she explained, shifting from foot to foot in a pair of four-inch-heeled sandals. "There have been crashers. People who were not invited and have no right to be here, just showing up to, like, steal food."

"Oh," I said. "That's…terrible." I pictured a troop of homeless people wandering around Avril's high-tech kitchen, trying to figure out which shiny white door hid the refrigerator and thus the promise of food.

"I know, right?" She jerked her head at some people arriving behind us. "Like these people. Who are they? Why do they think they can come here?"

I turned around, expecting some disheveled street person. Instead, there stood two girls I vaguely recognized from my history class.

"Clara!" One of them—Rachel—waved excitedly. "Hi!"

Avril looked at me, appalled. "You know these people?"

"Um," I said helplessly. I looked around for Bree, but she'd already gone in and was chatting animatedly with some hot guy I didn't recognize.

"We're in history together!" Rachel smiled brightly at me, and I tried not to make eye contact. I didn't want to raise the ire of Avril—not in her own home.

"Clara?" Avril's hands were on her hips. "Did you invite these people?"

"Invite them?" My eyes widened. "No!"

"We just heard there was a party," said the other girl, whose name momentarily escaped me. I cringed. The girl had a slight lisp; not the sort of thing Avril was likely to miss.

"We jutht heard there wath a party," mimicked Avril, exaggerating the poor girl's impediment. "Did you altho hear you need thomething called an invitation?"

Rachel's expression wavered. "Clara?" she said, her voice pleading. "We have history together."

Avril, meanwhile, had barred their path. "Sorry," she said coolly, "but having class with Clara doesn't mean you get to come to my party. If Clara throws a party, you can cry to her at her door."

Do I say something? I fidgeted nervously, avoiding eye contact with both Rachel and Liana, whose name I had just remembered. I didn't want to be mean. I wasn't the mean type. But I had worked hard to be the kind of girl who was invited to these sorts of parties. Years of watching what I ate, what I wore, how I spoke. Rachel and Liana would just have to work harder.

"Sorry," I muttered to no one in particular and ducked inside.

Avril put a hand on my shoulder. "No worries," she said breezily. "Not your fault you have groupies."

I blinked. *Groupies? Really?* Still, I said nothing. I wondered if Rachel and Liana also had assumed my apology was for Avril. Trying to shake off the guilt and shame, I gratefully accepted a drink from Bree, who had reappeared at my side.

"It's water," she said in a low voice. "You can pretend it's vodka."

Bree knew I hated alcohol. Just the smell of it made me ill, the likely product of years of behavioral conditioning from loathing Jacques and his ever-present martinis. "Thanks," I said gratefully, taking a sip.

"Did you see that guy I was talking to?" Bree gestured discreetly behind her, where Hot Guy was now talking to Mark Trainer, student council VP, basketball forward, and general Guy-Your-Mom-Would Love-You-to-Bring-Home.

"Um, yeah. Who is that?" I stole an appreciative glance at the mystery boy. He was dressed more formally than our classmates, in a starched-looking striped shirt and khaki slacks. The other guys all wore faded jeans and affected T-shirts adorned with things like the names of 1980s TV shows or quirky advertisements.

"Avril's brother," she said quietly.

"Brother?" I echoed, surprised. "Isn't Avril an—"

"Only child," agreed Bree, finishing my sentence. "But you know her parents split, right? Well, her mom just remarried."

I knew her parents had split. Everyone knew her parents had split. Avril's dad, once a high-profile human-rights lawyer rising up the New York political ladder, had been involved in a very public and very humiliating scandal involving compromising texts to and from a Columbia sorority president. There were rumors that, before her life became tabloid fodder, Avril had been a relatively nice and normal human being. It was tough to envision now, but what wasn't difficult to imagine was how having your parents' marriage unravel in *The New York Times* could harden a person.

"So he's a stepbrother," I said, interested. "Who's his dad?"

"No idea." Bree shrugged. "He's finishing up freshman year at Yale. In for the weekend."

I stared at the back of his head, admiring the longish golden curls. "He's really hot."

"You think so?" Bree turned to study him, frowning. "Not really my type. Too clean-cut and preppy."

"Maybe that's how college guys dress," I pointed out.

"Just in a Ralph Lauren catalogue." She grinned.

We wandered to the kitchen, where various friends waved hello. Alex Belloti and Johnson McCain were engaged in some kind of elaborate drinking game involving a pair of dice and a funnel. Emma Levy, perched precariously on the edge of an oversized granite kitchen island, gave a loud shriek as Erik

Peters tossed caramel popcorn at her. Andria Sawyer leaned against the spaceship-like stove, trying to hold the attention of Cameron Mehta, who everyone except Cameron knew she had a huge crush on.

Taking a carrot from a nearby veggie platter, I grabbed a stool and feigned interest as Bree struck up a conversation with Emma and Erik about the yearbook. I had nothing to add, and focused instead on my carrot, chewing laboriously. Carrots, I decided, were overrated. Night vision be damned. They took forever to chew, and the longer I did so, the more disgusted I became by the gritty texture. I took a gulp of water to try to wash it down, seeking somewhere I could dispose of the remainder.

"Excuse me." I turned around and came face to face with Hot Stepbrother. Nearly choking on my carrot sludge, I swallowed quickly, trying not to gag. Gagging in front of a hot guy was probably a quick path to social ostracization.

"Yes?" I said, trying to sound casual. I wondered if there were bits of orange stuck in my teeth.

"Someone told me your mom is Catherine Malcolm." He raised his eyebrows questioningly.

"Guilty," I said, trying not to move my lips much. *Were* there carrots wedged in between my incisors?

"I met her recently," he said. He reached past me to the kitchen counter and grabbed a handful of nachos. "At a campaign fundraiser."

"Oh?" I tried not to sound surprised. My mom is not a very political person. I'm not sure she's ever made it to the polls, even with me wailing at her about civic duty.

"Yes, she was with someone." He licked the salt off a nacho and then tossed it on the counter. I stared, fascinated. This was the sort of thing presumably most of us did, but generally limited to the privacy of our own homes. Though, I suppose this *was* his own home.

"That would be Jacques, I guess," I said, trying not to wrinkle my nose. "He's the ballet's director."

"Right." He chose another nacho, this time taking an actual bite. "He seemed like an interesting person."

"Interesting?" I echoed. I was tempted to ask him if by "interesting" he meant "asshole," but I held my tongue.

"Yes, very interesting." He dropped the half-eaten chip on the counter and I began to reconsider his attractiveness. There's only so much odd behavior that having adorable, floppy, curly hair will cover for.

"I'm Clara," I said finally. "You're Avril's brother?"

"Stepbrother," he said. "Spencer Caplan."

"Nice to meet you." I watched him take a third chip, and wondered what he would do to this one.

"I have a famous parent, too," he said conversationally. "My dad is Thomas Caplan."

"Oh," I said politely. I wracked my brain, but came up blank. I made a mental note to Google the name later.

"These nachos suck," he commented. He licked the nacho, and I fought the urge to knock it out of his hand. "I hate commercial nachos."

"Commercial nachos?" Another blank.

"Yeah. After you've had real, artisanal nachos, these are

just vile. Have you been to Hacienda?" He dusted crumbs off his preppy shirt, and I observed that he had cufflinks. I'd never seen a guy my age with cufflinks before. His were shaped like hashtags. I wondered if he had a Twitter fetish or something.

"No, I haven't," I said. I assumed Hacienda was a restaurant. "Did you just use 'artisanal' to refer to nachos?"

He wasn't paying attention to my response. "Come on," he said suddenly, taking me by the elbow. "Let's get some air."

I followed him out the patio door to the back deck, pausing to take an admiring glance at his butt. I wondered if this made me shallow, but then he did go to Princeton. Or was it Yale? Maybe I really was shallow.

The air was hot and humid. It would be June in a couple of days, and summer seemed to be off to an early start. Nearby, mosquitoes hummed loudly around the patio lanterns, their noises more like electronic static than something alive. On the other side of the deck, someone lit a mosquito coil. I inhaled deeply, enjoying the incense-like smell.

"You shouldn't do that," said Spencer.

"What?" I frowned.

"Inhale the coil smoke. It's dangerous." He waved his arms, as if he could banish the smoke with his hands.

"Thanks," I said awkwardly.

"It's true," he insisted.

"I've smoked worse, I'm sure," I said uncertainly. I thought of the things I'd done prior to my current clean-living streak. "You've never tried a cigarette? A joint?"

He looked affronted. "Never," he said primly. "Don't do

anything you don't want anyone else to find out about. That's my motto."

I stared at him. "Quite the planner, huh?"

"Of course." He fiddled with a leaf of ivy that had twisted its way around the deck post. "I'm a Caplan."

I didn't say anything. I still didn't know who his dad was.

"So Jacques Dubin," he said. "Would I be able to get his contact info?"

Was that why we were out here? Stung at the rejection, I stepped back. Was I not pretty enough? *Too fat?* The little voice nagged in the back of my head.

"Why do you want it?"

"Oh, you know." His tone was evasive. "Fundraising, that sort of thing."

"You want to help Jacques fundraise for the ballet?" I snorted. "Might as well just write him a personal check."

"What do you mean?" His voice was sharp and interested.

"Well, you have to know the guy." I made a face. "He's the most self-interested jerk on the planet."

"Really," he said. "Isn't he a friend of your mom's?"

"Less friend, more abusive pseudo-spouse." I yanked forcefully at a piece of the ivy. "He practically controls her."

"Wow," he said. In the shadows, his eyes glinted with sympathy. He put a hand on my arm and squeezed, gently. "That sounds tough."

I waited for him to remove his hand, but he didn't. The skin on my arm tingled; all the tiny hairs stood upright at attention. Maybe he wasn't just interested in Jacques.

"You have really great hair," he said softly. He leaned forward and brushed a few strands off my bare shoulder. I shivered. His hands felt surprisingly cool against my warm skin.

"Thanks," I said feebly. I felt my cheeks go pink, and Spencer pulled me closer to him, bending his head towards me.

The kiss was brief but exciting. He clearly knew what he was doing. No novice kisser, Mr. Yale. Or Princeton. I sighed and melted into him.

"That was nice," he said coyly, playing again with my hair. "We should go out sometime."

"Sure." I shrugged, trying to look nonchalant, as if college guys asked me out all the time. "I'm on Facebook."

"Great." He smiled warmly. "I'm glad I met you. I've got this thing at the Yale Club now, but I'll definitely be in touch."

He was leaving? Already? I tried not to look disappointed. "Okay."

He turned as if to leave and then paused. "Oh," he said, "could I have Jacques' personal cell? I really do want to help fundraise for the ballet."

"Huh?" I stared at his left cheek. He had an adorable dimple that showed when he smiled. "Oh, sure." I pulled out my phone. "Just tell him you're a friend of mine."

"Great," he said again, and gave me his number. "You can text it to me."

He put his hands on my shoulders and massaged them gently while I sent along Jacques' coordinates. I bit my lip and stared hard at the screen, trying to concentrate.

I heard the buzz from Spencer's pocket, signifying my text had gone through. He pecked the back of my head. "Thanks again. You're the best." Spencer patted his pocket and gave me a warm smile. "We'll talk soon, okay?"

"Sure," I managed. "Have a good time at the Princeton club."

"Yale." He grinned, activating that adorable dimple again.

"Right! Well, goodnight."

He disappeared into the kitchen and out of my life. *Would he call? Text?* I fought the overpowering urge to chase him into the brownstone and throw myself at his polished loafers.

"Get hold of yourself, Singerman," I muttered to myself. "Guys hate crazy."

I found Bree in the kitchen, frowning over a cupcake.

"Oh, hey!" She brightened. "Where have you been?" She held out the cupcake. "Try this. It's supposed to be bacon-flavored, but I think it just tastes like salt."

"Ugh." I shook my head. "No way."

"Come on," she said, wheedling. "Just a bite. Think how happy Marisa would be."

"It's Melisa. And, no. No normal person would want to eat a bacon-flavored cupcake. What's wrong with you?"

"Boo." She stuck her tongue out at me, then pushed the cupcake aside. "Where were you?" She hopped up onto a stool. "I had to talk to Andrew Patten for, like, ten minutes. He was trying to impress me by talking about car repairs."

"I was with Spencer," I said, unable to hide the delight from my voice. "You know. Hot college guy."

"What?!" Bree gawked at me. "Are you about to tell me you hooked up with the stepbrother?"

"Maybe." I relayed the story. Bree listened attentively, eating pretzels and looking increasingly excited.

"This is great! Do you think he'll text?"

I shrugged, trying not to look too hopeful. Both Bree and I had dated a lot of Spencer-esque boys, and we had devoted many hours over coffee to dissecting their behavior.

"He seemed nice. He'll call," she said encouragingly. "You know what? This party is lame." She lowered her voice. "Want to get out of here?"

I did. With Spencer gone, I didn't see any point in sticking around. We escaped into the still-humid night air, undetected by Avril. As we waited for Albert, it began to rain. Just a drizzle at first, but soon the skies seemed to open up. Bree ducked into a Starbucks for shelter, but I stood outside an extra moment, enjoying the cooling sensation of the downpour.

That night I had the cake dream. The cake dream is a recurring nightmare of sorts in which I am eating a chocolate birthday cake with colored frosting, and it is incredibly nauseating. The nausea isn't merely distaste, it's an all-consuming disgust, and I have both a headache and an urge to puke. Highly detailed and sensory, the dream always involves me slicing the piece of cake with a plastic fork and taking huge bites, despite feeling ill. When I wake I can recall the sensation of laboriously chewing it. I am always standing, surrounded by people who are watching me expectantly, waiting for me to finish, and I try to please them, though each bite is sickening. Then, without warning, the floor drops open beneath me and I fall. Down, down, down into the darkness, with no one to catch me.

"Wake up, Clara." My mother was standing at my bedside, shadowed in the darkness. "You're having a nightmare."

"Huh?" I blinked and struggled to sit up. "Was I yelling or something?"

"What? No. Just moaning and saying 'no' over and over. I thought I should wake you."

"Oh." I yawned and pulled the duvet up to my chin. We had the AC on full blast, rendering my room the approximate temperature of a meat locker. "How did you hear me then?"

"I came by to check on you. Make sure you got home okay." She tightened the belt of her robe. "It's freezing in here."

"You check on me?" I raised my eyebrows, surprised.

"Of course," she said, affronted. "What kind of mother do you think I am?"

Unspoken words passed between us, and I knew we were both thinking of Melisa and the restaurant and the rest of it. She looked down and tugged at a loose thread in her robe. "What were you dreaming about?"

I hesitated, wavering. Should I tell her the truth, or not?

"Nothing," I said, finally. I avoided looking at her. "I can't remember."

"Right," she said, nodding. Our eyes met and I knew she

didn't believe me, but she isn't the sort to push further. "Well, you should go back to sleep."

"Yeah." I sank back against the pillows. "Good night."

She rose, sliding back into her slippers. "Night."

"Mom?" I said, sitting up slightly. She paused in the doorway and turned around.

"Yes?"

"Thank you."

She nodded without saying anything, though I could see her gentle smile in the moonlight.

CHAPTER 5

"Your father has been calling for you." Mom hovered over me, dressed already in her warm-up clothes. "I told him to text you."

I looked up from my iPad. "Yeah," I said. I took a sip of my coffee. "I forgot."

She clicked her tongue. "Clara, he's your father. Please call him back." She walked over to the phone cradle, grabbed the receiver, and slid it forcefully across the breakfast bar at me.

I sighed, stopping it with my elbow before it could knock over my coffee. "I know, I know."

She grabbed a bottle of water from the fridge and tossed it into her bag. "Then call him now."

I waved my hand at her. "Later. I'm trying to read *The Hunger Games* here."

She wrinkled her nose. "Is that the one with the children killing each other?"

"It's not like that. It's genius."

"I'll take your word for it." She grabbed my iPad, ignoring my protestations, and placed it out of my reach. "Now, call your poor dad."

I snorted. "I barely know him."

"That's not his fault, though." She gave me a beseeching look. "Please. He's not a bad man, you know that. It was just... life."

Right—life. I knew the story. Shy-but-handsome bachelor surgeon treats promising (and much younger) prima ballerina. They fall in love. Unfortunately, she is only eighteen and is his patient, causing a huge ruckus both in the newspapers and at the New York State Medical Board. Long story short, she gets pregnant, they marry, he loses his medical license, they have me, marriage fails, he decamps overseas, where he starts over as an academic. Mom and I go on with our lives in New York; Dad eventually marries Mag, who wear socks with sandals and lots of beaded necklaces and has a PhD in Norse mythology.

"Since when do you care if I call Dad?" I frowned. My mother never bad-mouthed my father, but she didn't usually plead his case, either.

"Parenting classes," she admitted, not looking at me. "It's not just the food thing. We're working on lots of things. Empathy, involvement—"

"Ugh, please stop. I don't want to hear." I swiveled on my stool and slid off. "Did you talk to him?"

"Only briefly." She rummaged through the fruit bowl and selected a banana. "You can fill me in later."

"Hmmmph." I ignored the phone and took another swig of coffee. "Matinee today?"

"Yeah." She finished the banana in four quick bites. "At two. Evening performance at seven."

"All right, see you later." I spun the phone around on the counter, watching it travel slightly across the marble and hit the ceramic fruit bowl.

Mom looked up from tying her sneaker and winced. "Careful." She picked up her umbrella and unlocked the door. "Have a good day. And call your father!"

I waited for the sound of the door locking and sighed, looking longingly at my iPad then back at the handset.

"Fine," I muttered. I hit one of the preprogrammed numbers—no way could I remember the long string of digits that made up Dad's French *numéro de téléphone*—and took a deep breath.

"Allo?" Mag, affecting a French accent. Or maybe that's just how British people sound when they speak French. I don't know.

"Hi, Mag. It's Clara." I twisted a lock of hair around my finger, a habit from when I was little. I still found it emotionally satisfying to tug at my hair in stressful situations. Talking to Mag fell into that category.

"Clara! How are you? How's school?"

"Fine, thanks." I tried my best to sound polite without encouraging further conversation. I didn't mind Mag, but she always tried too hard with me. She reminded me of the kid in the playground who asks if you'll be their friend; the desperation is something of a turn-off.

"Anything interesting going on in New York? How's your love life?" She tittered.

"Nothing to report," I said automatically. "Is Dad there?"

"Yes. Just a second, I'll go get him. He's just in the loo, but he's been in there ages. He's got to be nearly done. David! Telephone! Clara!" The last words were shouted, and I turned away from the phone, cringing as images of my father on the toilet popped into my head, unbidden. I'm not a prude or anything, I just don't know my dad well enough to have reached the level of comfort where you can talk freely about poo.

"Clara?" Dad, finally. I wondered if he'd washed his hands. Probably, I figured. He is a doctor, after all. Or was.

"Hi, Dad."

"I hear you were at a party last night. Have a good time?"

"It was okay." I drummed my fingers on the countertop. I hated this small talk. It seemed silly and forced, given that we weren't that familiar with each other.

"And how's school going?"

I sighed. "Fine, Dad."

There was an awkward pause. I could hear his breathing on the other end as he struggled to find something to say.

"So, what are your plans for the summer?"

"I don't know yet, exactly." I didn't, either. Usually Mom and Jacques arranged some kind of summer job at the ballet, handing out programs or stuffing envelopes. I figured I'd probably end up doing the same this year. Bree was off to work as a counselor at some kind of fancy summer camp. She'd tried to convince me to join her, but I'm not really the outdoorsy type.

It would be lonely without her, but at least there would be no bugs or hiking.

"Well, Mag and I were thinking it might be nice if you came and stayed with us this summer."

I didn't answer. A whole summer, with Dad and Mag? And Alastair? No thanks.

"That's very nice of you, Dad, but—"

"It's Paris, Clara. You'd love it."

I pictured beret-clad girls on bicycles with baskets full of baguettes and croissants, the Eiffel Tower looming large in the background. Paris, the city of love or lights or something. Also the city of carbs and fatty sauces. What would I eat?

"I don't know, Dad." It wasn't just Paris; it was also two months with virtual strangers. There was a comfort factor involved. I thought of sharing a bathroom with Mag and cringed, imagining her hemp bras or whatever hanging to dry on the shower rod.

"Clara, we would really like you to get to know Alastair. He's your brother, and you've met him only a handful of times."

Ah, the guilt card. I pictured Alastair, freaking out over his orderly blocks. He had to be about five now. Or six? Seven? A real walking, talking kid. What could I possibly have to say to him? How would I get to know him if he was autistic or almost-autistic or whatever it was called these days?

"Clara?"

"I'm still here, Dad."

"We could use your help." His voice was pleading now. "Alastair could use your help."

"Help? With what?" I was wary. Was this whole thing a ploy for free summer babysitting? If I wanted to babysit, I could go to the Berkshires with Bree. And get paid.

"Well, you know Alastair is on the spectrum. He could use some…sisterly guidance. You're a popular girl. You could help him. Teach him how to fit in."

I groaned inwardly, closing my eyes. I felt a headache coming on—I'd gone too long before my morning coffee. "Dad, you can't teach someone how to fit in."

"You'd be surprised what you can teach a kid like Alastair. How much you could help. And we would all get to spend time together, and you'd get to see Paris."

"I'll think about it, okay?" I already knew my answer, but to refuse at this point was just rude. It would have to be a slow letdown. I slid off my stool, getting ready to end the conversation.

"Your mother says you're having eating issues."

I bristled. "She told you that?"

"Yes. I'm your father, and I used to be a physician. Of course she would tell me."

I kicked the stool with my foot. I didn't need lecturing from someone an entire ocean away.

"Look, it might be good for you to get away, Clara. Change of scenery. New experience. Your mom thinks it's a good idea."

"Mom knows?" I sat back down with a thud, winded at the betrayal. *How could she discuss this with Dad and not mention it?*

"I talked about it with her. We both think this is a good idea."

I felt my anger bubble to the surface. "Well! I'm glad you all had a great time planning *my* life."

"Clara, no one is trying to force you into anything. We just think it would be good for you—and everyone—to get away this summer."

I didn't answer. I kicked the stool again, harder this time. I winced as my toe throbbed from the impact.

"It would be good for me," he added quietly. "I would like to get to know you, Clara. I want to know my daughter."

I remained silent, but more because of his earnest tone. He sounded sincere. He also sounded as if he might cry, and that scared me. I didn't know him well enough for that. Really, I didn't know him at all.

"Okay," I said finally. "I'll think about it."

We had just hung up when there was a loud pounding on the door. *What now?* Annoyed, I went over to check the peephole.

"It's me," shouted Bree. I could see her blonde head, distorted by the magnification so that she looked like a parade-float balloon. She was frantically waving her hands, which were clutching two tall Starbucks cups.

"What's up?" I asked, unlocking the door. "I didn't know you were coming. Did I miss your text? I was on with my dad."

She thrust a cup at me. "It's a skinny vanilla latte," she said. "One Splenda."

"Thanks," I said. I sighed happily at the smell of roasted espresso wafting from the drink. "You've made my morning."

"Don't thank me yet." She looked grim. "I take it you haven't heard."

Baffled, I took a sip of coffee. "Heard what?"

"I think you should sit down." She kicked off her violet flip-flops and led me to the couch. "Sit."

"Bree, you're freaking me out. What the hell is going on?"

"Sit." She pushed gently on my shoulders.

I sat down hard on the couch.

"Have you checked Twitter today?" Her voice was calm, but her eyes were full of concern.

"No. I was exercising, then reading *The Hunger Games*." I felt my heart accelerate ever so slightly. "Why?"

Bree sat back against a handful of throw pillows and held up her phone. "I think you'd better have a look at this."

I took the phone from her and stared at the screen. Spencer, hot guy extraordinaire from last night, grinned back at me from a thumbnail-sized Twitter photo. Frowning, I read his latest series of tweets.

"Hooked up with @CatherineMBallet's daughter @ClaraSings last night. Hot but nothing like mom."

I made a small moaning noise before continuing to the next message, my voice now shaking.

"Plenty to say on NEBallet Director Jacques Dubin. Seems rumors of corruption may be true. Digging further."

For a moment, I said nothing. I felt deaf, mute, and blind, as if I were locked inside myself. I continued to stare blankly at the phone, at Spencer's evil smirk. I noticed his Twitter handle and dropped the phone in horror, realizing what I had done.

Spencer Caplan @CaplanJr. Caplan Jr, meaning son of Tom Caplan, star investigative reporter who had broken the story on Avril's dad. Who, apparently, had gone on to marry Avril's mom.

Bree hastily retrieved the phone and tucked it out of sight. "You didn't know, I guess." She sounded sympathetic.

"No." I avoided looking at her. "He kept saying stuff about his dad, but I didn't know what he meant."

"How could Avril's mom have married him? He ruined their lives." Bree shook her head, looking disgusted. She had her hair tied into two braids and they rocked back and forth vigorously like ropes on a playground swing.

"I don't know." Avril's family was the last thing on my mind. *Hot, but nothing like mom.* My cheeks burned with shame. I wondered if there was anyone who hadn't seen it by now. How would I ever face school on Monday?

"What an asshole." Bree put a hand on my arm. "I knew he was a jerk."

"You said he seemed like a nice guy." My voice was hollow. I still wouldn't look at her. Why would I ever have thought someone like him would be interested in someone like me?

"What are you going to do when Jacques sees it?" Now Bree's tone was tentative. She sank back again into the cushions and grabbed a cashmere throw, wrapping it about her bare shoulders.

"Oh my God. Jacques!" I jumped up, the terror plain in my voice. "He's going to kill me! He's going to literally kill me.

He probably already has someone on their way here." Panicked, I eyed the door.

"I doubt he'll actually kill you," said Bree reasonably. "It would upset your mom."

I glared at her. "This isn't a time for jokes."

She raised an eyebrow. "I was only half joking."

"Okay." I took a deep breath and tried to focus. "What do I do?"

"You need to fight back," she answered immediately. She sat up straighter, the throw falling back like a discarded cape. "Twitter war. Refute the accusations. And say something nasty about him. Like how he looks like a fake Ralph Lauren model or something."

I put my head in my hands. "This is a nightmare!"

Just then, the phone rang. My eyes met Bree's. It rang again.

"Are you going to get that?" she asked tentatively on the third ring.

I closed my eyes. "It's for sure Jacques. No one else would call the apartment at this hour."

We listened as the phone rang a fifth and final time. Then I rose and went over to the kitchen to check the Caller ID.

"Was it him?" Bree cowered under the throw.

I let out a sigh of relief. "No. Telemarketer. Dave's Ducts."

"Okay." She threw back the blanket and retrieved my phone, waving it. "Twitter war."

I stared at the phone, motionless. I wasn't the Twitter-war type. I was the girl-in-the-background type. Watching my mom onstage. Lady-in-waiting type to the popular girls like Avril. I wasn't smart or beautiful like Bree. I couldn't do this.

"I can't do this," I said, flatly. "I'm just going to have to, like, run away." I thought of my dad, in Paris. Éclairs or no, it was starting to seem like a good option. Mentally, I started to pack. I wondered if I could get some sort of pity exemption on the rest of my junior year.

Bree raised her eyebrows. "Run away? Where? Be practical. You have to fight back. You have to go to school on Monday."

School. I slumped further down on the couch, stuffing my face into a pillow to muffle my frustrated moan. "I'm finished," I said.

"You're not," Bree's voice was firm. "We are not going to let this sociopath ruin your life."

Bree liked to label people as sociopaths. She had once seen a TED talk on sociopaths and it had clearly affected her. Any guy who acted like a jerk—which was most of them—was automatically labeled a sociopath by Bree.

I sighed. "Not everyone can be a sociopath, Bree. If everyone you've labeled a sociopath were really a sociopath, it wouldn't be considered an anomaly anymore."

"But maybe it isn't an anomaly," she said meaningfully. "Maybe there really are tons of sociopaths."

"You're missing the point. If everyone were a sociopath, it wouldn't be pathological. It would be normal."

She sighed and shook her head. "I have no idea what you're talking about."

"I know. Never mind." I paused. "Anyway, you're probably right this time." I thought of Spencer telling me he liked my hair. "That asshole is a sociopath."

"See!" She gave me a triumphant look. "There are sociopaths everywhere. You have to watch that TED talk."

I groaned and buried my head in the pillow again.

"Sorry," she said. "Let's focus. Twitter war. We are going to bring this bastard down."

Limply, I took the phone from her and stared blankly at it. I had no idea how to respond. I was the sort of person to say nice, encouraging things to others, even when I didn't mean them. I wasn't sure I knew how to verbalize what I was feeling right now.

"I don't know what to say," I admitted.

"You need to channel your inner bitch," explained Bree. "How do you want him to feel?"

I thought again of his wording. *Hot, but not like mom.* My face burned once more. "I want him to feel humiliated and inadequate," I announced.

"That's better!" Bree looked pleased. "I knew you could do it."

"I don't know what to say, though. All I can picture is attacking him with something 'hot' and heavy like an iron."

"Open a new tweet," she instructed me. "We need to do this piece by piece."

"What do you mean?" I tapped on my screen. The empty box stared back at me expectantly.

"We take him down word by word," she said, rubbing her

hands together. "Okay, here you go. Start with this: '@CaplanJr, u call that hooking up? Ha.'"

I cringed, but typed it anyway. I felt sick, thinking about that kiss. I should have walked away. I recalled our conversation in the kitchen. The artisanal nachos comment should have been a red flag.

"Now, what next?" Bree drummed her fingers on her knee, looking thoughtful.

I was silent for a moment, then spoke up. "How about, 'You think you're clever but you're nothing like dad?'"

"Clar! That's brilliant!" She gave me an approving whack on the back. "It's perfect. See, I knew you had it in you."

I typed the nasty little message, carefully substituting shorthand to limit my virtual venom to one hundred and forty characters.

"Did you post it?"

"Not yet." My finger hovered over the send button. "You're sure?"

"Do it." Her eyes burned with anger. "He deserves it."

He did. I tapped and it was done. I swallowed, a sour-milk taste in the back of my throat.

"Good." Bree reached for her drink and took a long swig. "Jerk picked the wrong girl to Twitter-shame."

I grabbed the throw and pulled it right up to my nose. I had been Twitter-shamed, whatever that meant. By now, the entire school would have seen it. I wondered how people would react. People who were supposed to be my friends. Would they feel upset and outraged, or would they secretly revel in my humiliation, take pleasure in the *schadenfreude?* I remember when I first learned that word. Mrs. Blackwell, our ninth-grade English teacher had taught it to us in the context of some short story whose name I could no longer recall. *It's German,* she'd explained. *It means taking pleasure in the suffering of others.* At the time, I'd been baffled and repulsed by such a concept, but Twitter had long since eliminated any confusion around my comprehension of the term. Twitter, Facebook, Instagram—on some level, all of it evokes either envy or *schadenfreude*. I'd felt them when Emma had posted pics from her family vacation to the Amalfi coast, and when Simone accidentally tweeted topless photos of herself to the entire class rather than to her boyfriend. I felt it daily on Instagram when I tortured myself by purpose-fully searching out posts tagged "clean living" or "goals." Now, it was my turn. I thought of girls like Rachel and Liana, whom I'd studiously ignored and had failed to help out. They would be the most delighted by my fall, I supposed. I wondered if, on some level, I deserved this.

Bree was saying something, but, lost in thought, I had missed it.

"Huh?" I blinked.

"Jacques," she said urgently, waving her phone again, and I sat up, panicked.

I took the phone but couldn't bring myself to look at it.

"He's threatening to sue," she said cheerfully. "Defamation."

"Can he do that?" I wondered, shocked. I hadn't even considered that angle.

"Probably." She beamed at me. "Maybe Spencer will go to jail! With all the other sociopaths."

I frowned. "I don't think defamation is a crime."

"No?"

"No. He would just have to pay Jacques a lot of money, I think."

"Oh, well." Bree looked put out, but only for a second. "Still, it should kill his little aspiring-journalist enterprise. Asshole."

"Definitely." I took a minute to picture cocky Spencer Caplan crying like a whimpering preschooler as his dad reamed him out for being such a dumb-ass on social media. It gave me a fleeting-but-intense sense of pleasure.

"Jacques is still going to kill me," I said grimly. As if on cue, my phone buzzed. It was him. I closed my eyes, not wanting to look.

"Is that him?" Bree looked scared.

"Yes." I continued to avert my eyes. "Would you read it?"

"Do I have to?" She looked warily at the green bubble on the screen.

"Yes, you do."

Bree sighed. "Okay." She took the phone and cringed.

"How bad?" My heart was thumping.

Bree read aloud. "Clara what the fuck is going on? I'm getting calls about corruption from the *New York* fucking *Times*. I know you hate me but this is the fucking limit. You want me to go to fucking prison? I haven't fucking done anything." She lowered the phone. "That was a lot of fucks in one text."

"He's going to kill me," I said, resigned. I thought again of my father, in Paris. Sharing a bathroom with Mag was sounding better and better. What did I care if she used seaweed toothpaste, or whatever?

The phone buzzed again. This time, I took it and read it myself. "What did you fucking say to that fucking little prick? I want an answer, Clara."

Bree bit her lip. "What are you going to do?" She paused. "What *did* you say, exactly?"

I sighed. "I don't even know. Honestly. Something about Jacques being a self-serving asshole."

"So nothing out of the ordinary, then. Nothing about, like, corruption."

I felt my cheeks go pink. "There may have been a comment about not bothering to write a check to the ballet because Jacques would just take it for himself."

Bree winced. "Oh."

"Yeah."

I wondered if my mother knew what was going on, or if she was absorbed in her dance. Mom tended to be quite oblivious to anything unrelated to ballet, and social media in particular left her baffled. She had a Twitter account, but it was managed by some unfortunate underling at the company. My mother was a physical, tactile person who lived through movement and the body; the virtual world eluded her.

"Are you going to answer him?" Bree sounded uncharacteristically timid.

"I guess I have to." But how does one apologize for siccing *The New York Times* on an old family friend?

"Can I make a suggestion? Deny it. Deny all of it. It's Spencer's word against yours, and he's an asshole."

I contemplated this. It wasn't a bad idea. "So just lie, you mean?"

She shrugged. "Why not? It's his word against yours. And he's a sociopathic scumbag."

I pictured Jacques, red-faced and fuming in his office, shattering martini glasses against his signed Margot Fonteyn poster. He would never believe me, but he had no proof, either.

I grabbed the phone and texted back before I continued to overthink and lost my nerve. "No idea," I typed back. "Met asshole at a party. He's a liar and a sociopath." I was glad Bree had reminded me of the sociopath angle. It lent a medical kind of legitimacy to my claims.

He replied almost immediately. "I'm going to fucking ruin Tom Caplan and his little shit kid. They are going down."

"Okay," I wrote back, not knowing what else to say. I waited for a response, but none came. I settled the phone back down on the coffee table next to the now-tepid latte.

"What did he say?" Bree eyed the phone. "Did he buy it?"

"Not sure. Mostly he was ranting about Tom and Spencer. He's going to ruin them, he says."

Bree shrugged. "Well, as long as he's not screaming about ruining you."

"I guess." I paused. "My dad asked me to come stay with him this summer."

Bree's eyes widened. "Oh my God, Clar! Paris! You said yes, right?"

"I said I'd think about it."

Bree made a small noise. "What's there to think about?"

"Well, Mag and her Birkenstocks, for one. Alastair for another. Not to mention my dad himself. I barely know him."

"Exactly," said Bree. "You have to go. Get to know him, and your brother. And Paris!" She sighed contentedly. "It's magical."

I rolled my eyes. "You were there when you were nine."

"So? It was still magical." She stood and spread out her arms, motioning around the apartment. "You have to go. You can't sit here all summer, moping."

"I said I would think about it." I glanced out the window. The sun blazed in the late-morning sky. There wasn't a cloud in sight, and the people below on the pavement already looked as if they were melting.

Bree sighed, exasperated. "Fine, I'll drop it—for now." She peered towards the window, where I was staring. "It's hot out there."

"Yeah."

"Do you want to do something? There's a photography exhibit at the MOMA."

I hesitated, wavering. It would be nice to get out, but I hadn't finished my workout this morning. I had recently added a new routine, exercises targeted at achieving a thigh gap, that much-desired space between the inner thighs. I felt my own thighs rub against each other. I shuddered at the familiar friction, trying to suppress the ensuing wave of nausea.

"Don't tell me." Bree's tone was cool. "You have to work out."

I flushed, feeling defensive. "It's not just that."

"No?" Her hands were on her hips now, her eyes full of pity mixed with exasperation.

"No. I—I'm feeling overwhelmed." The words tumbled out, my voice sounding small. "The Twitter, and my dad, and Jacques…"

Bree's face softened. "Okay," she said. She sat down next to me. "We'll stay here." She put her hand on mine.

CHAPTER 6

I would go to Paris, I decided the next week. It was less than a decision, really, than a realization that I had no other means of escape. The Monday back at school after the party and ensuing Twitter War was unbelievable. *Everyone* was whispering about me, including the teachers, who at least had the decency to look embarrassed when they saw I was watching. There had been a small story in one of the lesser papers about the incident, and about Jacques retaining "Lawyer to the Stars" Allan Smitherman. Freshmen whispered and giggled as I walked by their lockers, kids who ordinarily treated me, a popular junior, with a quiet reverence. I'd once done a project on leper colonies. Clearly, I was experiencing a sort of social leprosy. In history class, I caught sight of Rachel looking at me. Our eyes met, and I looked away, embarrassed. I wondered if she felt vindicated by my swift social downfall. I wouldn't have blamed her if she did.

Strangely, it was Avril who showed me a hint of humanity, a side of her I'd never been exposed to. She showed up at my locker after fourth-period chem and wordlessly handed me a steaming paper cup.

"It's a mint tea," she said. "I would have brought chocolate, but I know you don't really eat."

Good old Avril, blunt as always. "Thanks," I said cautiously, accepting the drink.

"Spencer Caplan is a first-class asshole," she said quietly. She leaned against the locker next to me. "His father ruined my life. My idiot mother married him like some kind of lunatic with Stockholm Syndrome."

I nodded, not knowing what else to do. I took a sip of my tea. It was beyond hot, and I suppressed a gasp as I felt my tongue burn like I'd licked the stove element.

"Spencer is a wannabe. Thinks he's some kind of god because he's at Yale and his dad is famous. I hope that Jacques guy sues the shit out of them. I hope they go to jail."

I sighed. "You don't go to jail for defamation."

She waved her hand dismissively. "Whatever. I just hate them. And I'm sorry for you. He shouldn't have been at the party, but he lives in my goddamned house now." Her voice was bitter.

"It's not your fault," I said automatically.

She shrugged and laughed, a hollow sound. "Fault, whatever. Life sucks. I'm counting down the days until I get the hell out of here. I got accepted to USC."

"Congrats," I said, meaning it. I envisioned Avril out west, reveling in the sunshine. I wondered if it would help melt her icy persona.

"Thanks." She stood straight, hoisting her messenger bag back onto her shoulder. "Let me know if you need anything. And just FYI, I won't let anyone talk shit about you. I've told everyone Spencer is a pathological liar."

"Thank you," I stammered, shocked at this unexpected kindness. It wouldn't stop the looks and the whispering, but it might go a long way in restoring my tattered reputation.

Avril nodded and walked away. She looked smaller to me than she usually did, more vulnerable.

My phone buzzed. It was my mom, asking if I would prefer turkey or salmon for supper. I'd been afraid she'd be livid with me over the Twitter scandal, but she was blaming herself for the entire episode. She had decided it was somehow mixed up with the orthorexia and her supposed failures as a mother, so she'd been trying to compensate by constantly asking me if I'd "like to talk" in a tentative voice, as if she is worried I'll snap like an incarcerated psych patient. Now, it appeared she was going to try to make up for years of mild maternal neglect by cooking.

"Mom, do *not* touch the stove," I texted back. I pictured our kitchen in flames, my mother's hair ablaze as she frantically fanned a smoking turkey with a pair of charred oven mitts. Mom has no idea how to cook; it's something I've done since our old housekeeper had to go back to Puerto Rico to care for her elderly parents.

"I want to make supper," she answered. "I'll be careful."

"Wait for me," I wrote back, increasingly desperate. "We'll do it together."

She didn't answer. Worried, I pulled my calculus text out of my locker and shoved it into my backpack. Bree appeared at my side, angling her body to shield me from the passersby.

"You okay?" She grabbed my tea so it didn't spill as I slammed my locker shut.

"I guess. I didn't think I could survive everyone staring at me like this, but then I don't really have a choice. It's not like I'm going to throw myself off the roof or whatever."

"Well, that's positive." Bree put an arm around my shoulder as we walked down the hall together. My calc class was on the way to her advanced English seminar. "Besides, about half the people are saying Spencer is a crazy asshole liar."

I made a face. "And the other half?"

"Well…" She hesitated.

"Be honest."

"That you're trying to get attention." She didn't look at me.

"Attention-seeking slut, you mean."

She still wouldn't look at me. Her cheeks blushed bright pink as she pretended to be absorbed by a poster advertising last semester's drama production.

I balled my hands into fists. "All I did was kiss him. He made it sound like we slept together in a broom closet or something."

"I know. I know. I'm so sorry, Clara."

Overcome with rage, I kicked a locker. A startled junior looked at me and scurried away. I wondered if she'd tweet it and I'd end up looking like a violent lunatic, on top of everything.

That would just about seal things for me.

"I'm going to Paris," I blurted out. I hadn't yet broken the news to Bree. We were outside the math lab, and I still had a few minutes before class started. "I need to get out of here."

"That's amazing!" Bree looked genuinely thrilled. "When?"

"Right after my last exam next week. I'm not sticking around any longer than necessary."

At St. Andrew's, the last week of June was considered "enrichment," which largely consisted of field trips to the Met or watching lame movies like Kenneth Branagh's four-hour production of *Hamlet* on the classroom smart screen. It was nothing I needed to be present for—and my mom had agreed. She even offered to use her airline points to get me there.

"Paris." Bree got that dreamy look on her face again. "You'll probably meet some amazing French guy. And you'll learn to speak French!"

"I already speak some French," I pointed out. Bree had opted for Spanish as her language elective. "And I doubt I'll be meeting anyone. I'm going to help look after Alastair."

"Well, I'll be looking after kids and I definitely won't be meeting any French guys or strolling around the Eiffel Tower or whatever."

The warning bell rang. "I'll see you later," I said. I ducked into calculus, where three seniors I barely knew immediately started whispering, taking turns to stare openly at me.

"At least be discreet about it," I muttered under my breath. I slid into my seat and checked my phone. Only two hours of torture to go.

"Mom! What did you do?" I walked into the apartment and was instantly hit by an acrid smell. I coughed and covered my face with my hand, trying not to breathe through my nose. My mother hovered in the entryway looking apologetic and waving an oven mitt at the smoke alarm.

"I tried to make a turkey breast," she admitted, shamefaced.

"I told you to wait for me!" My eyes traveled towards the kitchen and landed on a smoking black lump. I shook my head in disbelief. "What did you do to it?"

"I don't know." She sniffed, looking put out. "I followed all the directions exactly. I was going to make us a nice, healthy supper."

I rubbed my temples; the sickening scent of charred poultry was giving me a headache. "Please," I groaned. "Next time, just stick to the Whole Foods counter, okay? Prepared food only."

"I feel like an idiot." She hung her head. "It was such a nice piece of meat. And the fire alarm went off and Henry had to come and make sure the building wasn't on fire or anything."

Henry was the doorman and assistant superintendent. Like most men who knew her, he was half in love with my mom. I doubted he'd have cared if she committed arson.

"Let's clean this up and order some sushi," I said with a sigh. I opened the cupboard under the sink and rummaged around for a garbage bag.

"That I can do." My mom grabbed the bag from me. "You

relax. Seriously, Clara." She searched my face, looking worried. I knew she wanted to ask how I was doing, how the day had gone after a weekend of Twitter Hell. But she knew better than to push.

"Fine." I handed her the bag and sank down on the couch. "I'll have some salmon sashimi, okay? And a wakame salad."

"Sure." Mom swept the ruined turkey into the trash bag and knotted it before grabbing the phone. "Miso soup?"

"Too hot." I yawned, and lay back against a soft cushion. I closed my eyes, grateful to be home.

Over dinner, Mom gently broached the subject of Jacques. "He isn't mad at you," she said, carefully spearing a piece of fish with her chopsticks. "He knows that boy took advantage of you."

I tore open a packet of soy sauce, carefully emptying only a quarter of it onto my sashimi. "Jacques hates me. If it weren't for you, he'd have hired an assassin to take me out."

"Don't be silly." My mother looked affronted. "He's not perfect, but he certainly doesn't hate you. Or want you dead. For God's sake, Clara."

"Hmmmm." I didn't answer. Mom didn't understand the mutual state of enmity between me and Jacques. She never had.

"His lawyer says they should be able to settle the whole thing fairly quickly," she added. "Apparently, the boy's father—the reporter—is furious."

That, at least, gave me some pleasure. I pictured the cocky Spencer being chewed out by his dad and took a satisfying bite of salad.

"So it will all blow over quickly, with no harm done." She gave me a wan smile. "No one will even remember it in a couple days."

I looked away. I wasn't so sure about that. People moved on swiftly, sure—inevitable in a world with non-stop Twitter feeds and Facebook updates. But would they forget? Unlikely. The damage would be done.

"I got your ticket today, too!" Mom brightened. "Jacques paid the extra to get you a first-class ticket. And you say he hates you."

I was fairly certain Jacques would have paid for a private jet if it ensured my absence for an entire summer, but I didn't say anything. Instead, I muttered some version of thanks and went back to poking at my supper. Usually I liked sashimi, but tonight it was making me nauseous.

"I spoke with Melisa this afternoon." She wouldn't look at me, and she was the color of a ripe tomato. "We talked about your going to Paris. She thinks it's a great idea."

I put down my chopsticks. "Melisa called you? Why?"

"Well." She fidgeted awkwardly with a bottle of water. "I called her."

"What?" I couldn't believe it. Mom had called Melisa? What the hell for?

"I was worried the Twitter thing would set you off," she said nervously. She still wasn't looking at me. "I wanted to make sure I was doing the right thing."

I stood up, furious. "I'm not some dying anorexic," I snapped. "I'm not about to fall off the wagon like an alcoholic and start starving and puking or whatever. I eat more than you do!"

Mom looked frightened. "I know. I know. I'm sorry. I'm trying to do the right thing here, Clara."

"And the right thing is…*conspiring* against me with some social worker." For the first time that day, my eyes filled with tears. Relieved at the release, I let them flow.

"Not conspiring." She grabbed my hand. "Just talking."

She held on to me, and I stared at her hand, at the long, bony fingers. It felt almost like my grandmother's used to feel, and I recalled the dismal bone scan. My mother was not yet forty.

"I'm sorry," she whispered. "I just want you to be okay."

I thought of the sashimi and Spencer, Jacques and exams. Alastair and Paris. I wanted to be okay, too.

CHAPTER 7

With little to occupy my time given my sudden social implosion, I hit the books and spent the week ensconced in the library studying. It was the perfect reprieve from the watchful eyes of the St. Andrew's student body; no one of any consequence spent any time there. I'm not a bad student, but I rarely put in the effort to go the extra mile for that A. I've always been more of a B-plus kind of girl, despite pleas from my teachers to "live up to my potential." However, hiding in the stacks, I studied harder than I ever had before. As a result, I ended up acing my exams. Since my early departure for Paris meant I would be missing the official exam-return day, Call-me-Jane phoned me personally to inform me of my results.

"Clara? Is that you?" She called on my cell phone.

"Yes?" I didn't recognize the voice or Caller ID at first.

"It's Jane."

Jane? Oh. Mrs. Cartwright. "Oh. Um…hi?"

"I know you're leaving, so I wanted to let you know how impressed we all are with your exam results."

I wondered who "we all" was. I had a brief image of the entire faculty sitting around the staffroom, eating their lunch out of Tupperware containers and gossiping about the students.

"You managed A's on all of your exams except Chemistry, which was an A minus. Congratulations."

A's on everything? Me? Stunned, I stammered some words of thanks, then ended the call as quickly as I could.

Bree was there when I hung up. "What was that?" We were in Central Park. Bree had had a post-exam urge to watch the sea lions being fed at the zoo and binge on Nuts 4 Nuts from one of the park vendors. She was already on her second bag.

"Call-me-Jane." It was uncomfortably hot. I fanned myself with my bag and fumbled with my bottle of water, enjoying the sensation of the cold plastic against my warm skin.

Bree stuck out her bag of nuts. "Is she calling about your healthy-eating disorder? Here, have some nuts. You can call her back and tell her you're having junk food."

I shrank away. Nuts were a good source of protein, but that value was lost once they were honey-roasted.

"She was calling to give me my exam results." I leaned against a fence. A crowd was gathering in anticipation of the feeding.

Bree looked apprehensive. "And?"

"Straight A's," I said, trying to sound casual. "Well, almost. A minus in chem."

Bree coughed, nearly choking on her candy-coated cashews.

"I know, right?" I shrugged. "Who knew it was even possible?"

"Wow." Bree grabbed my water and took a swig. "Straight A's, huh?"

"I guess." The sea-lion feeders came out with big buckets of fish, and the kids in the crowd clapped and cheered. I watched as a sea lion emerged, its whiskered nose sniffing eagerly at the fish-scented air.

"You know, if you kept it up and rocked the SATs you could go to, like, Harvard or something."

I raised my eyebrows. "Let's not get crazy."

The workers held out the fish on long poles, teasing the sea lions out of their pool. They wiggled onto the rocks and flapped their fins excitedly. I winced as the bait was dangled higher and higher, forcing the sea lions to jump and dance for their food

Bree made a face. "It seems kind of cruel, doesn't it?"

"It's awful. But you wanted to come here."

"I know," she said, abashed. "I have such fond memories of coming here as a kid. Was it always like this?"

"Probably." I turned away. "When you're a kid, though, you don't see the ugly part." I thought of Alastair, the brother waiting for me in Paris. Would he enjoy watching the sea lions turn tricks for food? Did they have a zoo in Paris? Probably. There were zoos everywhere. Human beings liked to watch others, be it animals in small cages or other humans in their own habitats online.

"I guess we're not kids anymore, then." Bree took a final look and turned away, too. "This is kind of sick. Let's go get some frozen yogurt."

I hadn't had any intention of eating, but to celebrate my exam grades, I decided to allow myself a small dish of plain yogurt. Bree, of course, opted for chocolate truffle and loaded hers up with an assortment of candy toppings. Taking a deep breath, I focused on the calcium and protein content of the frozen dessert before me and ignored the calorie count, trying to savor the sweet spoonfuls as they melted on my tongue.

"Need some help?" My mother leaned against my doorframe, her eyebrows raised at the mess of clothing strewn about the bed and floor.

"I've given up." I folded a tank top and placed it in the suitcase. "I'm taking everything."

"Everything?"

"Well, apparently the weather can be unpredictable." I gestured around me at the different piles of clothing that had accumulated. I had warmer, long-sleeved shirts and light-weight hoodies and jackets on the floor near my desk, tank tops, tees, and jeans on the bed, and an additional pile of dresses on an armchair in the corner. "Sometimes July is cool and rainy. Sometimes it's unbearably hot, and they don't have air conditioning."

Mom shuddered. Her Manitoban blood abhorred the

heat, a trait I'd inherited. "That's a good point. Tank tops, then. Lots of them." She came over and picked up a stack to help fold, settling down on the edge of my bed.

"How are things with Jacques?" I tried to keep my voice casual. Mom had done her best to shield me from the entire affair over the last two weeks, but it's hard to protect someone from *The New York Times*. Without proof and facing an army of lawyers, Spencer had been forced to recant his accusations. I had further learned from Avril that his father was so angry over the whole debacle that he had barred him from using any social media or else be cut off financially and otherwise. Personally, I would have welcomed being cut off from social media. It certainly wasn't making my life any easier these days, and it was proving to be a tough habit to kick.

"Jacques will be fine," she answered evasively. I turned away, guiltily fidgeting with a pile of socks. I loathed Jacques, but I hadn't wanted him to be falsely accused of corruption. It was bad for the company and the charitable donors it relied upon to survive.

"He must really hate me now," I said. I tossed the socks into a second suitcase.

Mom sighed. "He doesn't hate you, Clara." She finished folding the tank tops and neatly tucked them into a corner of the bag. "He just doesn't understand children. He lives and breathes the ballet."

"Whatever." I played with the suitcase zipper, tugging it back and forth. "I'm sorry for what I did. I didn't know what would happen."

"No one blames you," Mom said quickly. "That boy—it was his fault."

I grinned, picturing Spencer's reaction to being called a boy. He was so full of himself, play-acting the part of Big Important Reporter.

"Anyway, it will be good for you to get away for a bit." Mom placed another pile of neatly folded shirts into the suitcase. "Really get to know your father and your brother."

"Half-brother," I muttered.

She frowned. "What's the difference?"

"Nothing." I sighed. I didn't know why I'd said that. The idea of spending time with my brother—a brother I didn't know—unnerved me.

"It will be nice, to have a sibling. I was always sorry that was something you didn't have growing up. I used to have such fun with my brothers when we were little."

Mom's brothers, my Uncle Paul and Uncle Drew, both still live in Manitoba, where my mom grew up. Uncle Paul took over the family business—a local hardware store in a small town—and Uncle Drew is now some kind of major science-nerd professor in Boston. They're both nice, I guess; we only see them once a year, at Thanksgiving, and sometimes not even then, if Mom has a performance. I can't picture the three of them as kids, horsing around, but my mother assures me they got up to all sorts of mischief. Regardless, I doubt it will be that way for Alastair and me. I'm sixteen, and he's six. What could we possibly have in common?

As if reading my mind, my mother put a hand on my

shoulder. "It may surprise you, how nice it is to have a little brother. I used to feel very protective of Drew. He was almost six years younger than me."

"Yeah, but Uncle Drew isn't weird," I blurted out, then felt ashamed. "I mean, Alastair...there's something wrong with him."

Mom put down the jeans she was folding. "Drew was a math prodigy," she said. "He used to spend hours skip counting outside on a swing in the backyard."

"Skip counting?" I looked up, blank.

"Like counting by threes," she explained. "Or sevens. Drew loved sevens." She resumed folding. "They didn't have a name for it in those days, but I'm sure today he would have been diagnosed with something like what Alastair has."

I thought back to last Thanksgiving, when Uncle Drew had gone around the table to ask which way people preferred to hang their toilet paper in the bathroom and had taken notes. Sure, I'd thought it was strange, but then Uncle Drew had always been a little different. I envisioned a serious-looking miniature Uncle Drew on a swing, counting methodically. It wasn't that hard to imagine. I pictured Alastair with the blocks, and pondered my mother's words.

"Just give Alastair a chance," my mother said. "That's all I'm saying."

I nodded, but didn't answer. I resolved to do more research on what "the spectrum" was. I didn't really understand what it meant, but hadn't bothered to find out, either.

Mom stood. "I have to go," she said apologetically. "Performance tonight."

I tried to remember. "*Copelia?*" I guessed.

"*Swan Lake.*" She yawned. "I'm exhausted. I'd better get some coffee." She looked at me. "What are you doing later?"

"Gym, then sushi with Bree." I got up, too, and rummaged around for my gym bag. It was hidden under my ever-growing pile of makeup, shampoo, and body lotion. I made a mental note to pick up another suitcase. I'd need one for toiletries alone.

"Make sure you eat," she said automatically, and our eyes met.

"You, too," I said pointedly.

Her cheeks briefly turned pink before she left the room.

CHAPTER 8

"I can't believe I can't take you to the airport." My mother blew her perfect nose into a tissue and groaned, rolling over onto her side to look at me. "I feel terrible."

"Don't even think about it," I said swiftly. "You're in no shape to go anywhere."

It was true. Mom had contracted a summer cold that had left her eyes red, her throat sore, and her nose runny. She'd had to bow out of a performance yesterday—an almost unheard-of occurrence for her.

"Think how happy you've made the understudy," I'd joked as I prepared her a mug of tea with lemon and honey. "She probably crosses her fingers every day that you'll get a cold or eat expired mayonnaise or whatever."

Mom gave me a dark look. "You're kidding, but I wouldn't put it past her. She wants my job."

"Well, definitely don't accept any tuna-fish sandwiches from her, then."

We had spent the day under a blanket on the couch watching old movies and eating popcorn. Air-popped and butter-free, but it was something.

"I feel just awful thinking of you in a cab all by yourself." Mom sneezed violently.

I ducked, using my purse as a shield against the sudden explosion of airborne virus particles.

"Sorry," she said blearily.

"Don't go making me sick now." I lowered the bag and slung it over my shoulder. "Mag will force her herbal remedies on me."

"Clara." Mom gave me a warning look. "Don't be rude to Mag."

I snorted. "The last time she visited, you laughed at her earrings for a week."

Mom sneezed again, this time covering her face with a pillow. "I know. But that was before these classes with Melisa. Empathy, remember?"

"Fine. But in your defence, they were hand-made dream-catcher earrings. With pigeon feathers she had found in the park and dyed magenta."

I could tell she was trying not to laugh. "Really, though, Clara. Give Dad and Mag a chance. And Alastair. Be nice."

I sighed. "Of course I'll be nice, Mom. You act like I was raised by wolves."

She laughed, then sneezed again. I tossed her the box of

Kleenex and checked my phone. "The car is going to be here any second," I said. "Take care of yourself, okay?"

"Call me when you get there." She looked worried again. "And text or call whenever you can. Or email. Or update your Facebook page."

"No Facebook," I said, making a face. "I'm getting off of social media for the summer."

"Are you?" she looked impressed. "I guess the Twitter thing has left a bad taste in your mouth."

"Yeah," I said. I didn't mention the rest of it—that Instagram stars in skimpy bikinis clutching bottles of cucumber water were driving me slowly to madness. She would no doubt flip out and go running to Melisa.

"And, Clara," said my mother in a hesitant voice. "Eat. It's Paris."

I didn't say anything.

"Have a safe flight," she said finally, when she realized I wasn't going to take the bait. "I love you."

"Love you, too, Mom."

In spite of her cold, I hugged her goodbye.

I love airports. I love the anonymity of them, the absence of any real time or place. It can be dawn outside an airport, but inside you can still find someone to serve you a full-course meal. People wander around in any manner of dress, no matter what the season: skiwear in July, beachwear in January. Sometimes you spot celebrities in sweatpants with no makeup, and they look like regular people, possibly even uglier.

I also like shopping at the airport. Sure, you can buy headphones anywhere, but there is something particularly exciting about purchasing them from a vending machine the size of a bus shelter. It was also a good place to buy last-minute gifts, I realized guiltily once I'd cleared security. I chose a New York Yankees baseball cap for Alastair, and a large, fancy box of assorted chocolates for Dad and Mag. I had a vague idea that Mag only eats things she's grown herself in some kind of composting garden, but figured it was the thought that counts.

For myself, I bought a bag of rice cakes and an apple and idly thumbed through fashion and gossip magazines, something else I only do at the airport. I stared longingly at the slim silhouettes of the models, their perfect thighs flashing just the right amount of space between them. Self-consciously, I shifted from foot to foot, feeling my own thighs rub together in a pair of cotton leggings, despite a strict regimen of daily kicks and squats. If Bree were here, she'd remind me that these girls were either airbrushed or starving, but it was hard to not feel anything but envy at their perfection.

When it was time to board, a suspicious-looking flight attendant with large, red cat's-eye glasses stopped me.

"Executive-class passengers only right now, Miss," she said in a patronizing tone. "We'll be doing general boarding soon."

"I have an executive ticket," I said. I didn't know whether to be angry or embarrassed. On one hand, I wasn't fond of being talked down to by smug adults. On the other, I felt guilty that, at sixteen, I would be comfortably tucked in my pod and fawned over by a personal staff, while a woman with a baby and an elderly man with crutches would both be sucking it up in coach.

"It was a gift," I added lamely. It was the sort of thing I always said. Bree said I didn't have to apologize for having nice things, but my mother said it was my humble Manitoban roots poking through. Regardless, I hated the idea of the world perceiving me as an entitled, spoiled Manhattanite, born to a life of privilege, flying first class because my mother was famous. The flight attendant made a clicking sound with her tongue, but her face was like a mask, a perfect smile plastered across her scarlet-painted lips.

"Of course," she said smoothly, now all professionalism and politeness. "Go right ahead. Enjoy your flight."

I settled into my seat, surrounded mostly by businesspeople. There was also a family with two kids, a boy and a girl with matching heads of thick, curling sandy hair. They were speaking rapid-fire French. I wondered if they lived in Paris or were just ordinary American kids who spoke French with their parents. Then the rank-and-file economy passengers began boarding, and I concentrated on avoiding eye contact.

"Welcome aboard!" A red-headed flight attendant, maybe a few years my senior, appeared at my side, beaming. "I'm Julia. Here's a menu with tonight's offerings!" She thrust a pale-blue card into my hands, emblazoned with the airline's logo.

I took the menu and opened it. A choice of cream of asparagus soup or a green salad to start. Filet mignon with roasted potatoes, or salmon in some kind of mushroom velouté with rice. I chewed on my lip, wondering which was worse. I also wondered if my rice cakes and apple were enough to sustain me for the eight hours to France. The word *velouté* sounded suspiciously viscous, abundant with hidden butter and cream.

"Any decisions?" Julia reappeared, still looking bright and enthusiastic. I reopened the menu and pointed at the fish description.

"Would it be possible to get this without the velouté?" I asked.

"Of course," she said. She leaned in towards me and lowered her voice. "Is it just because you don't know what velouté is? Because it's just a sauce, apparently. It has cream, I think, so it's probably really yummy."

"I'm, um, lactose intolerant," I lied easily. I was good at lying about food. It came as natural to me as breathing. The recent increase in allergies and intolerances was a convenient excuse, and tended to shut down any further lines of questioning.

"Oh, no!" She put her hand to her mouth. "That's so sad. We have ice-cream sundaes for dessert!"

"Oh," I said, trying to feign disappointment. "That's too bad. Anyway, I'll have the salmon with no sauce, and the salad with no dressing, please."

"I don't think there's milk in the dressing," she said thoughtfully, her eyebrows furrowed. "Do you want me to check? Because it's a nice dressing, an orange vinaigrette—"

"No, no," I said hastily. "It's fine. Seriously."

Later, when we were well on our way, the ice-cream sundaes were rolled out and I couldn't help but stare at the glass dishes brimming with whipped cream and chocolate sauce. The French kids across the row eyed them greedily. I watched as the girl snatched her dessert from the flight attendant and dug in with the long metal spoon, her eyes half-closed in pleasure as she took that first bite.

She was about twelve, I guessed. Still skinny, but with a certain awkwardness that suggested a recent or impending growth spurt, and with the telling white strap of a training bra peeking out from under her T-shirt. I tried to remember the last time I'd had a sundae. It had to have been when I was around that age. While my mother had always made her thoughts on sugar abundantly clear, I had secretly indulged at friends' houses and birthday parties. I could remember going to Ben and Jerry's with Lorelai Parker after a sleepover, and that was back in sixth or seventh grade. Her parents had given us a ten-dollar bill, and we'd spent nearly all of it, selecting bowls made of sugar cones and topping the ice cream with things like hot fudge and maraschino cherries. It had to have been sixth grade, I realized suddenly, because I'd asked for a food scale for my twelfth birthday.

Four years, I calculated. Four years since I'd had a real ice-cream sundae. *A quarter of my life so far.* I pictured the flight attendant placing the glass in front of me and handing me the spoon. *Could I have eaten it?* I pondered the question, imagining the feeling of the whipped cream on my lips, the sensation of the ice cream as it slid down my throat, slowly cooling my body as it traveled downward…to my thighs. *Aye, there's the rub*, I thought wryly, grimacing at the unintended pun. I couldn't see the sundae as just a tasty treat. It was a concoction of calories and trans fats, insidiously working its way into my butt, my abdomen, my upper arms. Also my arteries, and my heart. I thought of my Bubbe Singerman, who had terrified me with her enormous bulk, dying prematurely from a dog's breakfast of diabetes, high blood pressure, and heart disease. As I gazed around at my fellow first-class passengers, I marveled at their ability to eat such large amounts of garbage with such reckless abandon.

"I have good news!" Julia was back. "I saw you looking around at everyone with their sundaes and I felt so bad. But I asked Shirley—she's been working this route forever—and she said they had *this!*"

Beaming again, she whipped out one of the tall glass dishes, filled to overflowing with some kind of frozen orange goop.

"Sorbet," Julia explained. "It's dairy-free!"

I poked at the sorbet with the spoon. "Thanks," I said weakly. "Wow. That was…really nice of you."

She gave me a huge smile. "Well, it's terrible to be left out of ice cream! I mean, what's the point of traveling first class if you can't eat all the delicious food, right?"

I gave her a wan smile as she bustled away, collecting empty dishes and soiled napkins.

I contemplated the sorbet. Sure, it was dairy-free—but it certainly wasn't calorie-free. Sorbet wasn't too high in sugar—I knew that from years of assessing the nutritional information at Baskin-Robbins while Bree waffled between Mississippi Mud and World Class Chocolate—but I'd already eaten the rice with my salmon—white rice, something I rarely allowed myself. White rice was a glutinous trap of useless calories, but I'd had a sudden urge and decided to treat myself since I was on holidays, sort of.

Still, I couldn't offend the flight attendant, who'd gone so far as to procure a lactose-free dessert on my behalf. Taking a deep breath, I scooped up a spoonful and swallowed it quickly, supressing the urge to gag. *There*, I told myself. *That wasn't so bad*. I took another, and then a third, wondering how many I would have to eat not to seem impolite. But by the fourth or fifth, something odd had happened. It wasn't sickening anymore. It was just sweet and cold and…good. I didn't even know how many bites I'd had when I finally put the spoon down, breathing heavily. This was why it was better to avoid desserts entirely. Eating "just a bit" turned quickly into "just one more bite." "Only a sliver for me," Bubbe would chortle about whatever cake or pie she'd bring out after supper. But then she'd have another sliver, and then another, until half the thing was gone.

Until half the thing was gone. I stared at the dish in front of me. It was half-empty. Horrified, I pushed it away.

"You don't want to finish that?" Julia again. She was starting to get annoying. I'd have to break out the headphones in a minute.

"It was delicious," I said politely. "But I'm so full from supper."

She whisked it away. "Can I get you something else? Coffee? Tea?"

"No, thanks," I said, gritting my teeth. "I'm going to try to sleep."

"Nighty-night!" she said brightly.

Relieved, I switched off my overhead light and lowered my seat. Grateful for the privacy, I took a moment to silently thank Jacques for his generosity. Spoiled or not, it was nice to have the space and seclusion. I flipped through the movie choices on my screen, looking for something to serve as a sedative. My plan was to drift off watching movies—I didn't have a great history of sleeping successfully on planes. I turned on *Lincoln*, which was something like three or four hours long and bound to be a colossal bore. Unfortunately, three hours later, I was an expert on the sixteenth U.S. president, but no closer to nodding off. For hours, I lay there, tired and fuzzy-headed, but unable to make the final descent into unconsciousness. When I finally drifted off, life-sized ice-cream sundaes danced across my mind, waltzing spoon-in-arm with my poor Bubbe, dressed as Odile from *Swan Lake*.

CHAPTER 9

The first thing I saw after I'd retrieved my luggage was a giant sign with my name plastered on it. I ventured a guess it was the first thing everyone saw. It was absolutely enormous, and yellow. Mag and my father held up opposite ends of the monstrosity, grinning and waving madly.

"Clara! Over here!" Mag shook the sign slightly to catch my attention, as if it were necessary in light of the veritable billboard she was clutching. I cringed and lowered my head. I was sure people were laughing.

"Hi," I said weakly, walking over. My father grabbed my bags and the sign fluttered to the floor. It was then I noticed the small boy standing behind it.

"Clara, you remember your brother, Alastair," my dad put his hand on the boy's head. He had thick, wildly curling hair in a color that was not quite red and not quite blond, but somewhere in between. His cheeks were rosy and freckled, and his eyes were huge and green.

"Half-brother," said Alastair. He stared at his feet. At that moment we had that in common.

"Hey, Alastair," I said. Awkwardly, I put my hand on his shoulder. "Good to see you."

Alastair didn't say anything, but shrank away. I wondered if I wasn't supposed to touch him. Bree said she'd once babysat for an autistic kid who would shriek and tear out chunks of his hair if you accidentally touched him.

"Did you like the sign?" Alastair suddenly looked right at me, his huge eyes sharp and alert.

"Er—yes," I lied. "Lovely."

"It was my idea," he said. He didn't sound as if he were bragging, or even proud, just stating the facts. "Otherwise we wouldn't have been able to find you. We don't know what you look like."

"Ah," I said, smiling. Maybe he wasn't so weird, after all. That seemed like a pretty cute six-year-old type of thing to say.

"I chose yellow, because black writing on a yellow background is one of the most pleasing to the human brain."

"I'm sorry?" I stared at him.

"I read it online."

"You read it online?" I blinked. "You can read?"

"Of course I can read," he said impatiently.

"We should get going," Dad said hastily. He put an arm around Alastair and steered him towards the exit. "We only paid for half an hour of parking." Mag fell in beside me, the sign trailing behind her.

"How was the flight?" she asked brightly. "I hear you flew first class."

"It was a gift from one of my mom's friends. He had a lot of frequent-flyer points," I said quickly. I didn't want Mag to think my mother and I were rich capitalist jetsetters. Mag had once lived on some sort of commune and had pretty strong ideas about the redistribution of wealth.

"Very exciting. Was the food as good as it looks in the movies?" Then her hand flew to her mouth. "Oh, my goodness, Clara, I'm so sorry."

"Why?" I stopped and looked at her, mystified.

"It's okay, Clara. You don't have to hide it from me. We're family."

"Hide what?" Feeling exasperated and confused, I walked through a set of automatic doors and outside into a light mist of rain. It was cool, too. I shivered and wished I had my windbreaker.

"Your anorexia." She put a motherly arm around my shoulders. "We're going to help you recover here."

"I'm not anorexic!"

"It's all right," she said soothingly. "It's not your fault. It's the media—"

Thankfully, we arrived at the car before she could say anything else. Inwardly, I fumed. Was that what my dad thought, too?

"Car's a bit short on space," he said apologetically, popping the trunk of the little gray Renault. "They make them smaller here." He tossed my bags in, and then slammed the lid shut. The whole car shook.

"Yes," agreed Mag. "No giant, gas-guzzling SUVs like you have in America."

I bit my tongue. Alastair turned to stare at me as he climbed into the backseat. "Do you have an SUV?" he inquired. I noticed for the first time he had a hint of a British accent.

"No. We don't even have a car," I snapped. I slid in the opposite door. "I walk. Or take the subway." I didn't mention Bree's driver. I was willing to bet Mag Would Not Approve.

I glanced over at Alastair, who was still staring at me. He didn't blink a lot, I'd noticed. I looked away, but I could still feel his eyes on me.

I remembered the gifts in my backpack, which I had with me in the back seat. Relieved at the potential distraction, I hastily unzipped it and rummaged through.

"Here, Alastair, this is for you," I said. "It's a Yankees cap."

"Thank you," he said automatically. He turned it over and over in his hands, then brought it to his nose and inhaled deeply.

Mag was watching through the rear-view mirror. "Alastair uses other senses to get input on his environment," she explained. "Senses we might not ordinarily use."

"Oh," I said politely. I wasn't sure how to respond. I'd never seen anyone sniff a baseball hat before.

Alastair carefully placed the hat on his head. "It smells interesting," he announced. "I like it."

"Great!" I said, trying to be enthusiastic. "Are you a Yankees fan?"

"I don't know what that means," he said.

"Yankees? You know, baseball?" I made a bat-swinging motion with my arms. Did they not have baseball in France?

Mag turned around. "It's a bit like cricket, Love," she explained to Alastair. "Very popular in America. Yankees are a New York City team."

"Oh," he said. "I don't like cricket."

"It isn't exactly like cricket," my father interjected. "It's much better."

"How is it better?" Alastair frowned, but he kept the hat on.

I sighed. "It's just a hat. You can wear it even if you don't like baseball."

"I do like the hat," Alastair agreed. "I don't know about the Yankees, though."

"That's fair," said Dad from the front. "Lots of people don't like the Yankees. Like, the entire city of Boston, for example."

"I also got this, for you guys," I interrupted. I wasn't interested in baseball politics. I took out the chocolates and handed them up to Mag in the front.

"Oh, lovely," she said. "Chocolate. You shouldn't have." Her voice implied that I really shouldn't have. Guess my instincts were right about the organic herb garden, because judging from the size of Mag's behind, it wasn't the calories she was wary of.

"Can I see the ingredients?" Alastair sat up straight, speaking loudly. "We need to check the ingredients."

"What for?" I asked, baffled. I wondered if Mag had him programmed. Nothing packaged in plastic, nothing with genetically modified ingredients. Organic only. I didn't go in for that stuff—I'd had a great ninth-grade science teacher who'd clearly demonstrated that the arguments for those things were mostly bunk. No evidence.

"Nuts," said Dad, Mag, and Alastair in unison.

"Alastair is allergic to nuts," explained my father.

"I have anaphylaxis," said Alastair. "That means my throat swells, and if I don't get my adrenaline medication, I die." His tone was matter-of-fact.

"I didn't know," I said, feeling guilty. "I'm sorry. I would never have brought chocolates."

"No, no," said Mag. "It's quite all right. We expect Alastair to take responsibility for his allergy. None of that nut-free nonsense you have in America. He needs to manage it on his own. Not," she added, "that it's as much of an issue. Children don't take peanut-butter sandwiches to school here. They eat proper lunches."

The anti-American rhetoric was starting to wear a little thin. I gritted my teeth in an effort to control my temper and stared out the window, looking for signs of France. So far, it didn't look much different than New Jersey.

"We live in the fifth *arrondissement*," Dad announced, changing the subject. "I don't know how much you know about Paris."

"Not much," I admitted. I'd intended to do some reading before I left, or even on the plane, but it had never happened. I figured I'd hit the ground running and learn on the fly.

My father went into full professor mode. I don't know what he was like as a physician, but I have no trouble picturing him in a college lecture hall. "Paris is divided into twenty different boroughs, or arrondissements, which spiral out numerically from the center." He met my gaze in the mirror. "Picture it a bit like a snail's shell."

"Okay," I said. In my mind, I saw a large snail painted the red, white, and blue of the French *Tricolore*, the Eiffel Tower perched precariously on its back.

"There are twenty arrondissements. The further from the center you go, the greater the number. We're in the fifth, near the university."

"It's a wonderful neighborhood," piped up Mag. "Home to the Latin Quarter and all sorts of lovely museums." She sounded like a guidebook.

"The *Métro* is excellent here," she added, "so you can get around quite easily wherever you need to go. It's very simple."

"Yes, I'm sure I can figure it out," I said patiently. "We have a subway in New York."

Sensing the edge in my voice, my father interjected again. "Alastair knows a lot about the city. He's very good at finding his way around. You'll make a good team."

"He's allowed out alone?" I recalled reading various articles on how much more independent kids were in France versus America—how they used the oven by themselves at three, or whatever. If a six-year-old could wander the streets by himself, I guessed that was all true.

"No, no. Of course not. I just meant that you'll be his chaperone this summer, but he'll be able to show you a thing or two. It will be more of a symbiotic relationship."

"Sure," I said, sneaking a look at Alastair. "Hey, Alastair."

His head swiveled towards me. "Yes?"

"When Dad was talking about the neighborhoods all coiling out like a snail shell, I kept picturing a giant snail with the Eiffel Tower on its back."

I don't know what I was expecting, but if it was laughter, I was definitely out of luck.

"Why?" asked Alastair. He stared at me intently.

"I don't know." I wished I hadn't said anything. Trying to explain a joke to someone who doesn't get it is a painful exercise. "I guess he just said 'snail' and the first thing that popped into my mind was a big snail with the most famous Paris landmark on top."

"The Eiffel Tower is in the seventh arrondissement," he informed me, without a trace of humor. "So it should be *in* the snail shell, not on top of it."

"I know," I said, even though I didn't. "I just meant it as, like, a joke."

"But it doesn't make any sense."

I closed my eyes. "Forget I said anything."

"I can't forget it. You just said it. It's too soon to forget."

"Alastair." Dad's voice was patient. "Clara is using an expression. What she means is, she doesn't want to talk about it anymore."

Alastair nodded and snapped his mouth shut. I avoided looking at him. *Was this what the summer would be like?* I didn't know if I could stand it.

"Getting into Paris proper now!" announced Mag. "Pity

it's such a dull day, the sights are so lovely. But not to worry, you're here all summer."

Yes, I thought grimly. *Yes, I am.*

I looked out the window, where the streets had become narrower and the buildings older and closer together. The architecture *was* charming, I thought grudgingly. I pressed my face against the glass and noticed a girl about my age sitting outside at a café, a lavender silk scarf draped casually about her neck. Under a striped awning, she seemed unperturbed by the weather, content with a steaming espresso cup and a book, and I wondered briefly what she was reading. All the cane-seated chairs were carefully arranged, just like in the movies, and in spite of myself I felt a little thrill of excitement. Alastair or not, this was still Paris.

CHAPTER 10

Dad's place was in a delightful ivory stucco four-storey walk-up with black wrought-iron balconies and trim. In other words, it looked exactly like a movie set or something out of a magazine article on where to go in Paris. I couldn't help but be taken in by its Old World charm, though I made a concerted effort to hide my pleasure from Mag, who I felt sure would make smug remarks about American architectural soullessness if I let on that I was impressed. The entire ground-floor level was occupied by various storefronts—a bakery, a small café, and something like what in New York we'd call a *bodega*: a small store selling groceries, wine, and odds and ends.

"We're on the next floor," said Dad, heaving my bag onto his shoulder.

"I can carry it myself," I said hastily, embarrassed. "Let me take it."

"No, no, it's the least I can do," he answered, and I wondered what he was referring to. *The least I can do since you'll be here with us all summer? The least I can do given I rarely see you? The least I can do given you're a sickly, starving anorexic?*

I grabbed the second, smaller bag and followed behind my father and Mag up a flight of red-carpeted steps.

"Well, this is it!" announced Mag. I stepped in behind her and looked around. Plenty of charm, certainly, in the form of polished oak floors, plaster mouldings, and antique-looking chandeliers. But plenty of clutter, too—books stacked in haphazard piles throughout, crumb-filled plates teetering precariously on sofa arms, spilled tea on the dining table.

"Very nice," I said, making an effort to be polite. I took a step sideways, trying to avoid stepping on what appeared to be a pair of beige Lycra underpants. I didn't say anything.

"Oh dear, how did that get there?" Mag hastily swept up the underwear and tucked it into her purse.

"My hankie," she explained. "I often drop them at the door."

"Right," I said, though I knew what I'd seen. That was no hankie. I hoped there was an explanation for the proximity of Mag's underwear to the entryway that did not involve her or my father in various states of undress. I shuddered inwardly at the mental image.

"It's rather cozy, I'm afraid," said Dad, spreading out his hands to demonstrate the apartment's limited size. "Just the living room"—he motioned to the main room with the stacks of books and dirty dishes—"the dining room"—he pointed to a table in the living room, and I wondered at the label of "room"—"and the kitchen." He pointed at a small galley kitchen with white wooden cabinets and what looked like half a stainless-steel fridge and about two-thirds of a matching stove. I stared, intrigued. They were a bit like miniature versions of what we had back home, and I had the sensation of looking into a dollhouse.

"I've never seen such a small fridge and stove," I commented. "Are they all like that here?"

Mag dropped her keys on the countertop and made a face. "They're European-sized," she said primly. "Smaller spaces equal smaller appliances. No room for one of your space-age refrigerators."

I bristled. "Our kitchen in New York isn't much bigger than yours," I said, "But you can at least fit a chicken in the oven."

"I can cook a chicken," said Mag. Her voice was dry. "Maybe not an American chicken, caged and overfed with hormones and—"

"Why don't you show Clara her room, Alastair?" Dad cut her off with practiced ease and firmly turned Alastair's shoulders in the other direction.

The place wasn't really that much smaller than our apartment back in New York, but I suppose there were twice as many people living under its Parisian copper roof, and it felt like it. I followed Alastair back past the living room to a small bedroom. There was another, larger, room opposite, and a decent-sized bathroom between them.

"This is my room," Alastair informed me, turning on the light. "Mum and Dad said you get to have it for the summer." He didn't look pleased.

"I'm sorry," I told him, feeling guilty. "I didn't know."

"You don't have to be sorry," he said seriously. "It isn't your fault."

"Um, right." *Be patient*, I told myself. *He can't help it.*

The room was, in shocking contrast to the rest of the apartment, very neat. Spotless, in fact. The double bed was tidily made, the blue duvet cover with its printed sailboats flat and taut. The books were all in bookcases, carefully displayed with their spines facing outward and, it appeared after a second and more-studied glance, organized by color. Toys were cleverly tucked away in baskets and drawers, hidden from view. There were three pictures on the wall, each in a shiny, white plastic frame: one of Dad and Mag helping Alastair blow out the candles on his first birthday cake; one of an unremarkable-looking pizza; and one of an overweight gray tabby cat.

"Is that your cat?" I nodded at the last photograph.

Alastair brightened. For the first time, it seemed like he might even smile, but then his face fell serious again. "That's Minou," he said. "She's my best friend."

"Ah," I said. I wondered if he had any human friends. Children could be cruel in normal circumstances. What might they do to a kid like Alastair?

"Here she is," he added, lifting a pillow from atop his bed. "She likes to sleep under my pillow during the day."

Sure enough, the pillow's removal revealed a large gray

feline, even more portly in real life than in the picture. She looked at me and rose up, hissing loudly in my direction. I jumped back about three feet, nearly tripping over the leg of Alastair's desk, which was set against a large bay window. The cat leaped to the floor and gave me a disgusted look. I stared after it, wary. I'd never had a cat.

"She doesn't like me," I observed.

"She doesn't know you," he said. "It's her instinct. She's an animal."

"Right." I watched as Minou darted behind a pair of faded curtains printed with yellow duckies, and left only her nose and whiskers sticking out. It was actually sort of cute, if you ignored the fact that she had tried to attack me just moments before. "So, if I'm taking your room, where are you staying?"

Alastair went over to Minou and picked her up, cradling her like a baby. She purred contentedly, giving no hint that she was anything but a docile pet. Her emerald green eyes met mine and narrowed, suspicious.

"In Mum and Dad's room. I have a tent."

"A tent?"

"Yes. I don't like any lights or noises when I'm trying to sleep, so Mum got me a special tent."

"That's kind of cool," I offered. I'd had a Barbie play tent that I'd sometimes camp out in, when my friend Emily would sleep over. We'd had matching Disney Princess sleeping bags. "Do you have a sleeping bag?" I asked Alastair.

"I have a weighted blanket," he replied. He set down Minou and picked up a large, green-and-white striped quilt that was folded neatly on a shelf and handed it to me. "It helps me relax."

"Oh, wow, this is heavy!" Caught off-guard, my arms sagged and the blanket fell to the rug. "What's in here? Lead?"

"Sand," he said, his voice matter-of-fact. "Lead is dangerous."

"I know. I was kidding." I picked up the blanket and carefully folded it. "I've never seen anything like this before."

"It helps me settle," he explained. "I have a hard time falling asleep."

I nodded, not sure of what else to say. Everything about Alastair seemed foreign—alien, almost.

My father poked his head around the door. "You two okay in here?" he asked. He looked nervously at Alastair, then me, and then back at Alastair.

"Yes," answered Alastair. "I showed Clara my blanket."

"It's helpful for kids like Alastair, who are on the spectrum," Dad informed me. "They have issues with their sensory processing. The weighted blanket allows them to relax."

"Right," I said. I glanced over at Alastair. He didn't seem to mind that we were talking about him as if he weren't right there. I felt annoyed on his behalf.

"I see you've met Minou," Dad commented, bending to scratch the cat's head. She was circling his feet, poking her nose at his ankles. "She can be a bit…excitable."

"I noticed," I said dryly.

Minou looked up and made a sort of squawking noise, her back arched. Then she jumped straight up and took off.

"Cats," said my father with a shrug as we watched her depart. "Unpredictable."

"So, this is a great room," I said, turning my attention back to Alastair. "Thank you for sharing it with me."

"I'm not sharing it," he corrected. "I'm staying with Mum and Dad."

"Borrowing, then." I paused. "I promise to keep it neat."

He nodded. "I would appreciate that. I don't like messes."

I wondered how he dealt with the rest of the apartment. Perhaps they kept it that way intentionally, as some sort of cutting-edge exposure therapy. I'd once seen a talk show where they brought in giant tarantulas to try to cure this guy of his arachnophobia. I don't know if it worked, though, because I'd been so freaked out I'd had to turn off the TV.

"Alastair," said Dad, "why don't you go feed Minou?"

Alastair frowned, glancing at the large red digital watch he wore on his right wrist. "It's not four o'clock. I always feed her at four."

"Water, then. You can refill her water dish."

Alastair didn't look convinced, but left the room. Dad quietly moved to shut the door.

"Thank you for being patient with him," he said. He went over and sat on the edge of the bed. "I know it can be difficult to get used to."

I shrugged, feeling guilty. I stared at the navy rug, subtly littered with fine gray cat hairs. I didn't feel like I had been patient.

"He's high-functioning, but he's on the autism spectrum," Dad continued. "He's also quite gifted, academically."

"Yeah, I guessed." That much I had noticed. I didn't think many six-year-olds read articles online. Not the one or two I'd babysat for, anyway.

"It's tough," he said, and I noticed his voice was tired. "He's bright, but he just doesn't grasp social norms. Things like slang expressions or humor are beyond him. And the other kids…" His voice trailed off.

"They're mean?" I went over and sat down next to my father. It felt odd; this was the closest we'd been, physically, in years. I inched away slightly, unnerved by the strangeness of it.

"They're mean. And he still has feelings, you know. He's just a kid."

I pictured Alastair as a teenager, exposed to someone like Avril. I couldn't help but shudder. Kids were merciless.

Dad said something else, but I didn't catch it. My eyes wandered around the room, taking in not only the tidiness, but also the decor, the furniture, the bric-a-brac.

"What's with the sailboats?" I asked, nodding at the duvet we sat on. I poked at one, embroidered in red thread on an ocean-blue background.

Dad looked puzzled. "I don't know," he said. "It's a blanket. What do you mean?"

"It's babyish," I said flatly. "Embarrassing. If you want him to be normal, you have to act like he's normal."

Dad still appeared confused. "I don't follow."

I stood, feeling exasperated. "This room. Those curtains." I pointed at the ridiculous parade of duckies decorating the bay window. "They're ridiculous. He's six."

"Oh." Dad nodded slowly. "What should they be?"

"I don't know. Batman? Angry Birds? Something cool."

He looked wary. "Mag isn't going to like that."

"Do you want him to get beaten up?" I felt angry. For a long minute, neither of us said anything. Avoiding my father's troubled look, I stared at the wall opposite and again noticed the hanging trio of pictures. "What's with the pizza?" I asked, pointing at the middle photograph.

Dad brightened. "He made it himself," he said. "He likes to cook. He loves knowing what ingredients go into something, or trying to guess by how it tastes." He stood and went over to the pizza photo, gazing at it fondly. "It started because of his allergy—asking about the ingredients, I mean. But then it sort of took on a life of its own. It's fairly common for people like Alastair to have a special interest," he added. "Something that they're preoccupied with." As if sensing my unease, he said, "We can talk more later. You must be tired. Why don't you go take a nice hot bath?"

I nodded, relieved. A shower sounded great, I told him.

"Oh," he said, looking awkward. "I should have mentioned."

I caught the tone of his voice and frowned. "Mentioned what?"

"We, er, don't have a shower."

"I'm sorry?" I stared at him blankly.

"A shower. We don't actually have one. Just a bath. It's quite common in Europe, you know."

No, I didn't know. *No shower*, I thought gloomily. *No*

shower for the whole summer. I unzipped my suitcase as my father disappeared into the hallway, eager to escape. I thought longingly of home, homesick for my bathroom and its American comforts. I wondered how one went about washing one's hair in a bathtub. Did you dunk under the water? It was going to be a long summer.

CHAPTER 11

"No," I moaned, as an unfamiliar man with red hair pushed the plateful of chocolate cake closer to me. "No."

Suddenly, the floor disappeared and I was falling. *No. Not again*, my body screamed. *No.*

I awoke with a start, my heart pounding. Gasping, I threw off the duvet and frowned. *Where was I?* I stared at the unfamiliar light fixture overhead, uncomprehending. Then I caught a glimpse of duckies out of the corner of my eye and groaned, pulling the sailboat duvet over my face.

Paris. Dad. Alastair. Mag.

I rolled over and reached for my phone. It was nearly eleven, according to the bright display. I wondered if Mag had already left; I had a vague memory of her mentioning an early seminar this morning. I crossed my fingers that she wouldn't be outside, waiting to pepper me with more passive-aggressive

120

comments. Yesterday over supper she had found my confusion over the bathtub absolutely hilarious.

"You can run the water to wash your hair, you know," she said, smirking, as I commented on the difficulties of dunking with a head full of suds. "I can't believe you've never taken a bath. Do you really let the shower run the entire time you're in? It seems so wasteful."

"Filling up a bathtub seems wasteful to me," I'd replied, stabbing a piece of overcooked chicken rather forcefully with my fork. "And sitting in one's own dirt is definitely odd."

Dad had intervened then, hastily steering the conversation back to my unpaid summer job as Alastair's de facto nanny.

"You can start your sightseeing tomorrow!" He said, trying to sound enthusiastic. "What do you want to start with, do you think? The Eiffel Tower? The Louvre?"

"Maybe the Louvre." I didn't particularly care. "Whatever Alastair wants."

Alastair didn't say much during dinner, focused as he was on his plate. He arranged his food carefully, ensuring that the chicken did not touch the rice, and that the rice did not touch the carrots. I watched him with a mixture of fascination and repulsion.

Now, I sighed and heaved myself out of bed, landing on something soft and furry. There was a loud screeching sound and I jumped. Minou glared at me reproachfully, back arched like a Halloween graphic. I glared right back.

"How did you get in here?" I asked her, annoyed.

As if understanding me, she turned towards the door and strolled out through the cat-flap.

Great, I thought. *Eight weeks of being stalked by an angry cat.* Maybe I could tape up the flap, but that might upset Alastair. *Do I get dressed?* I wondered. At home, I'd wander to the kitchen for coffee in my pajamas without a second thought. But here I felt awkward. Dad and Alastair would surely be dressed by now.

I looked out the window. No rain, but still gray. Even the people seemed gray, an undistinguishable sea of black and beige overcoats. I wondered if the sun ever shone here, or whether I'd spend the summer dodging grim skies and drizzle. Idly, I reached again for my phone and opened my weather app. *Sunny in New York,* I noted, and sighed.

I rummaged through my still-unpacked bags, and settled on jeans and a vintage blouse. It itched around the shoulders, but this was Paris. I didn't want to be sneered at for dressing in a faded NYU tee, no matter how comfortable it was. Resigned to discomfort, I unearthed my high-heeled boots and zipped them on.

Dad and Alastair were waiting in the living room. Dad had his laptop open and was frowning at the screen. Alastair was working intently on building some sort of spaceship out of Lego, the instructional pamphlet spread out in front of him.

"Morning," I said, feeling awkward.

Dad shut the laptop and grinned. "Morning! Or, should I say, 'almost afternoon?'"

I smiled weakly at the lame attempt at humor. "Sorry," I said. "Jet lag."

"I'm just kidding." He looked at Alastair, who had yet

to acknowledge me. "Alastair, did you say good morning to Clara?"

"Good morning," Alastair said automatically. He didn't look up from his Lego.

"Whatcha building?" I knelt down next to him, trying to be friendly.

"Starship *Enterprise*," he said, still not looking at me. He turned a page of the directions.

"Cool. That's from *Star Wars*, right?"

"No. It's from *Star Trek*. They're not the same." He sounded anxious. For the first time, he looked up at me.

"Right. Um, sorry. Anyway, it looks great."

I looked at Dad. "Is there coffee?" I eyed a mug on the coffee table hopefully.

"Yes!" Dad jumped up. "Where are my manners, you must be starved." He disappeared into the kitchen and came back with a chipped blue mug and a matching plate.

"Coffee and a fresh croissant," he announced. "From the bakery downstairs. Best in Paris, in my opinion."

"Thanks," I said. I took the plate and set it down on the coffee table. The croissant looked as if it had been prepared with approximately half a pound of butter. I took a sip of coffee. "This is good," I commented.

Alastair looked up at me now with interest. "We use a French press," he said. "Mum says it makes a superior cup of coffee."

I raised my eyebrows and laughed. "You sound like a commercial."

He gazed at me seriously. "I've never seen a commercial."

"No?" I looked around the living room and realized there was no television in sight. "Wait. Do you guys not have a TV?"

Dad looked up guiltily. "No," he said. "Mag doesn't approve."

I think my feelings must have been pretty obvious, because he started stammering something about being able to stream movies and shows on the computer if there was anything I wanted to watch. I waved my hand, irritated. "Never mind me. What about Alastair? What about *Star Trek?*"

Dad grabbed his own mug. He didn't say anything.

"I've seen some TV," offered Alastair. "I've seen movies at school. I liked it, but Mum says it isn't good for my brain. My brain is already different, you know. I read *Star Trek* books instead."

I didn't respond. I wondered if kids like Alastair weren't supposed to watch television. How did he interact with the other kids at school? Presumably the majority were permitted to watch SpongeBob, or whatever it was kids watched these days.

"Try the croissant," Dad said, changing the subject. "You'll love it."

I groaned inwardly. "Dad," I could feel my face grow hot and red with a mix of frustration, anger, and embarrassment. "I can't eat this."

He blinked, realization slowly dawning on his face. "Oh," he said. He took a deep breath. "I know I'm probably going to say the wrong thing here regardless, so I'm just going to go ahead. I think you should eat the croissant."

Alastair was frowning at me. "Do you have allergies?"

I sighed. "No."

"Diabetes?"

"No."

"Then why can't you eat the croissant?"

"It's not healthy," I said quietly. "I don't eat unhealthy food."

"Why?"

"Because I want to be healthy."

"You can eat unhealthy food sometimes and still be healthy," he informed me. "Mum says it's about moderation."

I tried not to snort. Mag didn't look like moderation was something that concerned her all that much. At dinner last night, she'd eaten two and a half chicken breasts and three servings of rice.

"Why don't you just try the croissant?" Dad picked up the plate and waved it under my nose. "You're in Paris. Come on. Just a bite."

Alastair stared at me expectantly.

"Fine!" I said, exasperated. "If you'll leave me alone after."

I grabbed the croissant and bit into it. The crispy, flaking exterior gave way to delicate and soft buttery innards. I chewed slowly, overwhelmed at both the perfection of the taste and texture. I swallowed and put the remaining pastry down quickly, alarmed.

"Well?" Dad grinned.

"It's a good croissant," I allowed.

"Best in Paris," he said again. "Jean-Pierre is a master of

his craft. And now he's teaching Michelle. Passing it on to the next generation."

I guessed that Jean-Pierre was the baker and Michelle his daughter. I wondered how Michelle dealt with the daily temptations of the bakery. She almost certainly wasn't fat. French women are never fat, apparently. There are actual books written on the phenomenon.

"Aren't you going to finish it?" Alastair was watching me again with his solemn green eyes. He had a way of looking at me that made me feel as if he could somehow read my thoughts. Unnerved by his penetrating gaze, I looked away.

"I said I'd just take a bite." I sipped my coffee.

"But if you like it, why not eat the whole thing?" He frowned again. He frowned a lot, this kid. I'm not sure I'd yet seen him smile. Maybe kids like Alastair didn't smile. The notion left me sad.

"I told you," I said patiently. "It isn't healthy."

"But you're only having one."

"Still. It's, like, ninety percent butter."

Alastair regarded me seriously. "It isn't," he said. "Michelle sometimes lets me watch, in the bakery. It's not ninety percent."

I felt the urge to close my eyes and rub my temples, the way perplexed parents do in the movies. "I just meant that there's a lot of butter in it."

"Butter isn't bad, though. It's a natural product," Alastair persisted.

I looked over at my father for help, but it seemed he was actually *enjoying* this. *Sure*, I thought angrily, *he thinks I have an eating disorder, and this is somehow going to help. Like I'm an alcoholic in need of an intervention.* I dug my nails into the waistband of my jeans.

"Butter," I said levelly, "is full of fat."

Alastair looked surprised. "But you don't get fat if you eat it."

"Yes," I said, gritting my teeth. "You do."

"I eat butter all the time, and I'm only in the twenty-fifth percentile for weight for my age. The doctor said so."

"Well, not all of us are that lucky," I snapped.

"Why is that lucky?" Now he looked puzzled.

"If I ate a lot of butter, I would get fat," I said flatly. "I'm not skinny like you. So I don't want to. Okay?"

He studied me, not saying anything for several minutes. "You are skinny," he said finally. "What percentile are you in?"

"I don't know!" I felt my temper and voice both rise. "Can you just drop it?"

"Drop what?" He looked at his hands. "I'm not holding anything."

That was it. "I'll be in my room," I announced, trying to stay calm. I grabbed my coffee cup. "I need to call Mom."

I didn't look back as I shut the door forcefully behind me. Taking a deep breath, I raised the coffee cup to my lips. There was a small croissant crumb on the rim. I caught it with the edge of my tongue, savoring its tantalizing flavor.

We went to the Louvre, the three of us. Alastair brought his camera, one of those that spits out a print right away. Dad reminisced about something similar they'd had back in the eighties called a Polaroid. I thought of Bree and her SLR and felt a pang of homesickness. I hadn't yet heard from her, though that was to be expected—her camp in the woods didn't have regular phone and Internet service.

The museum was incredibly crowded. When I had envisioned strolling the halls of the Louvre, gazing at famous works of art, I hadn't anticipated the throngs of tourists battling for prime viewing space in front of a Renoir or Matisse. As a New Yorker, I was used to masses of people and the ensuing pushing and shoving, but this was much worse than anything I'd ever experienced at the Met or the Museum of Natural History.

Alastair didn't take well to the crowds. At one point, he sat down in the middle of a gallery and started rocking back and forth, his hands over his ears. Alarmed and embarrassed, I stood helpless while my father swiftly moved him aside and retrieved a pair of noise-canceling headphones from his backpack.

"It's the sensory issues," he explained. "The earphones help with the noise. They soothe him."

"Right," I said, uneasily. How would I deal with this sort of situation on my own? Would I know when to break out the earphones?

"He also has a weighted vest," Dad said. "I didn't think to bring it. I didn't realize how busy it would be."

"It's crazy," I agreed. "Should we just go?" I glanced over

at Alastair, who had ceased rocking now that the earphones were on his head. He stared straight ahead, his eyes half-closed.

"No, let's go see the *Mona Lisa* first. We're already here."

Dad took Alastair's hand and I followed close behind, afraid to lose them in this maze of never-ending hallways. Dad had mentioned that you could spend months at the Louvre and not see everything, and I'd been skeptical at the time. I understood now.

"Through here," Dad said, motioning. He held Alastair firmly around the shoulders and steered us into a room teeming with people. We tried to make our way in closer for a better look, but it was nearly impossible. Alastair began to make small noises that reminded me of an injured bird I'd once come across in the schoolyard.

"I'm going to take Alastair over there." Dad pointed in the direction of an adjacent gallery space. "Have a look at *Mona Lisa* and meet us. Take your time, though."

Standing on my toes, I stared at the painting. It looked exactly like it did in books and movies. Nearby, an older woman wept as she gazed at the famous smile. I tried to concentrate and have some sort of spiritual moment. I waited for it, hopeful. Where was the thrill, the sensation of wonder at being in the presence of something extraordinary? I stared harder, but still felt nothing. I wondered idly if anything could evoke that response anymore, or if the Internet and smartphone had dulled my capacity for awe. Aware of my own cynicism, I stepped away.

CHAPTER 12

"Here," said Dad. He fished out a wad of euros from his wallet and handed them to me. "Take this. It should be enough."

"Thanks," I said, pocketing the cash. I shifted awkwardly from foot to foot, wincing as the heel of my left boot caught in a sidewalk crack. "So, you're leaving now?" I tried not to sound panicked.

"I have to go in to work for an hour or so," he said. "I'll meet you back at home by suppertime. Alastair knows the way—and here's a map." He fumbled in his briefcase, pulling out a faded and crumpled map of the city.

"Dad," I said, embarrassed. "It's okay. I have my phone." I held it up, as evidence.

He stared at it blankly.

"GPS," I clarified. "Google Maps. I'll be fine."

"Right." He shook his head. "I feel old."

He leaned over to ruffle Alastair's hair, but Alastair ducked out of the way, cringing.

"Okay, okay," said Dad. He sighed. "Be good. Have fun."

"Wait!" I cried as he turned to leave. "What are we supposed to do?"

Dad shrugged. "Whatever you want," he said. "It's Paris. Explore." He waved, then hastened off.

My anxiety rapidly mounting, I watched Alastair out of the corner of my eye. He was no longer wearing the headphones; they'd been tucked into the backpack, which I was now holding.

"Alastair," I said. "Here." I handed him the backpack.

He frowned. "Mum and Dad always carry the backpack."

"It's got your stuff in it," I pointed out. "Your earphones and your EpiPen. You're six. You should carry it. Don't you have one for school?"

"No," he replied. "We have a book bag for school. Everyone has the same one."

"Well, it's almost the same thing."

He held the backpack, looking dubious. "Okay," he said finally. He slid his arms through the straps. It was a bit big for him—it was an adult model—but he managed.

"See?" I said.

"It's for an adult," he said, frowning. "It's big."

I sighed. Alastair made me sigh a lot. "It's fine for now. But we'll get you a smaller one."

"We will?"

"Yes, we will," I said firmly.

Alastair looked uneasy. I had read that kids on the autism spectrum like routine and predictability. Still, he was six years old. He should carry his own backpack. I was starting to think Dad and Mag babied him too much. Ducky curtains were clearly just one symptom of a much larger problem.

I tightened the straps so the pack sat more firmly on Alastair's narrow shoulders, gazing beyond him at the glass pyramid that served as gateway to the Louvre. I felt a spark of something that had been noticeably absent at the *Mona Lisa*, and felt hopeful.

"Isn't it cool?" I said to Alastair, gesturing at the pyramid. He turned to look. "I don't know," he answered.

"Don't you like how new and modern it looks compared to the older building?" The juxtaposition of the intricate architecture of the ancient-looking palace, the former home to French royalty, and the stark, clean lines of the pyramid was startling.

Alastair didn't answer. He swayed gently back and forth. I wondered suddenly if he was as nervous to be with me as I was with him.

"So what's fun around here?" I asked him. "Is there a zoo? A park?"

Alastair stared at his shoes. "There's the *Jardin des Tuileries*," he said. "It's like a park. And there's a carnival there."

"A carnival! Perfect." I grinned at Alastair. "Have you been?"

"No." He shook his head. "I'm not supposed to go on rides."

I sighed. Nothing with this kid was ever simple. "Why?"

"Because of my sensory issues. Mum is worried I would react badly."

For a moment, I said nothing. Alastair continued to study his clunky, decidedly uncool shoes—they actually had buckles on them—and I watched a group of kids skip excitedly through the square, giggling noisily, backpacks bouncing. They were all about Alastair's age. One girl shrieked something in rapid French that I couldn't catch, and the others all burst out laughing. Two harried-looking teens about my own age were at the head of the group, trying to keep the kids walking in the same direction. A day camp, I thought. I looked at Alastair to gauge his reaction, but he hadn't even noticed them. Was he really that different from them? Could he really not ride a carousel?

"I think you should try going on rides," I said finally. "How do you know you'll react badly, if you've never tried? Maybe you'll like it."

"Maybe," he said. He looked hopeful. "I have always wanted to try the Ferris wheel."

"Great," I said enthusiastically. "I love Ferris wheels. You get such a great view." I paused. "You're not afraid of heights, are you?"

"I don't think so," he said, frowning. "I don't know. I've never been high up."

"What about on a plane?"

"I don't remember," he said. "I haven't flown since I was three."

I shrugged. "Okay, then," I said. "We'll just have to see."

He looked worried. "But what if I'm scared?"

I shrugged again. "If you hate it, we won't go again. But how will you know unless you try?"

Alastair nodded slowly. "That makes sense," he said. He took a deep breath. "Let's go."

The Tuileries Gardens reminded me a bit of Central Park. There was a similar vibe to both—a feeling of people brought together to enjoy a bit of nature in the midst of a bustling city. Alastair and I strolled through, pausing to stop and look at the colorful arrays of flowers.

"Do you know anything about flowers?" I asked him, bending to examine an assortment of bright yellow buds.

"No," he said. "Dad would know. He always stops to name the flowers. He knows their names in Latin."

"Does he?" I asked, surprised. "I didn't know that." I gently fingered the tip of a yellow petal.

"Well, you probably don't really know Dad all that well," Alastair said with his usual tact. "You don't see him very much."

I felt a pang at the truth of his statement, and wondered what other interesting things about my father I didn't know. I pushed the thought aside and bent over the flowers.

"Smell them," I said, inhaling deeply. "They smell amazing."

Alastair shook his head furiously and stepped back. "I don't like smells," he said anxiously.

"But it's a nice smell," I said, wheedling. "Come on."

"No." His voice was firm.

"Well, all right," I said, straightening. "Let's keep going, then."

"Wait," said Alastair suddenly. He swung the backpack to the ground and unzipped it, retrieving his camera. "I want to take a picture."

"Sure," I said. "Of the flowers?"

"Of you, with the flowers," he said. "Bending over like that. It looks nice."

I blinked, startled at this unexpected display of artistic sensibility. His expression and voice didn't change, but it was as close to emotional as I'd seen him so far.

I posed while Alastair stood, eyebrows furrowed as he composed the photo. I heard a click and a whirring sound as he snapped the picture, and a little black card popped out the bottom.

"That is really cool," I commented, watching as Alastair stared at the photo critically. "How does it look?"

"You have to wait a minute or so," he said. "It comes out dark and blurry."

"Okay," I said. I went to stand so I could look over his shoulder, peering at the little square. All I could make out was a dark blob.

"There," said Alastair, pointing. "That's you."

"Ugh," I said, joking. "Maybe I should start wearing more makeup."

He looked up at me. "It's not ready yet," he said seriously. "That's not what you look like."

"Right," I said, nodding. I didn't know whether I felt like rolling my eyes or hugging him tightly. I did neither.

The photograph slowly lightened to reveal me, laughing, with my hair falling in my face over a clump of yellow blooms. Alastair looked pleased.

"It's a nice shot," I said to him. "Good work."

"Thank you." He offered me the picture. "Do you want to keep it?"

"Really?" I took the photo in my hand. "You don't mind?"

"No."

"Well, thanks." Touched, I tucked it into my bag. I tried to think of something else to say, something meaningful. The sort of thing an older sister might say. I came up blank. Fortunately, Alastair didn't notice.

"There's the Ferris wheel," he said, gesturing.

We made our way over and bought tickets. The man selling them smiled kindly at my feeble attempt at French and answered me in perfect English. I blushed and thanked him, Alastair clinging nervously to my jeans.

"What's wrong?" I asked him, as we got in line. "Having cold feet?"

"Feet?" he asked, puzzled. He stared at his shoes,. "No, they're fine. I'm a bit nervous about the ride, though."

I resisted the urge to laugh. "Cold feet," I explained, "is an expression. It means to change your mind about something at the last minute."

"Oh," he said. His face didn't change. "I'm not very good at those. Thank you for telling me."

"No problem."

"My feet might be a bit cool," he said then. He was looking warily up at the Ferris wheel. "It looks so high from here."

"It's fun, though," I said. "I promise."

We advanced a few paces. I watched as the attendant loaded and unloaded people onto the ride. In front of us, two preteen girls ate pink candy floss on sticks and murmured in low tones. Behind us was an elderly couple speaking Spanish.

"Clara?" Alastair's voice was small.

"Yes?" I looked at his fearful expression and knew what was coming next."

"My feet are freezing." He pointed at them for emphasis.

"You don't want to get on?" I kept my tone light.

"No."

"You're sure?"

"Yes." His voice was barely a whisper now.

"Okay, Buddy." I put an arm around him, and noted that he didn't squirm. "Let's go."

We excused ourselves from the line, ducking under the ropes. Overhead, the sun peeked through and I felt my skin warm almost immediately.

"Sun's coming out," I observed, smiling. "That should warm up your feet."

"They're not really cold," he said. "It's just an expression, remember?"

"I know, but it is a lot warmer with the sun out." I looked around, trying to decide what to do next. "Why don't we try the carousel?" I suggested. I pointed at the merry-go-round, a beautiful antique specimen with both an upper and lower level. There were horses and cats, rabbits and elephants, all intricately carved and painted. It was filled with younger kids, mostly toddlers and preschoolers, and their parents.

He sized it up, his head cocked slightly to one side. "Could we stay on the first floor?"

"Absolutely," I said, eyeing the rickety steps to the top uneasily. I wondered just how old the carousel was.

"Okay," he said, breathing deeply. "I'll try it."

There was no lineup. We waited for the music to stop and the current riders to dismount. I handed our tickets to the attendant, and looked at Alastair. "Ready?"

"Yes." He looked around at the menagerie of animals. "I would like to ride the elephant."

"Good choice," I said. I helped him up. "You okay?"

"Yes," he said. He clutched the pole tightly, his eyes fixed straight ahead. "No cold feet."

"Awesome," I answered. I swung myself up onto a giant, grinning orange tabby cat wearing a hat and ruffled cravat. "I think you'll like this."

The melody started, an old-fashioned recording of loud, upbeat organ music. The ride began to turn and my cat slowly ascended. Straddling the oversized animal, I held the tarnished brass post and looked over at Alastair. His face was thus far expressionless, and I felt a swell of anxiety. *What if he couldn't handle it? What if he had an episode like he'd had in the Louvre, and ended up releasing the pole, tumbling head first from his mount?*

The carousel picked up momentum, turning faster and faster. The animals went up and down with increased speed. I watched Alastair's face. *Should I get off? Go stand behind him?* Again, I pictured him rocking back and forth on his elephant, falling in slow motion to the ground as he lost his balance.

But suddenly, Alastair laughed, and I realized I hadn't heard him laugh before. It was an odd, high-pitched but beautiful sound. His cheeks were flushed with excitement and his curly hair whipped about his face in the wind. I felt a surge of joy, a feeling in the pit of my stomach that had nothing to do with the merry-go-round.

CHAPTER 13

"We should stop and see Michelle," said Alastair. This was our third outing this week, and I was beginning to learn my way around the winding streets of the fifth arrondissement: the tree-lined Boulevard Saint-Michel, with its assortment of old shops and new, designer boutiques intermingled with used and rare bookstores, independent cinemas with trendy nightclubs; and the Boulevard Saint-Germain, where Armani competes for space with ancient cafés where famous writers and intellectuals once drank and waxed poetic about everything from politics to philosophy to science. Today, students crowd these same spaces, passionately debating the same topics. Alastair served as my translator, though at six he could only provide vague descriptions. My own high-school French had proved to be woefully inadequate.

"They're talking about love, I think," he said when we

stopped at the legendary *Les Deux Magots*. Dad said it's one of most celebrated cafés in all of Paris, and that I absolutely had to see it. I sat with Alastair at a small table under the famed white-and-green awning, his feet swinging off his chair as he stirred his juice with a straw. He had wanted a cookie, but I'd nixed the idea, fearful that something might secretly be harboring nuts. I don't know how to say "anaphylaxis" in French. Instead, he ordered a croque monsieur, which the waiter assured me was safe.

"Croque monsieur is my favorite food," Alastair had informed me earlier. "I've made it with Michelle. First, you take butter and melt it, and then flour…"

I tried to pay attention as Alastair reeled off the ingredients for his favorite, which basically looked like a ham and cheese sandwich with more cheese melted on top. Instead, I found myself eavesdropping on those around me. I sipped my coffee, feeling very young compared to the college students engaged in loud and earnest conversation.

"What about love?" I asked now, curious. There was a boisterous group at the table right behind us. I'd asked Alastair what it was they were going on about. They were speaking much too fast for me to catch anything save a word or two.

Alastair frowned and cocked his head, listening. "It doesn't make any sense," he said flatly. He took a large bite of his sandwich.

"Maybe I can help." I warmed my hands on my coffee cup; for July it was still awfully cool. The gray mist that had welcomed me off the plane had yet to subside and give way to any real sunshine. I'd purchased some funky faux-silk scarves from a street vendor and had become reliant on them for warmth, tying one loosely around my neck each morning.

"You look very French," Dad had joked. "*Trés chic.*"

"I just want to be *trés chaude*," I'd said.

Alastair fidgeted in his seat as he strained to listen to the students. "They're saying something like that you can't really love someone because you don't really know who they are. Because people act differently and pretend when they want someone to like them." He looked bewildered, his freckled cheeks flushed with the effort of eavesdropping.

"Ah," I said, nodding. "I kind of get it."

"You do?"

"I think so." I pulled my scarf tighter, trying to block the wind that had suddenly picked up. "They're saying that when you like someone, and you want them to like you, you act differently. Like if they like action movies, maybe you'll pretend you do too, so you have more to talk about. Or they'll pretend they like the same books as you. So if everyone is always doing that, always faking, how can you know who you really love, or if someone really loves you?"

Alastair's expression didn't alter, the confusion still readily apparent in his eyes. "I don't understand that kind of stuff," he said. His tone didn't change. "I don't pretend I like things." He pushed away his juice glass, now empty. "Dad and Mum have tried to explain it," he said. "That people don't always say what they're thinking, or that they mean something else. It doesn't make any sense to me. If I say something, I mean it."

"I know," I replied. I studied Alastair's earnest face, and

wondered what it would be like to exist without sarcasm or irony, without ever having to lie or suck up or feign interest. Maybe I shouldn't feel sorry for him; maybe he should feel sorry for the rest of us.

"Do you pretend a lot?" asked Alastair. He picked at the remainder of his croque monsieur, mostly crusts at this point. "Do you fake things?"

I gazed at him thoughtfully. "Sometimes," I said. "Not so much with you, really, though." I realized it was true. Alastair was frustrating, certainly—his candor could be infuriating—but it was refreshing not have to constantly engage in self-censorship.

"You don't pretend you're interested in things I like," said Alastair. "Like food. You don't like food."

I coughed, surprised. It felt a bit like an accusation. "Of course I like food," I said automatically.

"No, you don't," he answered. "You don't eat anything that tastes good. No sauces. No spices. No desserts. No *bread*."

"Not everyone likes bread," I said defensively.

He stared at me in that unnerving way of his, unblinking. "I think most people like bread. Maybe some people don't eat it, but I think most like it."

I thought of my mother, of our failed outing to Donatello's. The expression on her face when she'd sunk her teeth into that crusty bread, her eyes half-closing in pleasure. *It's been so long*, she'd said, or something like that. *I'd forgotten how good it was.*

"I don't really like it," I said lamely. I avoided his scrutiny and looked into my coffee. I was drinking it black; the café offered only cream, and I was too embarrassed to ask the scowling waiter for milk.

"You liked the croissant," he pointed out. "You just didn't want to eat it."

I sighed. "Look. Liking something and wanting to eat it are very different."

"Don't you feel sad, though? When you put down the croissant, or when everyone is eating a fresh baguette and you're just sitting there, watching?"

"No," I said firmly. "I don't. Because I know I'm doing the right thing."

"It's a baguette," he said, puzzled. "How can it be right or wrong? Stealing a baguette is wrong, but I don't think eating it is."

"I don't want to talk about this anymore," I said. I stared out at the street, my eyes focused on the passersby. The streets were nearly as busy here in the summertime as they were in New York, but people didn't move quite as quickly. Things were slower here.

He hesitated. "I heard Mum and Dad talking. They said you have an eating disorder. What does that mean?"

"I don't have an eating disorder," I said irritably. "An eating disorder is when you, like, starve yourself and make yourself throw up. I don't do any of those things."

"What does 'disorder' mean?"

"Like a disease. Do I seem like I have a disease?" I was upset now. I pushed my coffee away. I'd had too much, anyway; I could feel my heart racing in my chest.

Alastair looked pensive. "You're on the spectrum," he said finally.

"Excuse me?"

Alastair nodded. "I'm on the autism spectrum, but I'm not autistic. You're on the eating-disorder spectrum."

"I am not." I stiffened.

"I think you are. You're not normal." His voice was frank. "Normal people eat bread."

"Can you drop it, please, Alastair?"

"That means you want me to stop talking about this?"

I grit my teeth. "Yes. Yes, it does."

"Okay," he said simply. He slid off his chair, and that's when he mentioned Michelle. "We should stop and see Michelle on the way home," he said. "I always go to the bakery and help on Wednesdays."

I again imagined Michelle, a tall, slim blonde who effortlessly maintained a size-zero figure despite regularly indulging in *pain au chocolat*.

"I don't know," I said reluctantly.

Alastair looked anxious. "But I always go on Wednesdays. It's Wednesday. I have to go." His voice rose in pitch as his urgency mounted.

"Okay, okay." I dropped a few euros on the table. "Let's get going, then."

It was drizzling when we reached the bakery. "Maybe I'll just drop you off," I said. I looked longingly at the stairs. I wanted to check my email and my Facebook page, see if Bree had finally found the time and Internet connection to write. Maybe even call my mom. I'd spoken to her briefly that first day, but not since. She'd sent me several worried emails, but I'd been too busy to reply.

"No," said Alastair, worried. "You can't leave me. You have to come in."

"Fine," I sighed. I ducked under the awning as the rain picked up. "After you, then."

Alastair pushed open the door, setting off a small chime. The man in front was a bit older than Dad, with dark skin, a graying beard, and a bald head. "Alastair, *bonjour!*" he exclaimed. He had the sort of warm brown eyes that twinkled when the light caught them, and brown skin to match. He looked at me. "*Et c'est qui?*" He asked, smiling. "*Votre copine?*"

Even I could understand that he'd just asked if I was Alastair's girlfriend. I gave a small, obliging laugh, but Alastair shook his head furiously. "*Ma soeur,*" he said. "Clara."

"Clara, a please to meet you." His English was heavily accented. "I am Jean-Pierre."

"*Enchanté,*" I said politely.

He laughed loudly and called out to the back room, "Michelle!"

A tall guy, maybe a few years my senior, emerged from the back. Wearing a dusty apron and covered in flour, he beamed upon seeing Alastair. He had the same eyes as Jean-Pierre, but his skin was somewhat lighter. His head was a mass of unruly curls, not unlike Alastair's but decidedly darker in color.

"Bonjour," he said formally, noticing me.

"Bonjour," I stammered. Who was this insanely hot guy? How could Alastair fail to mention Michelle's delicious brother?

He reached over the counter and stuck out his hand. "Michel," he said.

Michelle? This was Michelle? My eyes widened, and inwardly I cursed my American ear. *Of course. Michel. Not Michelle.*

"Clara," I said weakly, shaking his hand. It was warm and surprisingly soft.

"The American sister," he said, smiling. "We heard you were coming." His English was much better than his father's.

"Yes," I said stupidly.

"Did you like the croissants?"

"I'm sorry?" I felt my cheeks go pink.

"Monsieur Singerman, he came by on your first day for croissants. For your breakfast. Did you like them?"

Oh, God. "Yes!" I said quickly. "Yes, they were delicious."

"You only had one bite," Alastair said, frowning. He turned to Michel. "Clara doesn't really like food."

"Yes, I do!" I kept smiling, and put an arm around Alastair. *Please*, I begged him silently. *Please, don't.*

I kept talking, desperate to change the subject. "Alastair says he comes here every Wednesday."

"Yes," said Michel. He smiled fondly at my brother. "He's a very good helper. *Un petit boulanger.* Great mind for ingredients."

"Right," I said. I paused.

"I'm being rude." Michel dusted some flour off the front of his apron. "Come this way." He said something in rapid French to his father, who nodded and waved us on behind the counter.

The back room was a large space that was a bit of a cross between a kitchen and a warehouse. Huge ovens flanked by oversized refrigerators lined the walls, and in the center of the room was a large workspace topped with marble and stainless steel.

"Today, we are making *le pain Suisse*," said Michel.

"Swiss bread?" I asked, hoping to sound clever.

Michel laughed. "Not quite," he said. He sprinkled some flour across a large marble board and smoothed it with his hand. "It is a kind of pastry, with chocolate and custard."

Custard. I pictured something like pudding and breathed deeply, feeling anxious.

"First, we shall prepare the custard." He reached up and retrieved a saucepan from an overhead pot rack. "Alastair, please separate the eggs." He nodded at a carton of eggs and a small dish laid out nearby.

"Can he do that?" I asked dubiously. Separating eggs—the act of isolating the yellow yolks—sounded difficult for anyone, let alone a child. I had enough trouble breaking an egg without getting bits of shell in the pan or puncturing the yolk.

Michel looked surprised. "Of course," he said. "*Naturellement.* Alastair has been separating eggs since he was four years."

"Huh," I said. I watched Alastair's small hands handle the

eggs with the grace and deftness of an expert. It was impressive.

"Now, Clara," Michel looked at me and handed me a stack of glass measuring cups. "I need one cup of milk and one cup of cream."

"Um, sure," I said, startled. I looked around blankly. "In the fridge, I guess?"

"*Oui*," said Michel. He winked at me, and pulled out a small knife and something long, black, and shriveled, like a kind of skinny prune.

"What is that?" I asked, interested.

He looked amused. "*Vanille*," he said. "Vanilla bean."

I looked closer. "Really? That's a bean?"

"*Oui.*"

I watched, fascinated, as Michel carefully sliced the bean lengthwise, opening it to reveal millions of tiny black seeds.

"Wow," I breathed. "So that's where vanilla comes from."

Michel paused and trained his sparkling eyes on mine. "Where did you think it came from?"

I shook my head. "I guess I never thought about it."

I found the milk and cream and did my part, carefully measuring the quantities as if I were in chemistry class. "There," I said. "One cup of each."

"*Bon*," said Michel. He had finished scraping the inside of the vanilla bean. "Please pour it in here." He held out the saucepan.

I added the liquid, watching the milk pour quickly and the cream, which was much thicker, drizzle slowly into the pot. When I was done, Michel added both the seeds and the bean to the mixture and transferred the pan to the stove.

"Medium heat," he said, looking over at Alastair. "And do not stop stirring."

Alastair came over and peered intently at the pot on the stove. Michel handed me the spoon and I obediently took over, while he retrieved a milk crate.

"Here," he said to Alastair, helping him up. "You try."

I handed the spoon to Alastair and stepped back. He stirred with the intensity I had come to expect of my brother. Michel took the opportunity to gather some other ingredients from around the kitchen.

"Now," he said, returning to the stove, "we remove it from the heat." Gently, he lifted the saucepan and placed it on a stainless-steel countertop.

"Now cornflour and *le sucre*, into this bowl." He handed me a well-worn copper measuring spoon and a dry-measure cup. "One *cuire de table* of the cornflour. *Un tiers de tasse* of the sugar." He pushed a large ceramic bowl in robin's-egg blue towards me.

Cuire de table, I translated silently. Tablespoon. Feeling victorious, I scooped out the proper amount and, seeing Michel's nod, overturned it into the bowl.

Tiers de tasse. Something of a cup, but what? Feeling too shy to ask, I held the dry-measure cup in one hand and the sugar in the other. Michel looked at me expectantly, but when I didn't move, his eyes softened. "I apologize," he said. "One-third."

Relieved, I measured the sugar and dumped it in. Next,

Michel had Alastair add the egg yolks. We watched as he whisked it all together, offering first Alastair and then me a turn. I tried to mimic his movement with the whisk.

"Now, we add the milk and cream." Michel grabbed a spoon and, after removing the husk of the vanilla bean, poured the hot mixture into the cool one, continuing to whisk. When he was done, he transferred the entire concoction into the pot.

"Alastair," he said, placing the pan back on the stove. "Please keep stirring this." Alastair nodded and set to work, his eyes never moving from the saucepan.

"Clara," he said. He motioned for me to join him at the marble slab. "Come help me over here, please."

I walked over and stood across from him. He shook his head. "Beside me, please." I went to stand next to him. I could smell him, a combination of sweat, vanilla, and shampoo. "I've already made the pastry," he said apologetically. "We will do that next time. But you can help me roll it out."

He lifted a bowl of fluffy-looking dough from the fridge and took out a large lump. "Feel it," he said. "It's much lighter and softer than it looks."

I touched it gingerly with my index finger.

"No," he said, shaking his head. He grabbed my hand, and I felt a jolt. "Really *touch* it." Using my hands as his own, he dug into the dough. It was cool and slippery.

"Better," he whispered. His mouth was close to my ear. I shivered.

Michel took out a large rolling pin and we worked together to shape the dough, rolling and flattening. Finally, he took the saucepan of custard from the stove and spooned it lightly on to the buttery dough. From the pantry, he retrieved a dish of dark chocolate chips and handed it to Alastair.

"Sprinkle it on," he said, demonstrating. Alastair watched carefully, then repeated the motions.

When he was done, we gently lifted the dough, forming a pocket of sorts, and, following Michel's lead, pinched it shut. Next, he sliced the entire thing into neatly shaped rectangles.

"Now," he said, "we bake it."

Michel handed Alastair another, smaller dish of chocolate chips. Alastair took it eagerly and went to settle down in front of the oven, watching the pain Suisse intently through the glass oven door.

"Chocolate?" Michel offered me a similar dish.

"No, thank you," I said politely.

He studied me. "Why do you not like to eat?"

I rolled my eyes. "That's just Alastair talking. Of course I like to eat."

"Do you?" His eyes looked deep into mine. For several seconds, neither of us spoke.

"I…" my voice trailed off. "I don't know."

I don't know what made me say it out loud. I took a step back, surprised. Afraid.

"I will help you," he said. He put a hand on my arm, and I felt my stomach flutter pleasantly.

"I don't need help," I said feebly.

"Then have some chocolate." He reached again for the bowl. "It's the best. Dark."

I stared at it. "No, thank you," I whispered. I turned away, not looking at him.

He touched my chin, turned my eyes back towards his. "I will help you, Clara."

This time, I didn't protest.

CHAPTER 14

I finally heard from Bree, who texted me on her day off from a pizza place in the town nearest to the summer camp. Naturally, she already had a boyfriend, a tall surfer dude named Carter from Santa Cruz who is a vegan. She sent me a selfie of the two of them from the restaurant, Bree smiling over a slice of meat lovers' and Carter giving a thumbs-up with one hand and digging into a salad with the other. I wonder if I would fit in better in California, where healthy eating was the order of the day and could be passed off as a denunciation of animal cruelty. I studied Carter with interest, noting his sun-kissed blondness as a direct counterpoint to Michel's dark good looks. Michel. I hadn't seen him since the bakery on Wednesday, though we had plans to meet him tomorrow to climb the steps of Sainte-Chapelle. I thought of his hands on mine as I kneaded the dough and shivered despite the humidity of the Paris restaurant.

"Who is that?" Alastair leaned in to study my phone, snapping me out of my Michel-induced reverie. It was pouring outside, and the two of us were taking temporary shelter at a café in the Marais district. I'd read online that le Marais was the place to go for cool shopping—vintage shops and eclectic finds. Mag had beamed at us when I'd informed her of our destination at breakfast.

"Excellent choice!" she'd exclaimed, slathering marmalade on a piece of toast.

"Oh?" I'd asked dubiously. I didn't think she was talking about fashion.

"I assume you're going to have a look at the Jewish museum," she said approvingly. "Good idea. Alastair doesn't get in touch much with his Jewish roots."

"Mmmm," I said politely, taking a sip of black coffee. I suppose we shared those Jewish roots. I didn't get in touch with mine, either, unless you counted the occasional indulgence in matzo-ball soup and the check for one hundred and eighteen dollars Bubbe had sent me when I turned twelve, notwithstanding the fact that I had not engaged in any kind bat mitzvah ceremony.

"In April we went to a communal Seder," continued Mag, pouring additional cream into her coffee. "It was a very interesting experience."

I looked over at Dad, who wasn't saying anything. He was leafing through the paper and staring at it intently, as if it might offer him salvation. I didn't blame him; I wouldn't want to engage Mag, either.

"Your father didn't like the Seder," explained Mag in a loud whisper, as if he couldn't hear her, when, clearly, he could. "He said it was too *alternative*."

"They had wasabi for the bitter herbs," he said, finally looking up. "My mother is rolling over in her grave."

"Your mother made tomato sauce with ketchup and ginger ale, dear," pointed out Mag reasonably. "She wasn't exactly a purist."

Ketchup and ginger ale? For once, I agreed with Mag.

"It was an old recipe," said Dad lamely.

"It doesn't sound good," said Alastair, who was finished his breakfast of cereal and repeatedly reading and rereading the ingredients on the side of the box. "What did it smell like? Did it smell like tomato sauce?"

It was a good question. Dad frowned, thinking. "She always made it with meatballs, so it always just smelled like ground beef. Like hamburger."

Alastair looked thoughtful. He pushed aside his bowl, empty now, though he had earlier informed us it contained exactly ninety-seven Cheerios. "It's strange," he said finally, "that if you eat hamburger with ketchup and have a soda to drink it's fine, but if you mix it all up it's not fine."

"Very clever," said Dad, reaching out to ruffle Alastair's hair. As usual, Alastair winced and pulled away, and I wondered why Dad kept doing that, when it was so clear Alastair loathed it. Was it some sort of primal fatherly gesture he simply couldn't surrender? I had a sudden urge to smack his arm.

"Soda isn't really fine," Mag said then, frowning. "Have you been drinking soda?"

"No," said Alastair flatly.

I frowned then, too, realizing the implication of this question. "Are you asking if I gave him soda?"

"Well—"

"Because frankly, I'm insulted." I stood up. "I don't even drink soda."

"I'm sorry—"

"You really have to decide, Mag, if I'm a starving anorexic or a soda-guzzling American, because, really, I'm not sure you can have it both ways."

"Clara!" Dad stood up now, an alarmed expression on his face. "Please don't talk like that in front of Alastair. And you're not being fair to Mag."

"What about her being fair to me?" I spluttered. "I never gave Alastair a soda or MSG or whatever else is on her no-fly list. I don't eat that crap, either."

"It's true," said Alastair, nodding. "Clara only eats healthy food."

"Alastair, stay out of this," said Dad sharply.

I glanced over at Mag, red-faced and silent, peeling a boiled egg. She had already eaten two slices of marmalade-saturated toast, and I wondered if she was a stress eater. Could anyone honestly be hungry after two pieces of toast?

"I'm sorry," she mumbled. "I don't know what I was thinking."

"Fine," I said through clenched teeth. "Me too." I didn't add that I thought Alastair could totally benefit from a few sips of Coke. For little kids it was cool to be allowed the occasional

Sprite, or at least to have tried it. Even I hadn't given up Diet Coke until last year.

"How did we get here, anyway?" Dad looked tired. He grabbed his mug and downed the last of his coffee. "Weren't we having a pleasant conversation?"

"The Marais," said Alastair automatically. "Clara said we were going to the Marais, and Mum said that was good for my Jewish roots, and then—"

"Thank you, Alastair," interrupted Dad. "I remember now."

"Enjoy *le Marais*," said Mag in an unnaturally friendly voice. "I think you'll really love it."

Damn. I wondered if, as a peace offering, I now had to actually go to the Jewish museum. How long would that take? I had other plans, both for my own benefit as well as Alastair's.

"I'll see you when I get back," she continued, still overly cheerful. "I'll be in London for two days."

"Right," I said, abashed. "I'd forgotten." I felt worse fighting with Mag knowing she was going off to a conference. It was like an unwritten rule that you weren't supposed to spar with someone before they left on a trip.

"I'll miss you, Alastair," she said, turning to him. She looked slightly sad, and a bit worried. "I'll call you."

"Right," said Alastair. He didn't look sad, and I felt badly for Mag. Having a child who couldn't be counted on to return your affections had to be tough.

"Are we going now?" he asked, turning towards me. "I'll go get my backpack."

"Sure," I said with a sigh. I glanced at the clock over the fireplace, an ancient-looking thing that lacked the charm to be labeled as an antique. The stores wouldn't be open for a while. *Museum it is*, I thought, sighing again.

"Grab your raincoat too, Alastair," I called, glancing out the window. There had been a trace of sunshine that morning, a tantalizing hint of promising weather to come. Now, however, the elusive star had retreated back to its usual Paris hiding place—behind a thick blanket of gray clouds.

"I'm ready," he said, returning in his yellow slicker, his oversized backpack making him look like a tiny mountain climber. I resisted a sudden urge to ruffle his hair and looked over at my father, who was staring at us both tenderly. I nodded at him as we exchanged a silent, mutual apology.

Outside, it began to rain again.

We had ducked into a café when the rain got too heavy. We were near the museum, but I needed to have a coffee and wring out my hair. Alastair, too, seemed relieved when I announced my intention to stop. His child-sized umbrella had blown inside out ten minutes earlier, and he was breathing heavily, distressed at his own wet hair.

"I don't like being wet," he panted, once we were inside. His breathing became more erratic. I hauled him into the bathroom, where I instructed him to put his hands over his ears and proceeded to dry him out under an electric hand-dryer.

"Feel better?" I asked, kneeling down to his level.

"I need my vest," he said by way of reply.

I scrambled for the backpack. "Here," I said, draping it over his shoulders. "You're okay."

He took several deep breaths before nodding. "Okay," he said. "I'm ready now."

I led him back out and we took a high table for two. I helped Alastair climb up, grinning at his dangling legs. The café was busy despite the rain and the fact that it was a weekday morning. In France, people took breaks seriously. Coffee was something to savor sitting down, both hands wrapped delicately around a real cup, not in cardboard on the go after having a fit because of the Starbucks line.

"*Oui?*" The waiter appeared, looking irritated.

"*Un café et un chocolat chaud,*" I ordered, proud of my French. I pointed to Alastair. "*Pas des arachides,*" I added, referring to Alastair's peanut allergy. The waiter made a face, but nodded as if he understood and decamped to the bar. That was when I got the text from Bree, and the subsequent photo of her and surfer-dude Carter.

"It's my best friend Bree and her new boyfriend," I explained in response to his query, enlarging the picture for Alastair. "See? That's Bree, there, eating the pizza."

He squinted and looked closer. "She's drinking a soda," he said, pointing.

I looked closer. It was true. Next to her plate was a can of Coke.

"Yeah," I said, shrugging. "Bree's one of those people who lives off pizza and cheeseburgers but stays skinny."

"And you aren't one of those people?" Alastair studied the photo intently, his eyes fixed on the soda can.

"I told you; I have to work hard to be thin. Anyway, I wouldn't eat that junk. It's bad for your body. Unhealthy." I took the phone back and typed a reply to Bree, but I didn't get a message back. I wondered if cellphone reception was spotty, even in town. The waiter arrived with our drinks, setting them down in front of us without speaking.

"How do you know you have to work hard to be thin?" Alastair asked thoughtfully, taking a spoon and skimming some whipped cream off the top of his hot chocolate. "Did you used to be like Mum?"

I coughed, spluttering. The coffee nearly came out of my nose, and I noticed the waiter shoot me a dirty look. "You can't say that!"

"Why?" Alastair looked puzzled. "Mum is large. She knows. It doesn't bother her."

"You can't talk about people like that. Seriously, Alastair." I dabbed at my mouth with my napkin in what I hoped was a discreet manner.

"But she always says her bum is huge," said Alastair. "She laughs about it."

"I doubt she actually likes her big bum," I answered, feeling my cheeks go red. I didn't like Mag, but I don't like describing anyone as fat—not out loud, anyway. It feels like bad karma, like the universe will exact its revenge and raise me by a dress size or two.

Alastair shrugged and went back to his hot chocolate.

"Anyway," he said. "If you've always been thin, you don't actually know that you can't eat food, like your friend."

I sighed. "I eat food."

We reverted to silence, Alastair licking at his sweet beverage, me sipping black coffee. The obligatory creamer sat between us, and I wondered what coffee tastes like with cream. I'd only ever drunk it black or with skim milk, having picked up my coffee habit when I started high school.

"Clara?" Alastair lowered his voice.

"Yeah?"

"Have you ever had a soda?" He was practically whispering.

"Of course I've had a soda, Alastair." I rested my feet on the bar of the stool. "Lots of people drink soda. Most people, even…maybe."

"Mum says it's full of chemicals." He gulped his hot chocolate. "And refined sugar."

"I think it's actually high-fructose corn syrup now," I said dryly.

"Does it taste good?" he looked at me earnestly, his eyes wide and innocent, and I felt a pang of affection so sharp and sudden I felt almost winded.

"Yes," I admitted. "It does." I paused. "Alastair, do you want a Coke?"

He stared at me fearfully. "I'm not allowed. And it's unhealthy. And full of—"

"We won't tell anyone." I felt reckless now, gleeful in my impending rebellion against Mag's draconian parenting.

"Okay," he said. He looked scared, and I felt bad.

"You don't have to."

"No," he looked determined. "I want to."

I signaled for the waiter. "We'll have a Coke, please." He made another face, but returned with a little glass bottle. I reached for it and popped the top off.

"Go for it," I said, sliding it across the table.

He eyed it warily and sniffed at it. "It doesn't really smell."

"No," I agreed. "That's true."

He took a deep breath and tipped the bottle towards his mouth, taking a small sip. "It's good," he said brightening.

"Sure it is," I said. "Coca-Cola didn't become a billion-dollar company for no reason."

"I would offer you some, but I don't share drinks," he said serenely. "Bacteria."

"It's okay." *When was the last time I'd had a real Coke? Four years? Five?*

I watched Alastair greedily down the bottle, and hoped he wouldn't tell Mag. He was fairly reliable, lacking the capability to lie, but he was still a kid, and Mag was still his mom.

"Well," I said. "What do you think?"

"It's good," he said again. "But I like hot chocolate better."

I felt a surge of warmth and wondered if this was love, the sort of love you feel for a brother or a sister. I felt suddenly lucky to have Alastair and a certain sadness for not having known him until now.

"What are the ingredients in Coke?" he picked up the bottle and began reading off the list of chemicals on the label, stumbling slightly over "caffeine citrate."

When he got to "flavor," he frowned. "It doesn't say what it is," he said. "Why?"

"Well, that's their secret," I explained. "It's a secret recipe."

Alastair looked horrified. "But there could be something *allergenic* in it!"

I blinked. I'd never considered that before.

"We should write a letter to Coca-Cola," he said, sounding indignant. "I think they're being dangerous."

"You're a good kid, Alastair," I said affectionately. I fished a few euros out of my purse and dropped them on the table. I tipped the waiter, even though Dad kept telling me it isn't necessary here. Maybe the waiters would be nicer if people tipped them. I think of it as a sort of "pay it forward."

I helped Alastair off the chair, and we headed to the museum.

The Jewish Museum of Art and History was housed in a palatial old mansion, former home to some count or another. Outside was a statue of Alfred Dreyfus, who had been falsely accused of treason in the late nineteenth century. I read out the Wikipedia entry on Dreyfus to Alastair, who listened intently, frowning.

"Why did they accuse him, if there was no proof?"

"Because he was Jewish. People hated Jewish people back then." I squatted down so that I could be level with Alastair. My heeled boots wobbled on the uneven cobblestones, and I struggled to stay upright.

"Just because they were Jewish?" He looked worried.

"Yeah. They needed someone to blame."

"Could that happen today?" He rocked back and forth slightly on the damp stones, and I could tell he was upset.

"I don't know. I'd like to think the courts are fairer, but today we have things like Twitter to wreck your reputation. Convict you in the court of public opinion." For the first time in weeks, I thought of the Twitter disaster that had driven me across an ocean.

"What do you mean?" Alastair gave me a puzzled look, and I reminded myself again that, no matter how smart he seemed, he was just a kid.

"Do you know what Twitter is?"

He straightened importantly. "Yes. People post messages on the Internet about what they are doing and what they think."

"Right. So a lot of the time, people post things without proving they are true. Even if later they fix it, they may already have hurt someone."

"Oh." He stared at the statue. "That's sad."

"That's social media," I said bitterly. I thought of Spencer and Twitter and shuddered, standing up. "Let's go inside."

We passed through various hallways and exhibits, examining and admiring artifacts that provided snippets of what it was like to be Jewish in Paris through the ages. Alastair was particularly keen on the paintings, which he examined with a concentration atypical not only of most kids his age, but of ordinary people generally. After fifteen minutes of staring at Chagall's *The Cemetery Gates*, I felt as if I needed to curl up for a nap on a nearby bench.

The final exhibit was entitled "To Be a Jew in Paris in 1939," and depicted the difficult life of the Jews after the Nazi rise to power and the victory over the French army. The exhibit ended in the courtyard, with a display of the names of Jews who had once lived or worked in the building and who had been deported under the Nazi regime.

"What does that mean?" asked Alastair, eyebrows furrowed. "Deported?"

Oh no. I stared at Alastair, uncomfortable. *What should I say? Do I tell him the truth?*

"Deported," I said carefully. "Like sent away. During World War Two. It was a huge war from nineteen thirty-nine to nineteen forty-five."

"Where did they go?"

"Um. Well, the Jews were sent to camps," I said lamely.

"Camps?" He frowned again, and I realized, fairly, that he must be imagining masses of Jews being shipped out to summer camps to play soccer and make friendship bracelets.

"A lot of them died," I said honestly. "They were killed."

"Because they were Jewish?"

"Yes."

We are both silent as we study the names in the courtyard. Raymond Freidman, *horloger*—watchmaker. Anna Scheidecker, *Concierge d'immeuble*—building concierge. What had they looked like? Had they been frightened to go? What had become of them?

"Clara?"

"Yes?" I fought the urge to take his hand. It seemed

natural, in the situation, but I knew Alastair didn't enjoy being touched, and I suppressed my own need for tactile comfort out of respect for his own, special needs.

"Why did people hate Jewish people?"

"I guess because they were different," I said honestly. I felt uncomfortable, being the one to explain this—particularly since I was rarely in touch with my own Jewish roots. My mother was a staunch atheist whose spirituality was limited to a Hallmark-style Christmas celebration. Also, I'd once been told by a Jewish classmate that you weren't really Jewish if your mother wasn't. I didn't understand what "really Jewish" meant—it didn't seem like a fixed trait like being tall, or having green eyes—but then I'd read that the Nazis labeled anyone who had even one Jewish grandparent as Jewish. Who got to decide?

"That makes sense," said Alastair, nodding.

Taken aback, I blinked, confused. "It does?"

"Yes." He nodded again. "I'm different, too, and the kids at school don't like me, either."

He said it simply and without much emotion, as if he were relaying something factual like the directions from here to the apartment. By contrast, I felt a surge of anger towards his classmates, accompanied by a wave of crippling pity.

"I'm sure they like you," I said feebly, then regretted it. I'm sure I even sounded like I was lying.

"They don't," he said tonelessly. "I don't do the right things. I don't say the right things."

That reminded me why I had originally chosen the Marais for our daily excursion.

"I'm going to help you with that," I said, putting an arm around him without thinking. He flinched and I quickly dropped it.

"How?"

I smiled at him. "We're going shopping."

We started at a street vendor selling purses and other assorted bags and luggage. The seller eyed us greedily, reeling off a list of "discount" prices as we approached. I ignored him, not understanding much of what he said anyway, and pointed at the selection of backpacks.

"Okay, Alastair," I said. "Pick one."

He looked at me uncertainly. "But I already have a backpack."

"But it's a grown-up backpack, and it's too big for you," I said flatly. "It's not cool. We're going to get you a cool one."

"Okay," he said, but he looked worried. He stared at the backpacks. "Which one is cool?"

There were six to choose from for a kid Alastair's age—three with superheroes, one with Anna and Elsa from *Frozen*, one My Little Pony, and one with French cartoon characters that I saw everywhere but couldn't remember the names of.

I surveyed the selection, immediately eliminating the ponies and the princesses. The world may be more accepting these days of boys who wanted to carry princess backpacks, but I doubted, sadly, that a boy like Alastair could do so and evade bullying. I considered the superhero options. Iron Man was a rich playboy who'd turned superhero when faced with a heart condition. Batman was another rich kid who'd only turned to justice after adversity. Then there was Superman, an alien sent to Earth to live amongst us, a creature with abilities and strengths ordinary humans couldn't fathom. I studied Alastair, and wondered if he ever felt like an alien, sent to live with lesser beings. Who decided what was normal, and what was not?

"Superman," I said finally. I unhooked the bag from the stall and handed it to him. "What do you think?"

He looked it over carefully, checking the straps, the zipper, the plastic "S" adorning the front. He brought it to his nose, sniffing deeply. "Smells fine," he said. The vendor blinked, eyeing us with frank curiosity.

"Do you like it?"

"Yes. Red is a very good color, and I am also fond of blue."

"We'll take it," I said to the confused vendor. I fished out a twenty-euro note and handed it to him, too pleased for Alastair to haggle over the price. The guy seemed almost disappointed to give me my change, as if he had been looking forward to a good fight.

"What's next?" asked Alastair, as I transferred his belongings to the new backpack. "Lunch?"

"Not yet," I said. I gestured towards a shoe store at the corner. "Over there."

Alastair trotted behind me in his ridiculous buckled shoes, looking uncertain. I wondered if he'd ever been shopping before, or whether Mag just brought him stuff home. I couldn't imagine a child ever choosing those shoes.

"Shoes?" he said dubiously, when we entered.

I looked around at a dizzying variety of styles and colors approvingly. There were green skater shoes and blue-and-white basketball high-tops and Star Wars sneakers that lit up when you walked.

"Shoes," I said firmly.

"Mum usually buys me my shoes," he informed me. "She says children need good shoes to walk in so their feet develop properly."

"No one needs shoes like those," I said frankly. "They have buckles."

"Buckles are bad?" His eyes widened.

"Do the other kids have buckles?"

He frowned, considering. "No," he admitted. "They have Velcro."

"Exactly," I said triumphantly. "Follow me."

With the help of a petite brunette with a pixie cut and bottle-green plastic glasses, we selected an assortment of six pairs for Alastair to try on. He insisted on putting on each pair himself, changing and fastening the shoes with slow deliberation. After each change, he walked around the room and stared at his feet in the full-length mirror.

"What do you think, Alastair?" I asked enthusiastically as he tried on a pair of black Converse running shoes. "Do you like them?"

He shook his head gravely. "I can't tie laces," he said. "I haven't met that developmental milestone."

I grabbed the flashing Star Wars shoes. They had Darth Vader's head on them, and they made weird, heavy breathing noises when I yanked on the Velcro.

"No!" shouted Alastair, his hands flying to his ears. "No sounds!"

"Sorry!" Hastily, I yanked the sneakers from his feet.

Alastair rocked back and forth in an effort to soothe himself, hands still cupped over his ears. I pulled out a pair of black-and-yellow trainers with double Velcro straps. They were cool and sporty-looking, and the tag said they glowed in the dark.

"Here," I said, handing them to him. "These glow in the dark."

"They do?" He seemed intrigued, or at least interested enough to stop rocking.

"Yes. And they're Velcro."

He pulled them on and rose, marching around the store before pausing at the mirror. He stood there for a long time.

"Well?" I asked, grinning.

"I like these," he said, smiling back. "I think they're cool. Do you think they're cool, Clara?"

"I do, Buddy."

"Can I wear them now?"

"Absolutely."

I paid for the shoes, putting his old, buckled monstrosities in the box and slinging the plastic bag over my shoulder. Alastair walked next to me, looking fiercely proud in his glow-in-the-dark sneakers and Superman backpack.

"Am I cool now, Clara?" he asked, his voice so full of hope that I felt my heart break clean in half.

"You were cool before," I said, feeling ashamed. Had I done the wrong thing? Wasn't it what was inside that counted, and all that? Was buying someone a Superman backpack tantamount to coercing him to be a follower, a sheep?

"No," he said firmly. "I wasn't."

"You're the coolest person I know," I said guiltily.

"The other kids made fun of my shoes," he whispered, looking relieved to have admitted this to me. "The St. Clare twins hid them at recess once."

"That's awful." I felt the tears prick my eyes.

"But now they won't bother me." His eyes met mine, and I felt the guilt abate, somewhat.

"Thank you, Clara," he said, and he put his hand on my arm, just for a second. I knew it was for my benefit, and I resisted the urge to grab him into a bear hug.

"Thank you, Alastair," I said. "It was a lot of fun. Hungry?"

"Yes!"

"Let's go get some lunch." I held the door open and Alastair hopped down the step back into the street. "What do you want?"

"Croque monsieur," he said promptly.

"You always get a croque monsieur," I said. "You don't like to try new things? I thought you liked to cook?"

He looked at me seriously. "I do. I like to cook croque monsieur."

I laughed and we set out in search of a café.

CHAPTER 15

Dad didn't notice the backpack until the next morning. "Superman?" he asked, surprised. He picked it up and studied the large plastic "S" adorning the front.

"Alastair chose it," I said firmly. I stepped into a pair of silver ballet flats. It was, at long last, a nice day, and I was eager to wear something other than boots. I'd also finally been able to don a summery dress, albeit with a jean jacket. Still, it was nice to discover I still had legs.

"Right, and you had nothing to do with it." Dad raised his eyebrows and leaned against a beam, his arms crossed against his chest.

"Dad." I sighed, leaning in so that Alastair, next door in the bathroom, couldn't hear. "The kids at school make fun of him. He needs to fit in better. Isn't that why I'm here? To help Alastair?"

Dad frowned, and the little lines around his eyes creased with worry. "I didn't realize it was that bad," he said, sounding upset. "Maybe Mag and I should talk to the school. Mag did go in to talk to the class about the autism spectrum and being sensitive. Maybe it's time for another visit."

Oh, my God. I stared at my father in abject horror. "Mag went into the class? With Alastair there?" I put one hand against the wall for support.

"Yes, why?" He looked puzzled at my expression

I closed my eyes, massaging my left temple with my free hand. How could anyone not understand the social suicide that was having one's mother come in and give a lecture on *any* topic? Just having my mom come on a field trip would have been enough to make me feign a fever, and my mother was a beautiful celebrity. I tried to explain this to Dad.

"Mag wouldn't understand that," he admitted to me. He riffled through the coat rack for his own jacket and shoved it into his worn messenger bag. "She won't understand the Superman, either. She thinks Alastair should be who he is, and the other kids should accept him."

I felt angry. "Alastair has enough to deal with without having ugly shoes and a massive backpack," I snapped. "The least you can do is try to make him cool."

I could see in his eyes that he was listening intently and contemplating what I had to say, but I could also tell he was conflicted. "Mag won't like it," he admitted quietly.

"I'm not saying he shouldn't be himself," I said, bending to reach for my own bag, a vintage pink leather purse I'd bought for myself yesterday in the Marais after lunch. "He's a great kid. But there's nothing wrong with making an effort to be liked and to fit in. When he's an adult, you won't be there to protect him. He needs to figure out how to function socially."

Alastair appeared in his slicker and new shoes. "I'm ready," he said, reaching out for his new backpack. "Is Michel here yet?"

"We're meeting him downstairs," I said, feeling my cheeks go slightly warm at the mention of Michel in front of my dad.

"Michel?" My father looked interested. "From the bakery?"

"He's coming with us to Sainte-Chapelle," I explained. Now my face felt outright hot. "He invited us when I took Alastair there last Wednesday. He said it's his favorite place in Paris."

"I take it you two hit it off, then," said Dad slyly. He winked at me.

I groaned. "Dad, did you just *wink* at me?"

"I did. I apologize." He grinned broadly. "Still, he's a nice boy. I'm glad that you—"

"Bye, Dad," I said loudly, interrupting him, unlocking the door.

"Have fun, kids," he said, handing me another fistful of cash. He held the heavy wooden door open for us, his eyes traveling downward to Alastair's feet. "I see you went to the shoe store, too."

"Yes," I agreed. "Now the rotten little monsters won't be able to hide those awful buckled ones at recess anymore."

He winced. "Don't mention it to Mag when she calls."

"She's going to find out sometime, Dad." I felt exasperated.

Dad leaned in to hug me, but I ducked out of the way at the last second, pretending I didn't notice his outstretched arms. We were getting along well enough, but I didn't feel quite ready for that. You didn't erase years of missing one's childhood in a couple of weeks. Instead, I nodded goodbye as we spotted Michel. I was sure Dad would call out something embarrassing, but he just waved briefly at Michel before heading off to work. Maybe he'd taken my comments about parental humiliation to heart—or maybe he was hurt by my brush-off. Pushing the thought out of my mind, I turned my attention to Michel.

Michel looked even better than he had at the bakery. Leaning against the stone wall of the building, he could have been a male model posing for a photo shoot. In basic jeans and white tee, he looked right out of a Calvin Klein ad.

"Bonjour," he said to us, smiling.

"Bonjour," I replied, blushing both at his liquid brown eyes as well as my own terrible pronunciation. I could never remember to drop the final *r* sound slightly in bonjour, making me sound like a stereotypical American. Which I guess I am.

"You are ready for the Sainte-Chapelle?" Michel put a hand on my shoulder, and I wondered if it was because he wanted to touch me, or just because he was French and Europeans are more touchy-feely.

"Yes," I said, nodding. "Even Alastair has never been. We're looking forward to it."

"It is my favorite place in Paris," he said. "And it is a beautiful day."

"It is," I agreed, gesturing at the clear sky. "It's finally sunny."

We started to walk, me alongside Michel with Alastair in tow, and I felt a rush of pleasure at the sensation of sunshine on the back of my neck. The copper-topped buildings of the city sparkled in the sunlight, and the birds emerged from their hiding places to treat us to their warbling. Paris was lovely in any weather, but there was a special magic to it when the sun decided to grace the city.

"When my father moved here from Algeria, he found the weather the hardest thing to get used to," commented Michel. "Where he grew up, it was always hot and sunny. Sometimes he still wears sweaters well into July."

"He wouldn't like New York winters very much then," I said. "Freezing and lots of snow."

"I like the snow." Michel grinned. "Like icing sugar, from the sky."

I smiled at the imagery: the domes of Les Invalides, topped with white, like frosted cupcakes. "It must be pretty here. In the winter, I mean."

Michel winked at me. "It is always pretty in Paris."

We lapsed into silence, and I realized that we had just spent upward of five minutes chatting about the weather. I wondered if that was a bad sign, as far as conversations with French guys went. Were French guys different than New York guys? I thought of Spencer Caplan. The Twitter debacle had long blown over—thank God for the twenty-four-hour news cycle—but the sting of his treachery and my own bad judgment lingered.

"You okay, Alastair?" Guiltily, I looked over to make sure he was still next to me.

"Yes."

"Isn't it a nice day?"

"Yes."

He didn't seem interested in pursuing conversation, so I turned back to Michel. "When did your father move here from Algeria?"

"In his twenties," answered Michel. "His parents had died and he wanted to start over."

"That's sad," I said. I thought of what it would be like to lose both parents in only a few short years and shivered as we waited to cross the street.

"Yes. He has had a tough life, my father. First my grandparents, then my mother."

"Your mother?" The light was green now, but I didn't move. "Michel, I didn't know. I'm so sorry."

"Come." He took my elbow with one hand, and held Alastair's in the other as we crossed the boulevard.

"It was a long time ago now," said Michel. We were back on the sidewalk, but he was still lightly touching my elbow. "Five years."

"Still," I said. "That's so hard."

"Michel's mom died of cancer," said Alastair matter-of-factly.

"Alastair!" I said, scandalized.

Michel grinned. "It's okay, Clara," he said. "I explained it to Alastair myself."

I shook my head. Would I ever get used to Alastair's bluntness? Just when I thought I was immune, he shocked me all over again.

"It was in her large intestine," added Alastair solemnly.

Michel nodded sadly. "Colon cancer," he translated.

"I'm sorry." I put a hand on his arm briefly, then quickly removed it, feeling awkward.

He nodded again, but said nothing. I walked alongside him, trying to think of the right words. I realized there were none, and remained silent.

We descended the steps to the Métro, and Alastair clasped his hands together. "I love the train," he said happily.

"You do?" I asked, surprised. I had thus far insisted on long walks or used taxis to get around with Alastair, afraid that he would have a panic attack or some other episode on the Métro. "You never told me."

"You never asked," he said simply, his eyes round and innocent.

"Right," I said. My eyes met Michel's and we both grinned.

We gave Alastair the change for the tickets, allowing him to approach the booth himself. Proud and excited, he handed us each a Métro card. We swiped our cards and headed for the platform.

The train was surprisingly cool and airy. Given that nothing else in Paris seemed to be air-conditioned, I was surprised. I said as much to Michel, who looked thoughtful.

"I'd never thought about it," he confessed.

"It's not exactly air conditioning," piped up Alastair. His

face was pressed up against the glass. "It's a sort of air circulation system."

"How do you know that?" I asked, impressed.

"Wikipedia," he answered, as if it were obvious. Michel and I looked at each other again over the top of Alastair's head and exchanged another smile. I was glad Alastair was there. Michel was great-looking and seemed nice, but I didn't know him at all. Having Alastair as chaperone helped break the ice.

"Your English is really good," I commented to Michel, my stomach lurching as the train sped out of the station. I watched as the scene outside became a blur of white tiles and then, finally, darkness. "Did you learn it at school?"

"Some," he said, leaning back against the faux-leather seat cushion. "But mostly from movies and TV."

"Really?" I asked, surprised. "You don't watch them in French?"

"My mother was adamant that I should learn English," he answered. "She was a stage actress. She loved Shakespeare. So when I wanted to watch *Aladdin, par example*, she made me watch it in English."

"My mom's a performer too," I said, seizing on the commonality for something to talk about. "A ballerina."

"A ballerina," he repeated. His eyes traveled over me, and I felt the urge to pull my jean jacket closed. What was he looking at? Was he thinking I couldn't possibly be the daughter of a ballerina? I stared at my bare thighs, repelled by how they spread out against the plastic cushion. Digging the balls of my feet into the floor, I yanked my dress down farther towards my knees.

"Catherine Malcolm," I said. "She's famous."

"I'm not familiar with ballet," he admitted. "But it cannot be easy, having a famous mother. My mother was a good actress, but she was not famous."

"It's okay," I said automatically, but my voice shook slightly. Involuntarily, I flashed back to the infamous tweet. *Hot but nothing like Mom.* Even now, it felt like being punched in the gut.

Michel raised his eyebrows, and looked as if he wanted to say something more. He remained silent, however, and then it was our stop.

"*Cité*," announced a drone-like female voice. "*Station Cité.*"

I grabbed my purse and Alastair's hand and followed Michel through the station. Alastair tried to pull his hand free, whimpering slightly at the prolonged contact, but I held it firmly in my own.

"I don't want to lose you in the subway station," I said firmly. "Hold my hand until we get outside."

Alastair flinched but didn't pull away. When we were outside again, our blinking eyes unused to the sunlight, Alastair turned to me. I thought he was going to tell me off over the hand-holding, but instead he said solemnly, "Subway is the best name, I think."

"Sorry?" I stared at him blankly, squinting slightly. I fished my oversized sunglasses out of my bag for the first time since I'd touched down at Charles De Gaulle Airport.

"Well, *Métro* isn't really very clever because it's just short for *le train métropolitain* and neither is Underground, really. I think Subway is the cleverest because it describes exactly what it is: a way to travel underneath the ground."

"That," I said finally, "is very true and very smart."

"I agree," intoned Michel, patting Alastair's backpack. "It is also creative." He pronounced creative the French way: cray-ah-teef. It was pretty much the same in both languages, but sounded much more romantic *en français*, thereby emphasizing its meaning. I stole a glance at Michel's curly dark hair, now rustling gently in the breeze, and felt my stomach lurch for the second time that morning. This time, it had nothing to do with the train.

"This way," said Michel, pointing, and I looked over to see Sainte-Chapelle. It looked lovely from the outside, plenty of stone and spires, but I privately wondered why this was Michel's favorite place. Surely Notre-Dame or Sacré-Coeur, with their giant domes and palatial size, were even more impressive, if churches were your thing?

As if reading my mind, Michel ushered us towards the door. "Wait until you see the inside," he said, sounding excited. I smiled at this display of boyish enthusiasm, and was about to make a comment when we entered through the heavy doors.

"Oh!" I exclaimed. My breath caught; I had never seen anything so beautiful. Endless arches of stained glass, each so intricate in detail that it must have taken months to complete just one small section. The sun shone through the windows, treating us to a dazzling spectacle of every imaginable color—scarlet and violet and what seemed like an endless array of shades in between.

"Wow," I managed, turning to Michel. "This is the most beautiful thing I have ever seen."

"Is it not?" Michel spread his arms out towards the domed ceiling. "To think that people made these. Real people, working their craft. It is humbling."

It was indeed. I stared at the majestic display before me, noting scenes from the Bible. Next to me, Alastair was silent, fidgeting with the straps on his backpack.

"Isn't it wonderful, Alastair?" I asked him. "Have you ever seen anything like it?"

Alastair shrugged. "I suppose," he said. He shuffled from foot to foot, and I wondered if he was just too young to appreciate the beauty of the stained glass.

Michel noticed Alastair's expression and turned around, pointing. "There are the stairs," he said. "It's a great climb and a great view. Come."

Alastair looked considerably more interested as he trotted along behind Michel. We began our ascent, the wrought-iron steps becoming increasingly more narrow as we climbed the spiraling staircase. Feeling out of breath about five minutes in, I vowed to lengthen my evening exercise routine. I'd become complacent since arriving in Paris, often so tired in the evenings that I only did twenty reps instead of thirty when doing my nightly kicks, squats, and crunches. I would have to do better than that.

Ahead of me, Alastair was breathing heavily too, exhaling noisily with each additional step.

"You okay, Alastair?" I asked, pausing. I put a hand on the "S" of his Superman bag.

He froze, then, very slowly, turned around so that I could see his face. It was devoid of all color, a ghostly white even in the shadow of the turret.

"I am not," he said quietly. "It's too—small in here. I can't breathe." Now that the words were out, the confession made, his breathing became louder and faster. "I can't breathe!"

Michel whirled around, tripping slightly, and I gasped as he wobbled on the tiny step. "It is all right," he said firmly, grasping Alastair by his shoulders.

"Careful," I said, scared. "He doesn't like to be touched."

Michel shook his head. "This is different. It is like his vest. The pressure is calming."

Right. I'd forgotten Michel knew Alastair well, better than I did. Behind me, a group of German tourists asked in polite-but-irked tones if we would please keep moving.

"I don't think we can," I said apologetically. "My brother... isn't well."

Alastair began keening then, rocking back and forth on the heels of his new sneakers. The gaps between the stairs were considerable, and it wasn't hard to imagine a child-sized leg slipping through.

"Alastair!" I cried. "Don't move like that."

Alastair moaned loader, his voice echoing in the ancient tower.

"Michel," I said desperately. "Get his vest. The backpack."

Michel unzipped the bag and found the vest. He handed the backpack down to me and helped Alastair into the vest. Once it was on, Alastair's shoulders visibly relaxed, but he

184

continued to whimper and refused to move forward. Beneath us, I heard the rumblings of irate tourists.

"We need to get him out of here," I said to Michel in a low voice.

"I will handle it," he said swiftly.

Michel cleared his throat and announced in a commanding voice that everyone would have to clear the stairwell due to a sick child. He then repeated his words in French. There were plenty of angry noises in response, but slowly, people began heading back down.

"I can't move," said Alastair. His eyes were full of terror as he stared at the steps below. "I can't!"

Michel crouched down to Alastair's eye level. "Alastair," he said calmly. "I want you to climb on my back. I will carry you down."

Alastair made a small, squeaky noise. "I can't."

"Alastair," Michel's tone was firm, "you must. On the count of three. One. Two. Three."

Michel grabbed my brother and hoisted him onto his back. I shuddered as I looked down. Alastair wasn't wrong. The steps were even more terrifying going down, the space between them much more readily apparent. What if I fell?

"Clara," said Michel in the same voice he had used with Alastair. "You have to walk now."

He was right; the Germans had long disappeared. It was time to go.

"Okay," I said in a small voice. "I'm going."

I took each stair carefully, one at a time, making sure both feet hit each step before attempting the next one. My feet were sweaty inside my ballet flats, and my heels slipped in and out. I cursed the fashion industry for making woman's footwear totally impractical, leaving me vulnerable to falling to my death because I had wanted to look nice. When I reached the bottom, I felt like kissing the cold stone floor.

A large crowd was milling about, muttering impatiently. When Michel descended with Alastair, they all stared at him, as if looking for proof that he was sufficiently ill to have warranted this disruption to their holiday.

"He doesn't look sick," I heard an American girl with a Texan accent whisper to her boyfriend. I felt like shouting at her, but held my tongue. What did they want? To see the poor kid soaked in vomit? Covered in boils?

"Excuse me," I muttered as I pushed my way through the crowd. Michel held on to Alastair and followed close behind me until we were outside. Michel then released Alastair who sat down on the pavement and rocked back and forth gently, his eyes squeezed shut. I started to approach him, but Michel put a hand on my arm.

"Give him a minute," he said quietly. "That is how he soothes himself."

I nodded, fighting the urge to collapse down right next to him.

"I guess we should have known he might be claustrophobic," I said, exhaling.

Michel shook his head. "I feel terrible," he said. "I never would have suggested it."

"You didn't know." I watched my brother, whose rhythmic rocking was becoming slower.

"You are also claustrophobic?" asked Michel. He looked concerned and wracked with remorse. "You should have told me."

"I'm not, really. It was just those stairs…so much space between them. I was scared of falling. I have this recurring dream…" I stopped. What was I thinking? I couldn't tell Michel about my dream.

"Go on," he said softly.

I looked over at Alastair, who still hadn't signaled his readiness to move on. Before I could stop myself, I told Michel everything. The cake, the disappearing floor, the falling.

"The falling I understand," he says thoughtfully. "It's being out of control. You're afraid of losing control."

"I am?" I frowned. "Maybe I'm just afraid of falling to my death."

He laughed. "That, and losing control."

I pondered this. Maybe he was right.

"Now, the cake, that is strange," he continued. "At first I thought, maybe it is a symbol? But you do not like to eat."

"That isn't true," I protested feebly.

"You would not eat my best chocolate."

"I like to eat healthy!" I didn't look at him. Instead, I looked over at a group of pigeons fighting over a scrap of bread.

"Healthy is about moderation. It is not about denying pleasure."

He was about to say more, when Alastair rose slowly, shuddered, and came over to us.

"I am ready to leave," he announced. "I would like to eat now."

Michel nodded and then clapped his hands together. "I have the perfect idea." He stood up. "Come with me."

Michel led us back to his apartment over the bakery, which was a mirror image of Dad's. In fact, I realized, looking around, it was opposite in nearly every way. It was spotless. It was also organized: everything seemed to have its own place, and there were special receptacles and shelves placed in strategic places throughout the flat to contain any potential clutter.

"Wow," I said, raising my eyebrows. I studied the hall closet, which Michel had opened to retrieve hangers for our jackets. The contents were hung shortest to longest, and it looked as if they were color-coded as well. "Did you plan on having us back here and spend, like, half the night cleaning it up?"

Michel laughed. "*Non*," he said, untying his sneakers. "It is my father. He is, as you would say in America, a neat freak."

"Neat freak doesn't quite cover it," I said, amused. "Is the color-coding in the closet coincidental?"

Michel blushed. "It is not."

We followed Alastair into the kitchen, which boasted ultra-modern stainless-steel appliances. They looked like, if you pressed the wrong button, you might end up in a parallel dimension.

"Which one do I press to beam me up?" I joked, running my hand along the handle of the dishwasher.

Alastair let out a barking laugh, and both Michel and I started, turning to stare at him. He so rarely laughed.

"I get it!" he said, excited. "Because they look like they're from space, or the future!"

"Yes!" I said, beaming at him. "*Star Trek* reference."

"I know!" He looked very pleased with himself. I helped him up onto a stool at the kitchen countertop, which was the same marble as down in the bakery.

"A chef needs a proper kitchen," said Michel, gesturing at the shiny counters and appliances. "When the bakery started doing well, we used the money to renovate."

"It looks great," I said, and I meant it. "In New York, people spend a fortune putting this sort of stuff in, and then they never use it. They go out to dinner every night or eat take-out sushi."

Alastair looked puzzled. "Why?"

I shrugged, sliding into the stool next to him. "They like the way it looks, I guess? The function is irrelevant."

Michel shook his head. "What a shame."

"I'm hungry," said Alastair, cutting off Michel. I gave him a meaningful look—*don't be rude*—but he just blinked at me.

"I apologize, Alastair," said Michel gravely. "Let's get started. Today, we make our own pizza."

"Pizza!" Alastair's voice was squeaky with excitement, and the way he squirmed happily in his seat reminded me of an untrained puppy. "I like pizza. I like to make pizza. It's my second-favorite thing. The first is—"

"Croque monsieur," said Michel and I at the same time. We both smiled.

"I thought pizza would be more fun, today," explained Michel. "Clara, do you like pizza?"

"Of course!" I lied smoothly, my voice full of false cheeriness. My heart picked up its rhythm ever so slightly at the fib, and I hoped my cheeks weren't bright red. I hadn't had pizza in ages. It was close to the top of my list of banned foods, right behind ice cream and before bacon.

"Excellent." Michel reached into the enormous refrigerator and retrieved a large stainless-steel bowl. Setting it down, he pulled off the makeshift lid of plastic wrap and pushed it towards us. "Here is the starter for the dough."

Alastair and I leaned forward, looking into the bowl. A weird, colorless clump of goop stared back at us.

"Er—what is this, exactly?" I asked politely.

From beside me, Alastair piped up. "It's a starter," he said, as if it were the most obvious thing in the world. "Yeast. To make dough."

"Right," I said, nodding, even though I wasn't any clearer on the goop than I had been moments earlier. Michel must have caught the expression on my face, because he grinned and leaned forward on his elbows towards me.

"So, in French we call this starter *levain*. When we bake, we keep a bit of dough each time, and add flour and water. Smell it." He pushed the bowl towards me.

Cautiously, I leaned forward and took a whiff. "It smells like beer," I said.

"That's the yeast," said Michel, nodding. He smiled. "So we take some of the starter, and we add flour and water to form the dough. Alastair, will you please assist me?"

Alastair scrambled down from his chair and knew exactly which cupboard doors to open to retrieve flour and a set of measuring cups. Carefully, he measured out the appropriate amounts of flour and water and assisted Michel in stirring with a large wooden spoon.

"Clara," said Michel. "You will help me with the next part."

"Okay," I said warily. "What do I do?"

"Knead the dough," he said, pushing the bowl towards me. "Get your hands in there."

I wrinkled my nose slightly, but my desire to please him won out over my distaste for the smelly yeast and mushy dough. I removed my rings, washed my hands, and let my fingers sink into the mixture. I recalled Michel assisting me with the *pain Suisse* and eyed his own hands, hopefully.

He did not, however, join in this time, but rather encouraged me while he went about collecting ingredients and saucepans for phase two of the pizza-making process. "Feel the dough," he said, reaching for a cluster of tomatoes on an open shelf and handing them to Alastair. "Close your eyes and really touch it."

Michel helped me divide the dough, and showed me how to roll and pinch it into a circular shape. "Not too thin," he explained, "or you'll have to start over."

Alastair was busily working next to me, apparently a proficient expert at pizza-dough manipulation.

"Does Alastair come here a lot?" I asked Michel, watching my brother's face as he carefully pinched the crust of his pizza.

"Besides Wednesdays when he helps me at the bakery? Sometimes I babysit him. We are old friends, me and Alastair." He smiled as Alastair finished with his dough and stood on his stool, leaning across the counter in anticipation.

"That's really nice of you." Michel took out a set of knives and handed one to Alastair. I flinched.

"Are you sure that's safe?" I asked, wincing as Alastair began expertly skinning a tomato.

Alastair spoke up. "I have been using knives since I was four," he informed me. "I learned at school."

"They have knives at your school?" I asked faintly.

"At my old school," he explained. "It was a Montessori. They teach practical life skills."

"Apparently," I said, bemused.

We added the tomatoes to the pot with olive oil, sea salt, and fresh basil. Michel closed the lid and asked Alastair to fetch peppers, mushrooms, and some Italian salami.

"No pepperoni?" I asked jokingly.

Michel made a face. "Pepperoni is an American concept," he said. "In Italian it means 'small red peppers.' They use salami."

Michel divided up the toppings, and we each set to work. Michel showed me novel ways to cut peppers—to slice them so that they uncoil like a roll of parchment, making it simple to cut strips. He also demonstrated how to cut a mushroom so that you only had to lift your knife ever so slightly each time.

Next to me, Alastair chopped his salami with the skill of a Food Network chef. I took a moment to snap a photo of him with my phone, hunched over a green pepper. I sent it to my mom, with whom I'd been a poor correspondent. Because of her schedule, email and texts were easier than phone calls, but they were also much more abrupt, more devoid of detail and emotion. I resolved to set up a time to hear her actual voice.

When the sauce was ready, Alastair showed me how to spoon and spread it across my pizza dough, then how to sprinkle just the right amount of mozzarella on top.

I hesitated, and grabbed my phone again.

"What are you doing?" asked Michel, frowning. He peeked over my shoulder.

"Nothing," I said hastily. I hit the home button so he couldn't see what I was doing.

"Why were you Googling 'mozzarella and nutrition'?"

I shifted nervously in my chair, as if I'd been caught by a teacher for passing notes during class. "I need to know the fat and calorie count," I said in a low voice. I felt uncomfortable.

"Why?" Michel shook his head. "Just follow Alastair. The key is to put just enough, not too much. If you eat the right amount, it is not unhealthy."

I shook my head. "I need to measure it," I whispered. "Do you have a food scale?"

Alastair had stopped what he was doing and was watching us. "Why do you need a food scale?"

"She doesn't," said Michel. He leaned against the counter and crossed his arms against his chest.

"You don't understand." The two of them stared at me, and I felt as if I were shrinking somehow—growing smaller and smaller with each look my way.

"Tell me, then." Michel looked at me expectantly.

"I need to know exactly what I'm eating," I explained. I was fighting back tears.

"Why?"

"She is on the eating disorder spectrum," announced Alastair.

"I am not!"

"Yes, you are. I heard Mum and Dad talking about it. It's called orthodontia."

The tears were flowing freely now, and I had what Bree referred to as "the cry" in my voice: the warbling sensation that you were about to launch into heavy-duty bawling. In spite of this, I smiled. "Not orthodontia. Orthorexia. They think I'm obsessed with healthy eating and exercise. It's not even a real disease, I don't think."

Michel came over and placed his hands firmly on my shoulders. "I told you," he said. "I will help you."

"You don't understand. I'm not sick. I'm not anorexic," I said, and even to my own ear it sounded feeble, almost desperate. "I'm just trying to be healthy."

"Whatever it is…" Michel came back around to the stove. Forgotten, the leftover tomato sauce had started rattling in its pot. He removed it from heat and lifted off the lid, jumping back so as not to get splattered. "Whatever it is," he repeated, "I will help you."

I took a deep breath. I wanted Michel to like me. "Maybe," I said slowly.

"We start by putting cheese on this pizza. No scale."

I swallowed and stared at the bowl of shredded mozzarella. I turned my head, so as not to gag. "Okay."

I scooped out a handful of cheese. Gritting my teeth, I sprinkled it around my pizza as if it were an art project. When I was done, Michel nodded with approval.

"Try the cheese," he said to me.

I paled, staring at the bowl as if it contained a thousand squirming maggots as opposed to an innocuous dairy product. Usually, the only cheese I permitted myself was ricotta. I couldn't remember the stats on mozzarella. Was it a relatively low-fat cheese? High? How bad was the sodium content— should I expect to swell up like a balloon?

"Clara?" Alastair was watching me, waiting. I went ahead and picked up two tiny fragments and placed them on my tongue. *Definitely high-sodium*, I thought grimly.

"Good," said Michel approvingly. Relieved that he didn't mention the minute portion I'd conceded to, I decorated my pizza with an assortment of mushrooms and green, red, and yellow peppers.

"Salami?" Michel pushed the bowl towards me.

I shook my head. "Not today," I said. Michel's eyes met mine, and he nodded slightly.

"Next time," he said lightly.

As the pizzas baked, the aroma in the kitchen became

intoxicating. Even I couldn't deny the pleasurable smell. Alastair stood in front of the oven, breathing deeply.

"They smell so good," he said. "I love pizza because it smells good while it's cooking."

"Is that unusual?" I watched as he knelt to look through the glass door at the rising crust.

"Some things taste good, but smell bad in the oven," he informed me without turning around. "Also, some things smell bad, but taste okay."

"Like what?"

"Fish. It smells terrible, but it tastes okay." His nose was now pressed against the door, leaving streaks of his condensing breath behind. "I think they're ready," he announced.

Michel peeked inside. "You're right, Chef," he said dramatically. Alastair didn't giggle, but instead nodded seriously.

When the pizzas had been cut, Michel caught my eye and pressed a knife and fork into my hand. "One slice," he whispered.

"But—"

"*Un tranche.* One slice. Slowly. Savor each bite. Clear your mind."

I sighed and let my mind go blank. I cut a square the size of a thumbnail and took a bite. It was delicious. You could taste the basil in the tomato sauce, fresh and aromatic. The dough was the perfect combination of chewy and crispy. The peppers, roasted from the oven, tasted smoky and retained a slight crunch.

"Do you have to eat pizza with a knife and fork?" asked Alastair. He was holding a slice in his hand, frozen halfway to his open mouth.

"Of course not," I told him. "In America, most people eat it with their hands."

"Show him," said Michel casually. I shot him a look that clearly said, *I know what you're doing*. He stared right back at me with a look that said. *Good, I don't care.*

I lifted the slice and folded it over, New York-style. "Like this," I said. I took another tiny bite, this one enhanced by the sandwich effect of the crust.

"Why do you fold it?"

"Maybe because it's less messy that way? I don't know, you just do."

Alastair and Michel both followed my lead, folding their pizzas like sealed envelopes. Michel's eyes bored into me as I discreetly tried to put my slice aside. Reluctantly I picked it up again. *Clear your mind*, I told myself. *Focus on the senses.*

I took another bite, making an effort to appreciate the taste and smell. And then another, and another. Soon, the slice was gone. Triumphantly, I placed my cutlery down on the table.

"That was not much," said Michel doubtfully, looking at my plate.

"Baby steps," I answered. "And you said one piece."

"But it's so good. Is it not good? Do you not want more?"

I sought the words to explain. "It is good," I assured him. "Of course it is. But—I can't. There's saturated fat in cheese. And—"

"Shhh," said Michel. He put a finger to my lips and I felt a jolt in my stomach that had nothing to do with the tomato sauce, excellent though it was. "You're right. Baby steps. That is what we will do."

I watched Michel and Alastair devour the remainder of their lunch and stared at my own plate with a sense of both accomplishment and self-blame. *It's going to take a lot of crunches to fix the damage you've done*, a little voice whispered in my ear. I tried to ignore it, but it pestered me the remainder of the day.

CHAPTER 16

That night, my back straight against the wall as I repeatedly squatted down to Alastair's nautical-themed rug, I told myself I didn't have to double up on exercise just because I'd eaten a slice of pizza. The problem was, I didn't entirely believe myself. When I thought of the cheese, melted, gelatinous, and likely to take up permanent residence in my thighs and belly, I recoiled and wanted desperately to increase the pace of my exercise. Did my "baby steps" promise to Michel include scaling back on kicks and crunches? It wasn't clear.

Alastair appeared at the door dressed in a pair of footed Paddington Bear pajamas that made him look much younger than his age. "Sorry," he said. "I'm just looking for my colored pencils."

"No problem," I answered, breathing heavily. I wiped the sweat from my brow. "Go ahead."

He didn't move. "What are you doing?"

"Exercise. I do it every night." I reached for my water bottle and took a long swig.

"That's what you do when your door is closed?"

"Yes."

"Oh." He shifted from foot to foot, and I wondered, with a surge of irritation, where one even found footed pajamas for someone Alastair's size. "I always thought you were talking with your mother."

"I should be, actually," I said, feeling guilty. I had planned to try and talk with my mom that night, but hadn't gotten around to it. I avoided Alastair's intense gaze, focusing instead on the ridiculous duckies that adorned the curtains. I had a sudden urge to rip them down.

"Do you ever talk to her?" He paused. "I don't like to talk on the phone, but whenever Mum or Dad goes away, they make me."

"We've…texted. Emailed," I said feebly, turning my attention back to Alastair. "It's tough, with the time difference."

"Do you miss her?"

More guilt. I loved my mother, but if I were honest, I'd have to confess that I was enjoying this break. I had also begun to see that, if I had any intention of sorting out my relationship with food, my only hope was to stay away from home, at least temporarily. Did I want to face the issue? Was that why I kept putting off calling her? Was that why she wasn't making more of an effort to call me?

I looked at Alastair, "I do miss her, but when you're older, it doesn't feel so bad. To be away from your parents."

"You're always away from Dad," Alastair commented. "Does that make you sad?"

I sighed. No conversation with Alastair was ever simple. I struggled to find the right words. "It will now, I think," I said. "Now that I've lived here. I'll miss you, too." Startled, I realized I actually meant it.

Alastair looked anxious at this statement, so I quickly changed the subject. "What are you drawing?"

"Drawing?"

"With the pencil crayons." I bent down into another squat, concentrating on keeping my back erect and bending only my knees.

"I'm not drawing," said Alastair, as if it were an outrageous proposition. "I need the colored pencils to do my math work."

"You have math work? It's the summer." I frowned, confused.

"It's for fun. Mum buys me extra books."

"You do math for fun?"

"Yes." He still hadn't moved towards his closet, where the art supplies were stored. "Can I watch you exercise?"

"What?" I blinked. "Why?"

"I don't know. I want to see." He still hadn't moved. I felt badly asking him to leave—it was, after all, his room.

"Um," I tugged at my tank top. "I guess…why not? Have a seat."

"Thank you." He went over and climbed up on to the bed, careful to smooth out the duvet as he crossed his legs. "What are you doing with the wall?"

"Squats. See?" I demonstrated, descending slowly and then rising back up, arms balanced carefully out in front of me.

"Why do you do those?"

"Exercise is healthy," I said quickly, repeating the squat. *Ten more*, I told myself grimly. My calf muscles burned with the effort.

"But can't you do another kind of exercise?" Alastair watched me repeat the squats. "Those look hard."

"They're good for your leg muscles," I explained. "I want to have nicer legs."

"How could they be nicer?" He looked puzzled, and scanned my legs up and down as if wondering how one could improve upon a pair of limbs. At Alastair's age, making something nicer involved painting it or covering it in stickers.

"Well, I want them to be firmer, and ideally I would like a space here," I said, motioning between my thighs."

Alastair looked alarmed, and I realized that talking to a six-year-old about thigh gap was probably bad form. If he mentioned this to Mag, I'd probably be carted off to a mental-health facility. Apparently health care was free here, so it would be easy. One call, and I'd be an in-patient.

"Never mind," I said quickly. "It's a grown-up thing."

"No, I want to know," he said. "If you want a space between your legs, can't you just stand with them apart?"

If only it were that easy, Buddy, I thought wryly. I motioned towards my legs, standing heel to heel. "When standing with them together," I elaborated.

Alastair regarded me and my legs in silence for several moments. Then he got off the bed, walked over to the bookcase, and retrieved a large, hardcover tome.

Thinking he'd lost interest, I went back to my squats, but he opened the book on the duvet and called me over.

"Look," he said, pointing.

It was an anatomy text. I wondered why a first-grader would need an anatomy textbook, but I guess if you enjoy recreational math, finding biology entertaining made perfect sense. Alastair was gesturing at a skeleton, stabbing his index finger against its waist.

"What?" I asked, baffled.

"See this?" he circled the skeleton's middle. "That's the pelvis."

"I know what a pelvis is, Alastair," I said.

"But, Clara," he said. "Your legs can't have a space between them because your pelvis isn't that big."

I started to laugh. "Alastair," I said, "what do you know about pelvises?"

"But, look," he said, sounding upset. "See how the leg bones connect to the pelvis?"

This was beginning to feel like an intervention. If I didn't know better, I'd think Bree put him up to it. She was always insisting that thigh gap was something genetic, something particular to some bodies and not others.

"Also, why would you want a space between your legs?" Alastair thrust the book at me, and I backed away.

"It's…a fashion thing," I said lamely.

"I don't understand."

"Yeah, well, fashion is like that."

"I don't understand that, either." Alastair looked both earnest and worried, his head cocked slightly to one side as if trying to puzzle it out.

"That's what I'm saying. Fashion is weird." I shrugged and released my hair from its ponytail. I was starting to get a headache.

He stared at me blankly for a moment, then shook his head. "Can you make me a hot chocolate?"

I looked longingly at the wall. I still had eight squats to go, and I hadn't even started on kicks. "Can't Dad do it?"

"He's snoring on the couch."

"Shouldn't your mom be back by now?" I glanced over at the clock. If I remembered correctly, Mag's train should have arrived an hour ago. Where was she?

"She's delayed."

"Okay," I said, sighing. I'd be up late now, finishing my set. Then I realized something else. "Alastair? I'm not sure I know how to make hot chocolate, exactly."

"I do," he assured me. "I'm just not allowed to use the stove by myself."

In the kitchen, Alastair pushed over a dining-room chair to the workspace and clambered up so that we were nearly shoulder-to-shoulder. I watched as he measured out milk and cocoa powder and sugar, then assisted him by lighting the burner and stirring gently. Alastair hovered next to me, watching the pot intently.

"You know, they say a watched pot never boils," I joked, running the long wooden spoon around the inside of the pan. It felt slimy, as if the milk were sticking to its sides. Mildly repulsed, I stirred faster.

"We don't want it to boil," said Alastair. "It's milk. We just want it to get hot."

"Right," I said, feeling foolish.

"Now," instructed Alastair, motioning for me to remove the pot and turn off the stove. He climbed onto the counter and fetched two mugs from a cupboard high over the stove.

"Careful," I said nervously. I didn't like him climbing on the countertops. I had visions of him sustaining third-degree burns on his adorable footed pajama feet. I gave him my hand, but he politely avoided it, setting down the two mugs.

"Pour, please," he said. He leaned forward towards the pot and inhaled deeply. "It's a good batch."

"You can tell from the smell?"

"Of course."

I poured the hot chocolate, which was thick and viscous and highly visually appealing. It did smell good too—it reminded me of Christmas as a kid, when Mom would let down her guard and make me pancakes and cocoa. Not for her, of course. I ate alone.

Alastair took the mugs to the table while I deposited the pot in the sink. He cleared a stack of books and loose papers so there was room to sit down, then set out two woven placemats I was sure Mag had made herself out of recycled cloth.

"Should I go wake Dad?" I asked, running a sponge along the inside of the pan.

Alastair seemed confused. "Why?"

"For his cocoa." I nodded at the mug and turned off the faucet.

Now he looked injured. "It's for you," he said.

I wiped my damp hands on my workout shorts. *Hot chocolate? Could I?* I thought of Michel's face earlier as he watched me eat the pizza, of my promise to try. "Okay," I said finally. I slid into the chair across from him and warmed my hands against the mug. Cautiously, I took a sip.

It was nothing like I had remembered, though of course, when Mom had made it, she had bought it in chemical-filled packets laced with artificial sweeteners. This was thick and creamy and delicious. I felt my heart beat faster as the calories and fat content of milk appeared—unbidden—in my mind's eye. I blinked fast, trying to rid myself of the unwanted mental image.

"This is really good," I said firmly, taking another sip.

"Yes," Alastair agreed simply.

We sat beside each another in silence, thoughtfully sipping our drinks. I stared ahead at the dining-room wall, at a family portrait of Dad, Mag, and Alastair dressed in matching white shirts. I felt a pang of sadness. Not only was I not in that portrait, I had never been in any family portrait. Why had Mom and I never posed for photos together?

"Clara?" Alastair's voice was hesitant.

"What's up?"

"Is this your first time eating chocolate?"

"What? No. No, of course not." I laughed. "Why would you say that?"

Alastair fidgeted in his seat and tapped rhythmically on his mug. "You never eat it."

I didn't respond. I stared into the pool of remaining hot chocolate as if it were a mug of tea leaves, hoping it would provide me with answers.

"If you can eat something good, I think you should eat it," he went on. "I can't eat peanuts and peanut butter or lots of chocolate bars with peanut stuff in them, and everyone says how good they are. Peanut butter even *smells* good."

"I'm working on it," I said. I took another sip of my hot chocolate, ignoring the mocking voice inside my head warning me that, if I kept this up, I would end up in elastic-waist pants. "And by the way, peanut butter is overrated."

"Really?" he asked, sounding hopeful.

"Absolutely."

"Let's take a picture together," I said suddenly. I retrieved my phone. "Come closer."

Warily, Alastair inched over to me, his chair scraping against the hardwood floor. Carefully, without touching him, I raised my phone just above both our faces.

"Smile!" I said. "Say, '*fromage*.'"

"*Fromage*," Alastair chanted obediently. I lowered the phone and showed him the picture.

"Good shot, don't you think?" I asked. It was, too. Alastair was rosy-cheeked from the hot chocolate and looking directly at the camera; I was laughing and looked genuinely happy.

"We should print it and put it on the wall," he said. He pointed at the family portrait. "With that one."

I wanted desperately to hug him, but restrained myself, busying my hands instead with once again raising the cocoa mug.

A

When Mag came home an hour later, Alastair and Dad were already asleep in their room. I was busy on my phone exchanging emotionally charged texts with my mother.

–How is the eating going?

–I had a hot chocolate today AND a slice of pizza.

–That's wonderful! Melisa will be thrilled.

–Are you thrilled?

–Of course, why wouldn't I be?

–Embarrassing 2 have fat daughter?

I didn't know why I'd typed that. Part of me wanted to push back, to get the old disapproval. *Suck it in, Clara.*

–Do I deserve that? I do, don't I?

–Forget it.

–Can I call you? Please?

I looked up and noticed Mag in my doorway. Her mouth was pulled tight and she was carrying the Superman backpack. She did not look pleased.

–Can't now. TTYL

I put the phone face down on the bed to avoid responding to Mom's inevitable next text and raised a hand to Mag. "Hey," I said casually. "Welcome back. How was the conference?"

"Fine," she said coldly. She held up the backpack. "I suppose this is your doing? And those shoes?" She spat out "shoes" as if it were a dirty word.

"Alastair and I went shopping, yeah," I said lightly. I was determined to try and keep my cool.

"Alastair had—has—perfectly good shoes. Shoes that will help ensure his back and legs develop properly."

For a second, I was thrown off. "I didn't realize he had back and leg problems."

"He doesn't—because he's always worn proper shoes!"

I rolled my eyes. I couldn't help it. What decade was this? Besides, the sneakers he'd chosen were Walkrights, a fact that I pointed out.

"They're ridiculous," she said, ignoring my comment about high-quality sneakers. "You're trying to make him someone he's not."

"He chose them," I said. Forgetting my earlier resolve to keep things civil, I slammed my fist down on the bed. "Why is my trying to help him look like a normal kid forbidden, but your trying to make him some sort of freak perfectly fine?"

"Excuse me?" her face was bright red. She looked as if she'd spent an hour too long in a tanning booth.

"The kids in his class make fun of him. They used to hide his shoes at recess."

"The other children bully Alastair because he isn't neuro-typical. I've been in to talk to the—"

"Yes," I cut her off. "I heard. You want to help Alastair? Stop showing up and talking at his school. And stop buying him ugly shoes and decorating his room like a nursery." I made a sweeping motion with my arm, drawing her attention to the roomful of duckies and sailboats.

"So he should be someone he's not, just to be *cool?*" She said the word disdainfully. "To *fit in* with silly children not nearly as bright as he is?"

"*He* didn't pick the buckle shoes," I countered angrily. "And he didn't choose these duckies. So *now* who's making him someone he's not?"

She didn't answer. She was still in her coat, and was per-spiring heavily.

"And being bullied sucks," I added. "Why would you want that for him?"

"You really think *shoes* are going to help Alastair," she shook her head, chuckling to herself. "I would use the word shallow, but—"

"Excuse me." I jumped off the bed, crouching as if we were in an actual boxing match instead of a verbal one. "I love Alastair. He's great. I wouldn't change him. But Alastair hates being bullied. And kids *do* care about shoes. That I know, be-cause, as you say, I am shallow."

We stood facing one another, both of us with our hands on our hips. The Superman bag sat on the floor between us like a referee.

"I think I'll go to bed, now," said Mag, breathing heavily. A bead of sweat trickled down her forehead and down the bridge of her nose. "We can discuss this tomorrow."

"Fine," I said angrily. When she left, I slammed the door. Alastair's pizza photo rattled precariously, as did the overhead light fixture. Fuming, I threw myself back on the bed and picked up my phone. There were three messages from my mom.

–Just 5 min pls.

–Clara?

–I guess you've gone to sleep. Maybe tomorrow. Xo.

I deleted the texts and rolled onto my side, angry at my mother for always caring too much about what others thought when I was growing up, and at Mag for caring too little. Feeling lonely, I opened my Facebook page despite my vow to avoid social media. Nothing new from Bree, who clearly was still in no man's land as far as wi-fi went. There was an update from Spencer Caplan, the first in ages, indicating he was living with his grandparents at a retirement community in Arizona for the summer, teaching technology classes to the elderly. He didn't look particularly pleased in the picture, which was of him seated at an ancient PC desktop, a group of white-haired people hovering in the background.

Karma, I thought to myself, with a certain grim satisfaction. *It's a bitch*.

My mood considerably lightened by *schaudenfreude*, I flipped off the lights and waited for sleep to claim me.

CHAPTER 17

"What are you doing with your clothes?"

I jumped, startled out of my outfit-planning reverie. "Alastair," I said, turning around to face him in my doorway. He was wearing a different pair of footed pajamas, these printed with images of Thomas the Tank Engine and his weird vehicular pals. "You've got to stop sneaking up on me like that."

"Sorry," he said quickly. He took a step back, looking very small in his sleepers, but I shook my head and waved him in.

"It's okay," I said. "Come, you can help me."

"With what?" He looked curiously at the clothing spread out on the bed. "Are you packing?" His voice was small and fearful, and he began to fold and unfold his fingers.

"What? No. No, of course not. I don't leave for ages." I gestured at the two outfits I'd laid out: one, a pair of skinny jeans with a lacy, loose-fitting pale-rose top, the other, a vintage-looking yellow dress, sleeveless, with a trio of large plastic buttons down the front. "I'm going out with Michel."

Michel had texted yesterday, asking if I would like to accompany him to the carnival at the *Jardin des Tuileries*. That was the word he used, "accompany," like we were characters in a Jane Austen novel who happened to own iPhones.

"I'm trying to decide which looks nicer," I explained. "We have a date."

I was excited and nervous for this first real, just-us date with Michel. How would he feel once he really got to know me? How would I feel about him? Would his reverence for food be an issue? Right now, it both attracted and repelled me. I felt thrilled at the thought of Michel's hands deep in a bowl of dough, his hands intertwined with mine, but also repulsed, as though we were standing on opposite sides of a well-defended border guarded by tall-hatted chefs wielding rolling pins.

Alastair made a face at the word "date." "Are you in love with Michel like Daddy and Mummy?"

I smiled and poked around my makeup bag for my liquid eyeliner. "I wouldn't say in love," I answered, trying to think of how best to explain it. "I would say strong like."

"Are you going to kiss him?"

"None of your business," I said jokingly, but Alastair stiffened and began rocking slowly in place.

"That's an expression," I said hastily. "Like, I'm teasing you. Because kissing is private."

"Oh." He stopped rocking and went over to examine the yellow dress. "I didn't know."

"So?" I held up the lace top against my body and waved it slightly at Alastair. "This one, or the yellow one?"

"How should I choose?" He frowned with concentration.

"Which do you think would make me look prettier?" I tossed aside the pink and grabbed the yellow dress, holding it against my shoulders.

Alastair shook his head. "I don't understand. You'll have the same face. Your face doesn't change when you wear different clothes."

I laughed out loud, wondering what the fashion industry would have to say about Alastair's comments. He stared back at me, his eyes wide and serious.

"Okay, so which do you like better? Just looking at them. Does one look nicer to you?" I was interested to see what he thought. Did being on the spectrum affect his perception of style? Of color? What would he think? Did he actually like those silly Thomas the Tank Engine PJs, or were they yet another manifestation of Mag's babying? I longed to ask him, or at least surprise him with some Minecraft pajamas or something, but Mag and I were in a cold state of détente after the shoe fight, and I didn't want to rock the boat.

"I think I might wear the trousers, if it were me," he said finally, nodding at the jeans. "Because if you wear a dress, there is a chance he might see your underwear. And that would be very embarrassing."

So much for assessing Alastair's aesthetic; he had responded the way any normal six-year-old boy would, reducing the issue to whether one's underpants would be exposed. The ultimate kindergarten calamity, as I recalled. Then I thought of the Ferris wheel and wondered if Alastair perhaps had a valid point.

"You know," I said gravely. "That's very true. I think I will wear the jeans."

Alastair beamed at me, looking pleased to have successfully participated in the endeavor. He perched comfortably at the end of the bed and watched me hang up the dress.

"Here you go," he said helpfully, handing me the lace top.

"Thanks." I paused, waiting, but he made no move to leave.

"Uh, Alastair?" I gave him a sidelong glance.

"Yes?"

"I need to get changed now? Remember? Privacy?"

He stared at me blankly, showing no signs of moving from atop the sailboat bedspread.

I sighed, clarifying. "I don't want you to see my underwear."

"Oh!" he jumped up. "Sorry, Clara."

"No problem," I grinned, shutting the door behind him.

I'd told Michel I'd meet him outside, but he showed up at our door. With flowers. Real, live flowers—pink ones. I wasn't sure what they were called, but they were beautiful and smelled great.

"Wow," I said, taking them from him. Stunned, I brought the bouquet to my face. "These are so pretty."

"Good." He looked awkward, hands stuffed in the pockets of a faded leather jacket. "I am glad you like peonies."

"What?" I asked, shocked. "What did you say?"

"Peonies," he said, startled. "The flowers? They are called peonies?"

"Oh," I said, relieved. "I thought—well, never mind."

Alastair, who had been hovering in the background piped up. "I think she thought you said penis."

"Alastair!" I exclaimed, scandalized.

Michel burst out laughing. "Oh, I am sorry. My accent—"

"No," I interrupted. "I'm not up on my flowers. I know roses, tulips. Maybe daisies. I didn't know what these were called. They're so beautiful."

My dad appeared with a vase. "Shall I take those for you?" he asked.

"Thank you," I said, handing them over. "Much appreciated."

No one had ever brought me flowers on a date, unless you counted various half-squished corsages produced by homecoming dates. I wondered if bringing a girl flowers was a French thing, or an older guy thing, or merely a nice-person thing. I suspected it might just be the latter.

"Ready?" asked Michel, and I nodded, grabbing my purse and a silk scarf from the hall closet.

"Goodnight," I called over my shoulder to Dad and Alastair. Mag, who was studiously avoiding me, was nowhere to be seen.

I waved at Alastair and let the door click behind me, overtaken by a sensation of relief. I hadn't been out without Alastair since I'd arrived in Paris. I told Michel, who shook his head.

"*J'adore* Alastair but he is not easy to care for. You need to relax more. Get out, have fun." Michel held various doors for me until we arrived outside. Each time, I marveled at his gentlemanly manner.

"I know," I said. "Thank you for suggesting this tonight."

"Have you been to the *jardins?* The carnival is perhaps a bit tacky, but also fun."

"I have," I assured him. "I took Alastair. He went on the carousel."

"He did?" Michel looked surprised but pleased. "That's great!"

We walked together in the direction of the Eiffel Tower, and I realized that I'd barely been out at night. Mostly, I'd been inside exercising or sparring with my mother via text. Clearly, I had been missing out. Paris had an energy at night that had to be observed to be fully understood. The streets were bustling with as many people as during the daytime, but the atmosphere was more relaxed. It seemed very different from New York, where everyone moved with purpose, in a hurry to get wherever they were going. In Paris, people strolled. The walk, one sensed, was the destination, and the goal was to enjoy it rather than hurry it along.

As we walked, we chatted about our parents, our friends, and our plans for the future.

"I would love to get experience in New York," said Michel. "Work at a restaurant there, or a bakery." I loved the way he spoke the word *bakery*, with an emphasis on the final syllable instead of the first.

"Really?" I asked. "I was just thinking it would be nice to live here. To come here for college. I think there are English classes at some of the universities."

"You could also learn French," he pointed out, grinning. "It is not so hard."

"I don't have your gift for languages," I said, shaking my head. "I can never even remember the word for 'bill.' I wave my hand in the air like a lunatic."

"It's *l'addition*," said Michel. He pronounced the word *la-dee-see-on*. "It's easy to remember, because it makes sense. *L'addition*—'the addition.'"

I hadn't made the connection until that moment that the string of sounds was spelled *l'addition*. I felt myself blush, and kept that to myself.

"Do you miss your mother?" he asked me.

I shrugged. "Yes. And no. I don't know." I sighed. "It's complicated. Everything with my mother is complicated."

"What is she like?"

I exhaled, thinking. How to adequately describe the great Catherine Malcolm, principal dancer with the world-renowned New England Ballet? I got out my phone and scrolled through my photos.

"Here," I said, thrusting the camera at him. "That's her."

It was a beautiful photo, a backstage snapshot of my mother dressed for her role as the lead in *Romeo and Juliet*. Her hair was braided with flowers and her eyes shone with pre-performance anticipation. Thin and willowy in her costume, she looked almost ethereal, and I felt the familiar pang of envy.

Baby steps and osteoporosis and Melisa were all very well, but there was no quick and easy remedy for the childhood I'd spent in my mother's impossibly lean shadow.

"She is very lovely," said Michel diplomatically. "But what is she *like?* As a person?"

"Well, she's a dancer," I said lamely. "And she has a major eating disorder that's left her with osteoporosis."

"I see," he said. He looked grim.

"She wasn't a bad mom," I said fairly. "She gets an 'F' on the food report card, fine, but otherwise—I'm being unfair. She's not a bad person."

"No one is perfect," he answered. "My mother was not perfect, either. She also sometimes did not eat. Before a play would begin its run, she would diet. It drove my father crazy. What kind of baker has a wife who will not eat? He would bake her croissants and she would snub him. Maybe she would take two bites, but no more."

"Huh," I said, surprised. He hadn't mentioned that until now. So he knew, then, what it was like, having a mother who performed. Who was a slave to costumes and cameras and directors full of passive-aggressive comments about "healthy eating."

"When she got sick, she began to lose weight," he continued. "She was happy at first." His face twisted with these words, and for the first time he looked almost ugly. "Happy." In the moonlight, the bitterness in his eyes was readily visible. I flinched, wondering if my mother would have thought the same. If I would have.

"Then came the chemo, and she could not eat at all," he

concluded. "I remember, she asked me to bring her a *pain au chocolat*. She tried to eat it, but she could not. She couldn't swallow."

I knew what the message was, why he was telling me this. I felt ashamed and guilty and resentful and angry all in one. Everyone, it seemed, had something to say on food, on eating, on weight. It didn't make it any easier for me.

Michel must have sensed I wasn't entirely pleased with the direction of our conversation, because he took my arm and changed the subject. "Look," he said, pointing at a sea of lights ahead of us. "There's the carnival."

The rest of our exchanges that night were light-hearted. Michel played—and lost—four silly carnival games of balloon darts before finally winning a small stuffed horse with a rainbow tail and purple wings.

"It's adorable," I said, clutching it in a dramatic hug. "Thank you. I love unicorns."

Michel grinned. "It is not a unicorn. It is a Pegasus."

I frowned, staring at it. It looked back at me with huge, solemn black-plastic eyes. "What's the difference?"

"A unicorn has a horn." Michel motioned to his forehead, miming the shape of a horn. I fought the urge to laugh. "A Pegasus is a winged horse."

"You're sure?"

"Yes."

"Huh." I tucked the Pegasus under my arm and, feeling brave, linked my other one through Michel's. "You learn something new every day."

"Yes," he said gravely, pulling me closer to him. "I am full of useful information."

We passed by the merry-go-round that had made Alastair shriek with laughter, and got in line for the Ferris wheel.

"I tried to ride with Alastair," I told Michel, as we handed over our tickets. "But he freaked out."

"He got scared?"

"Yes." I nodded. "Heights and small spaces are hard for him."

"I feel for him," said Michel. He leaned next to me so that our shoulders brushed against one another. "It cannot be easy, to be so different. Children are cruel. I used to get called all sorts of names. Many people in France are still very racist."

"That's awful," I said, feeling surprised—both at Michel's revelation and at my own reaction to it. Why was I shocked that black or mixed-race kids would be subject to insults and slurs? It wasn't as if the U.S. didn't continue to battle its own racist demons.

"Even tonight," he added, guiding me forward as the line inched ahead. "At least three people have stared at us. Why is a black man out with a white girl?"

"Really?" I looked around, feeling uneasy. Who amongst these people had looked at us, silently judging? And how had I missed it?

Michel tucked an errant curl behind his ear. "I have learned to live with it," he said, his face a mask of indifference. I wondered how he really felt, on the inside.

"That is enough about me," he said, his shoulders once

again brushing up against mine. "We were talking about Alastair." We climbed the steps as the ride emptied out, and the next round of passengers was loaded up. It still wasn't our turn. Sensing his desire to change the subject, I used the opportunity to tell him about Mag and the Great Superman Backpack Incident.

"You should try talking more to your *belle-mere*," he suggested. "Why is she like that? Maybe she has had her own troubles."

"Maybe," I said doubtfully. I hadn't thought of that. Mag was the sort of person who seemed inherently adult, as if she had been born at the ripe old age of thirty or so. Had she been picked on as a kid? I couldn't picture her as anything other than Alastair's mom in her dream-catcher ear-wear.

When it was our turn, Michel helped me into the carriage, and we settled onto the bench side by side. As the wheel began to climb, I watched the carnival and the Jardins des Tuileries disappear beneath us, the carousel looking more and more like a toy.

"It's a great view," I commented as we neared the top. I could see not only the Eiffel Tower, but the spires of Notre-Dame and Les Invalides. Lit up for the evening, they looked nothing short of magical. "So beautiful."

Michel, however, was looking at me. "Yes," he said softly. He brushed the hair from my shoulder, and it was as if every nerve in my body was suddenly alert, alive. Combined with the height and the swaying motion of the Ferris wheel, his touch was exhilarating.

He put an arm around my shoulders, and I snuggled into him. I waited for him to make some sort of move—to kiss me, or more—but he seemed content to remain that way, and I didn't know whether to feel disappointed or relieved at his restraint.

We stayed at the fair until it closed for the evening, finishing off with a large cone of pink and blue cotton candy.

"I can't believe you eat that," I said, eyeing it. "Is it not offensive to someone who makes real desserts? Real food, I should say?"

"*Non*," he said laughing. He popped a handful into his mouth. "It's delicious." He held out the cone to me and I took some, looking wary.

"Have you never had it?" he asked, gaping. "Go on, try it. In French we call it *barbe à papa*."

"Huh?" I held the fluffy cloud of sugar, staring at it skeptically.

"Papa's beard. See?" He held a piece up to his chin, and I couldn't help but grin.

"You look ridiculous."

"Try it."

"Okay, okay." I popped a bit into my mouth. It dissolved immediately. I frowned, taking another bite.

"Well?"

"I can't decide if it's yummy or disgusting," I admitted. "Maybe both?"

"Fair enough," he said, laughing again. "Let's get you home."

At the front door, he took both my hands in his and spoke hesitantly.

"May I kiss you?" he asked shyly.

I blinked. No one had ever asked permission before. "Yes," I said breathlessly. "Yes, of course."

He leaned forward, and I closed my eyes.

CHAPTER 18

Usually either Dad or Mag had to do some kind of work on the weekend, so we hadn't yet done anything as a group. Yesterday, however, Mag announced that we would be going on a "family outing" to the Museum of Natural History.

"Family outing?" I echoed. Having grown up the only child of a busy single mom, to me a family outing generally constituted a trip to the sushi place around the corner or going with my mother to buy new tights. Taking me to museums had been the purview of any of the number of *au pairs* who'd lived with us when I was little. I had vague memories of the New York Museum of Natural History—dinosaurs in cheesy-looking habitats, an Easter Island statue replica, dioramas of Native Americans.

"Yes, a family outing," my father had said firmly, shooting warning glances at both me and Mag. We hadn't argued again, but our exchanges had been perfunctory and our silences prolonged. "We're all going to have fun."

"Right," I said politely. My vision of wandering around Paris for a day alone in a silk scarf looking for vintage dresses vanished.

"It's a fascinating museum," Dad added. I recalled the New York stegosaurus in what was essentially a giant box full of plastic greenery. My less-than-enthusiastic expression must have been apparent to Dad, because he grinned and clapped me on the back.

"It's really different from its New York counterpart," he assured me. "Just wait until you see it."

"Right," I said doubtfully. I failed to see how such a place could be more than vaguely interesting.

I was wrong. The moment we stepped into the exhibit hall of the *Muséum national d'Histoire naturelle* I gasped.

"This place is *creepy*," I said, gaping at the array of skeletons and specimens on display. No silly dioramas or faux-Jurassic forest here: just rows and rows of cases, samples, and bones.

Alastair ran from skeleton to skeleton, examining each with great curiosity. "Look, Clara," he said, pointing. "A buffalo!" He ran over.

It was a huge skeleton, with black horns added to it for effect. I stared at its massive ribcage, and tried to imagine it alive, covered in thick, brown, shaggy fur.

"Its teeth are a lot like ours," he said, standing on his toes to get a closer look. "Not sharp and pointy-like."

"I think that's because it ate plants," I said, making a

valiant effort to dip into whichever corner of my brain harbored my second-grade curriculum memory reservoir. "It was a...." I struggled to find the lost word. "A herbivore!" I felt triumphant.

"But we eat plants and meat," said Alastair.

"Right," I said. "Humans are omnivores—we eat both plants and meat. But the predators, like tigers and lions and T-Rex, those are the carnivores. They eat meat only." I pointed at the sharp teeth on a nearby panther skeleton.

Mag and Dad lagged slightly behind us, also pausing to examine various specimens. Once or twice Mag called out to Alastair—*don't run, come look at this*—but I could hear Dad whispering to her, and eventually she quieted down. I wonder if Dad had taken some of my comments about babying Alastair to heart.

We wandered through the garden of skeletons, me following Alastair's lead. When he reached a shelf of large jars, he stopped short and took several steps back. "Clara," he said, looking terrified. He began to rock back and forth in place.

"Alastair? What's wrong?" I jogged over and saw immediately what the issue was. The jars had preserved specimens of what appeared to be mutant fetuses. I noted a two-headed duck and a cat with seven legs. *Monstres*, the exhibit was labeled.

"Are they monsters, Clara?" Alastair's words were barely audible. He continued rocking back and forth on the soles of the buckled shoes Mag had insisted he go back to wearing.

"No," I said quickly. "Just...mutants. Sometimes something goes wrong with a baby before it's born." I remembered his biology textbook. "Do you know what genes are?"

"Yes," said Alastair importantly. "They're like blueprints. They say what color your eyes will be and stuff."

"Right," I agreed, nodding. "So, sometimes something goes wrong. The blueprint gets messed up. So you get a cat with extra legs, or whatever."

"And they call those monsters?"

"Mutant," I said quickly. "Not monsters."

Alastair stopped rocking. He stood next to me silently, looking at the unusual and admittedly frightening specimens. I glanced back to see if Dad and Mag were nearby, but they were some paces behind us.

"Clara," said Alastair suddenly. "Am I a mutant?"

"What? No!" I jumped back from a grotesque-looking rabbit with three eyes. "Why would you say that?"

Alastair looked serious. "My genes are different. I'm not normal. I don't have two heads, but inside my brain isn't like other people's."

"That's true, but you are not a *mutant*, Alastair. You're just different."

Alastair didn't say anything. I put my hand on his backpack—he was allowed to carry the Superman one, as a concession—and steered him away. "Come on," I said. "Let's go see something else. Some dinosaurs, maybe."

As we walked away, though, I heard a shrill voice shout out in a British accent, "Look, it's *Alastair*."

We looked up. The voice belonged to a girl about Alastair's age. Her red hair was pulled back into a neat French braid and she wore a peacoat paired with a denim skirt and little black boots. The miniature *fashionista* put her hands on her hips and narrowed her eyes as she stared at my brother. Another kid appeared and made a face. This one was a boy in jeans and a T-shirt, with menacing eyes and a mop of curly red hair. *Twins*, I realized. Then I remembered Alastair's story. *The St. Clare twins*, he'd said. They were the ones who'd taken his shoes and hidden them in a tree.

Alastair stiffened next to me, and I stepped in front of him, shielding him protectively. "What's up?" I said casually to the pair. I looked around for some sign of parents, but there was none. "Where are your mom and dad?"

"Still in the café," said the girl, looking bored. "Alfie and I aren't babies, though. We don't need a *babysitter*." Next to her, Alfie snickered.

"I'm Alastair's sister," I said coldly. "Not his babysitter."

The girl frowned. "Alastair doesn't have a sister."

"Yeah, he does. I live in New York, with my mother." I put my hands on my hips. I didn't enjoy fighting with a seven-year-old, but someone had to put this kid in her place.

"You're from New York?" she looked impressed, despite herself.

"Yup." Next to me, Alastair was still stiff and silent. "Are you friends of Alastair from school?"

Alfie snorted. "Charlotte and I aren't *friends* with Alastair," he said, making a face. "We just know him."

I resisted the urge to lean forward and grab the rotten kid by his shoulders. "That's really rude," I said instead. "I think you should apologize."

Dad and Mag came up behind us, Mag smiling brightly at the sight of the twins. "Look, it's Alfie and Charlotte!" she exclaimed. "Alastair, look! Your friends from school!"

Charlotte snickered at this, but didn't say anything. Alfie, however, shook his head. "We aren't really friends," he muttered.

"Where are your parents?" continued Mag, looking around. I wondered if she had heard him, or whether she was selectively deaf. "Maybe we could all get a biscuit together in the café."

"We've already eaten," said Charlotte, nudging her brother. "Let's go."

"But—" Mag was about to say something else, but I put a hand on her arm.

"Enough," I said in a low voice.

Charlotte gave us a big fake grin. "We need to be off," she said airily. Then, as if she couldn't help herself, she gave Alastair a once-over and smirked, her eyes lingering on his shoes. "Nice shoes, Alastair," she said. Alfie started to laugh, and the two of them dashed off. I watched them disappear behind a woolly mammoth skeleton.

Dad, who hadn't said anything until that point, put a hand on Alastair's shoulder. Surprisingly, Alastair didn't recoil.

"They didn't seem very nice," Dad said in a low voice. "Are they mean to you, Alastair?"

Alastair nodded almost imperceptibly. "Yes," he whispered.

"They stole his shoes and threw them in a tree," I elaborated angrily, turning to look at Mag. "That's why I bought him the new ones."

Mag, for once, was speechless. She looked flummoxed, staring alternately at Alastair's feet and the retreating St. Clare twins.

"I don't understand," she said finally. "I spoke to the class about bullying." Her voice sounded far away.

"You can't talk kids out of bullying," I said, exasperated. "It would be nice if you could, but some kids are always going to be mean. That's why he needs the shoes. He needs to blend in a bit more. It's not about changing who he is," I added. "It's about...self-preservation."

Mag stared at me. For a long time, she said nothing. "Alastair," she said finally. "Why didn't you tell me they stole your shoes?"

Alastair shrugged. "You didn't ask," he said simply.

Mag looked as if she might cry, and for the first time, I felt sorry for her. It can't have been easy, mothering a boy like Alastair, and she had only been trying to do the right thing. Still, I thought, staring at Alastair's hideous footwear, the orthopedic shoes had been one over the line.

Mag took a deep breath. "From now on," she said, "you'll wear the runners. The ones you bought with Clara." Her eyes met mine, and I sensed an understanding pass between us.

"Good," said Alastair. "I like those better."

"Yes, they're very...stylish," said Mag, her nose twitching with the effort at suppressing her disapproval.

"They're also more comfortable," said Alastair. "I can run faster in them."

Dad made a small noise from behind me, and I turned to

look at him. His eyes were twinkling, and I could see he was trying not to laugh. Determined not to look smug, I pretended to be suddenly absorbed by a nearby display of early mammals.

"I could use something to eat," said Dad then. "Shall we head to the café?"

Alastair nodded. He shifted from foot to foot, the Superman backpack swaying with him. "I want a croque monsieur."

"Good idea," agreed Mag, looking relieved. She took a final look at the red-haired twins, as if wanting to go over and try to mediate. Our eyes met again, and I shook my head slightly. Some things, I knew, were best left alone. If Alastair and the twins were going to work it out, it would have to happen on its own, organically.

"Sound good to you, Clara?" Dad put a hand on my shoulder.

I wasn't hungry, but I thought of my promise to Michel, and to my mother. "Yes," I agreed finally. "I'll have something to eat, too."

CHAPTER 19

Michel had booked the day off to take us to the market, to the *Marché Bastille*. He wanted me to understand how Parisians shop for food, to appreciate their way of life. I imagined the three of us clutching wicker baskets as we paused at stalls to feel the apples or squeeze the tomatoes. For the first time, I wondered where Dad and Mag shopped for groceries. Did Mag hit the market daily? Probably, though I doubted she carried a basket. Mag was more a reusable shopping bag kind of person.

We met Michel outside, where he waited for us with a shopping cart. I stared at it in frank dismay. "Where are the baskets?" I asked, unable to hide my disappointment.

Michel laughed. "This isn't Hollywood. The cart is easier."

"But the baskets are so romantic," I said wistfully.

"How can a basket be romantic?" Alastair frowned. "It's a basket."

The sky was gray, with only a shadow of sun visible through the clouds. The weather channel had promised sun for later on, but I was skeptical. I pulled my denim jacket tighter around me, against the morning chill. Michel had insisted we depart at the ungodly hour of seven o'clock.

"Otherwise," he had intoned, seeing the look of horror on my face, "we will have to fight the crowds. It gets very busy."

I thought of Alastair at the packed Louvre, rocking back and forth in his weighted vest. "Okay," I had said with a sigh. "Seven it is."

Alastair tapped on my arm, still waiting for a reply on his question about the baskets. "Clara?"

"Sorry, Alastair." I yawned into my sleeve. "Baskets make me think of movies or novels about Paris, which make it seem like a foreign and romantic place where you come to find love and excitement."

"Oh," Alastair nodded. "So, like you and Michel?"

My yawn morphed into a cough of embarrassment. "Alastair!" I felt my face grow hot despite the chill. I made a concerted effort to avoid looking Michel's way, but he nonetheless managed to catch my eye and grin broadly. Did nothing embarrass him?

"I have coffee," he announced suddenly, reaching into the granny cart for a large paper bag. "And croissants."

"Bless you," I said gratefully, accepting a cup.

"Croissant?" offered Michel, handing one to an eager Alastair and then holding one out to me. His eyes were questioning. "Try more than a bite this time."

I took a deep breath. "Okay," I said. Trying to reassure myself that eating breakfast kick-starts the metabolism, I nibbled the edge of the flaky pastry. It was even better than I remembered. Michel watched me as I took a second, larger, bite.

"Okay?" he said, and I wasn't sure whether he was asking about me or the croissant.

"Delicious," I admitted, savoring the buttery taste. Determinedly, I took a third bite.

Alastair was watching me carefully. "Does this mean you're cured?"

"Cured?" I raised my eyebrows.

"Of your orthorexia. I heard Dad tell Mum that he thinks you're getting better."

I thought of Dad discussing me with Mag and made a face. What did they know of me and my life, really? They didn't know what it was like to be the mostly-ordinary daughter of a celebrated dancer. They barely even knew me at all. Resentfully, I washed the croissant down with more coffee.

"I'm getting better," I assured Alastair. I decided not to tell him that, only seconds ago, I had contemplated peeling off the flaky outside of the croissant and sacrificing the doughy interior to minimize calories and saturated fat. Instead, I bravely took a fourth bite. I had eaten almost half a croissant. I resisted every impulse to Google the average caloric content of a butter croissant, French-style. Anxiously, I chugged my coffee, grimacing suddenly.

"Does this have cream in it?" I asked, peering through the tiny sipping hole in the lid.

"And sugar," said Michel firmly. "That is the way coffee is meant to be drunk."

"I don't know about that." We were walking now as we ate, a practice common enough back home, but almost unheard of in Paris. Here, people sat to enjoy their coffee, whatever the time of day.

"No?" he cocked his curly dark head towards me. "Does it not taste good?"

"It does," I conceded, "but some people like their coffee black. I often just have it black."

Michel made a face. "Everything is better with cream."

"Spoken like a pastry chef," I said, amused.

Michel grinned. "Guilty," he said dramatically. I grinned back, and wondered if he was thinking of our kiss the other night. I hadn't seen him since, but we'd texted plenty, and even spoken on the phone twice. I also wondered if he hadn't had the cart, whether he'd have taken my hand.

Alastair finished his croissant and handed me his empty, crumb-filled bag and dirty napkin, something I've noticed all children do. Apparently, a grown-up is a person who desperately wants to relieve you of your trash. I asked Alastair and Michel to wait a moment while I went to toss the garbage. Standing over a nearby bin, I hesitated. Did I keep the rest of the croissant and risk eating it? Or did I dispose of it, and let the others think I ate it? Wasn't half enough? Surely it was.

Guiltily, I dropped in the remainder of my breakfast. I caught the eye of a nearby pigeon, who gave me a knowing look. "Enjoy," I whispered.

We rode the Métro, which was packed with briefcase-clutching commuters heading off to work. Perspiring in their suits, they piled in at each stop. I managed to find Alastair a seat, and hovered over him protectively.

"Are you okay?" I asked him. "Do you want your vest?"

"No," he said. He sat very straight, his arms at his sides as if he were reporting for military duty. "I think I can do this without it."

"That's great, Alastair," I said, feeling really pleased. "I'm so happy to hear it."

"You ate the croissant," he said, looking at me. "I'm trying to get better, too."

My stomach turned. I felt like a rotten liar, like the worst person imaginable.

"It's different," I mumbled. "You don't need to get better, Alastair. We love you the way you are."

"No," he said firmly. "I don't like it when the other kids laugh at me. I want it to stop. Like the shoes." He proudly held out a sneakered foot.

"Right," I said guiltily. "You know, though, you can take it one step at a time."

I felt Michel's eyes on me, and I wondered if he knew I'd disposed of the croissant. I kept my attention focused on Alastair, unable to meet Michel's gaze.

When we reached the market, I understood Michel's determination to arrive early. It wasn't even eight, and already it was looking crowded.

"This way," he instructed us, motioning. The market was

a sensory wonderland, an overwhelming hodgepodge of colors, smells, and sounds. We headed towards a group of vendors hawking fresh fruits and vegetables: plump red tomatoes, elegantly slender zucchinis, peppers so brightly colored they looked as if they had been shaded using Crayola markers. I inhaled deeply, enjoying the scent of the market air—in one breath, I caught whiffs of strawberries and apples, with a hint of cucumber.

I felt a tap on my arm, and noticed Alastair, looking pale. "I don't like it here," he said quietly. "Everything smells."

I'd forgotten Alastair's sensitive nose. I ran a mental inventory of the backpack contents, but couldn't think of anything that would help. I wondered why Dad didn't include nose plugs along with the earphones. Maybe something to do with the ability to breathe?

"What is wrong?" Michel turned around and noticed us.

"Smells," I informed him.

"Oh," he said. He looked worried. "I forgot. I didn't think of it."

Alastair began his rocking, and Michel and I stared at each other helplessly. All around us, people bustled about with shopping bags and baskets, politely uttering their *excusez-mois* each time we were inadvertently bumped by a leg or shoulder.

Michel snapped his fingers. "I know!"

He reached for my neck, where I'd tied one of the scarves I'd picked up in the Marais. Michel untied the scarf, and I tried to ignore the electric-like sensation of his fingers brushing against my collarbone.

"What are you doing, exactly?" I asked politely.

"This!" Triumphantly, Michel shook out the scarf and carefully wrapped it around the lower half of Alastair's face. He tied it loosely in the back and looked questioningly at Alastair.

"Does that work?"

"Yes," said Alastair, his voice slightly muffled. "Now I just smell the scarf."

"Is that okay?" I asked nervously. With Alastair, it was just as possible he would be offended by the smell of a fake silk scarf as by fruits and vegetables.

"Yes," he said again. He turned to me and looked me square in the eyes. "It smells like you, Clara."

Touched, I rested my hand on his backpack as we continued on. Michel led us to a tomato vendor and asked for three in rapid-fire French.

"You don't pick your own?" I asked curiously. I reached to grab a tomato, to squeeze it gently the way I might have at the Stop 'n' Shop back home. Michel grabbed my arm, shaking his head.

"*Non, non,*" he said. "You cannot touch."

"Really?" I asked, surprised. "But then how do you know you're getting good ones? What if they're squishy?"

The vendor, a small, older gentleman with sparse white hair and wire glasses, looked offended. Obviously, he had understood what I had said. He shook his head quickly, waving his arms back and forth and muttering something that included the word "squishy."

"He says he would never sell someone squishy tomatoes,"

Michel informed me. His eyes twinkled, and I could tell he was trying not to laugh.

The man, who had placed the tomatoes in a paper bag, looked mutinous.

"*Je suis désolée*," I told him apologetically. "I am sorry, really."

"Hmmph," he answered, taking Michel's cash and making change. Clearly, I wasn't to be forgiven so easily.

I didn't make the same mistake with the cucumbers or mushrooms that came next. We went from stall to stall, collecting produce.

"There's nothing like fresh fruit and vegetables," Michel informed us. "Here, try these."

He handed us each some white grapes. They were tender and juicy, and both the taste and the texture were superior to anything I had ever had at home. It was the same for the carrot I sampled, and especially the tomatoes.

"Oh, my goodness," I said as I bit into a tomato. I closed my eyes. "This is nothing like the tomatoes we have in our supermarket in New York."

"These are real tomatoes," Michel said, full of enthusiasm. "Tomatoes in most parts of the world are bred for size and color, but here you can still find ones bred for taste."

It was true. The tomatoes weren't as bright or enormous as those I was used to, but the flavor was rich and aromatic. Alastair, who was unused to anything else, smelled and tasted his tomatoes obediently, but did not demonstrate the same level of excitement as I did.

When we moved on to cheese, I warned Alastair to try to breathe through his mouth. Stinky cheese could be tough to take even for a seasoned foodie.

"Cheese can be pungent," I cautioned him. "Even through the scarf."

"It's okay," he assured me through his makeshift mask. "I like the smell of cheese."

I shook my head, amused. "No one could accuse you of being predictable," I said.

"I like Camembert," he continued, gesturing at a nearby stall. "Can we get some?"

"Sure," I said. Who'd ever heard of a six-year-old with a penchant for Camembert? I looked over at Michel, but he didn't seem to find this remotely odd, so I chalked it up to a cultural difference, one of those French-kids-are-awesome things you read about in *The New York Times*.

We purchased some Camembert—I was careful not to touch any, lest I raise the seller's ire—and Michel herded us over to the meat area, suggesting we select some sausage to go with it.

"This smell I don't like," announced Alastair, freezing in place when we'd reached the butcher section. Behind us, a tall, blonde woman with a toddler in tow gave us a filthy look as she nearly crashed into Alastair.

"You know what," I said to Michel. "I'm not crazy about this smell, either. Alastair and I will wait over there." I gestured to a nearby bench.

"All right," he said, looking disappointed. "I will just pick up some *charcuterie* and be right back."

Relieved, I ushered Alastair over to the bench. The sun was out now, and the air was warm. I shed my jean jacket and suggested Alastair remove his raincoat. I also helped him untie the scarf mask.

"You don't like the smell of raw meat, either?" Alastair had a revolted expression on his face.

"Not really," I said. It was true; I hadn't eaten anything approaching a sausage in years. In fact, I didn't eat much red meat at all. I told Alastair as much.

"Are you a vegetarian?" he asked me, looking serious. "My teacher was a vegetarian. She didn't want to hurt animals."

"I'm not," I told him honestly. "I eat chicken. I just don't eat much other meat."

"Because it's not that healthy?" guessed Alastair.

"I don't even know anymore," I admitted. "I thought so, but the science…it's always changing."

Alastair nodded. "It's true. Mum used to make me take all these disgusting fish-oil tablets, but now she says they're rubbish."

All around us, people have shed their jackets. Nearby, a couple of backpackers in their twenties spread out a blanket and a picnic of assorted cheeses, berries, and a baguette. They paused every few bites to kiss or hold hands, which made me feel both envious and as if I wanted to gag.

Michel reappeared, his cart even fuller than before. Under one arm, he clutched a long baguette, half-wrapped in red, white, and blue paper.

"Isn't that, like, sacrilege?" I asked, nodding at it. "What would your father say, eating another baker's baguettes?"

Michel burst out laughing. "Sacrilege!" he repeated. "Really, Clara, you are so funny. No, we would call it lunch."

I glanced at my phone. "It's not even ten!"

"A snack, then." He pointed at the canoodling couple. "Let's have a picnic."

"We just ate croissants!"

"But the bread is warm and fresh! We must try it." Alastair shrugged off his windbreaker and spread it out on the ground like a picnic blanket.

"Here," he said, tearing off a chunk. "Alastair, try it with some of your cheese. Wait, I'll get it for you."

Michel rummaged through the cart and retrieved both the Camembert as well as an apple. "Here," he said, carefully dividing the cheese with his Swiss-army knife. He handed us each a portion, then used the same knife to slice the apple. A light spray of apple juice reached us.

I stared, dismayed at the food in my lap—the still-warm bread melting the soft cheese ever-so-slightly, the apple, ripe and sweet-smelling. I had just eaten half a croissant. How could I possibly indulge in this so soon?

"It's really good," said Alastair happily. He had piled up the bread, fruit, and cheese into a sort of open sandwich. "Try it, Clara."

"Yes, Clara," echoed Michel, tearing off another hunk of bread for himself. "Please try it."

Resigned, I took a small bite. I chewed thoughtfully, taking in the assortment of tastes and textures. The bread was crusty and the apple juicy, but the cheese had an unpleasant tang to it.

"You know," I said, sniffing at it cautiously, "I don't think I like Camembert."

Michel looked skeptical.

"It's true!" I protested. I glanced over at the label, which provided the milk-fat percentage. Sure, it was high, but I could honestly say the taste of the soft cheese was not to my liking. "It tastes...I don't know. Sort of sour?"

"It's an acquired taste," admitted Michel, slicing another chunk of apple and passing it to Alastair.

"What does that mean?" asked Alastair, politely declining the apple and accepting more cheese.

"It means Michel thinks I have an unsophisticated palate," I said dryly, making a face at Michel. "I haven't built up my taste buds."

Michel elbowed me playfully in the ribs. "Sometimes, you have to try things a few times before you like them," he told Alastair. "That's all I meant."

"I liked Camembert the first time I tried it," Alastair informed him, and I grinned, sticking my tongue out at Michel.

"There you go," I said triumphantly. "Acquired taste, my foot."

Michel put an arm around me, and I felt my cheeks go warm. "I stand corrected," he said. He tucked a loose strand of hair behind my ear. I glanced over at Alastair; would he feel uncomfortable?

Alastair, however, seemed oblivious and unconcerned. He took another crust of bread. Michel pulled me closer, and I snuggled against him.

"What should we do next?" he asked. He glanced at his watch. "The day is still young."

I had no desire to leave the spot I was currently in. I stared lazily at the sun in the sky, enjoying the warmth against my face. Soon, though, Alastair would grow restless.

"We could go back to the carnival," I suggested. "Alastair likes the merry-go-round."

Alastair's face brightened. "Yes!" he said. He sat up straighter. "Could I try the Ferris wheel again?"

Michel and I exchanged a smile. "Of course," I said.

"I'm not going to get cold feet this time," he informed me.

"That's great," I said, grinning at him. "I'm very proud of you."

Alastair and Michel finished up the bread and apple, and Michel carefully rewrapped the cheese in its thick, waxy paper.

The market was thinning out now; the crowds had peaked. Michel explained that it was only open in the mornings. By the afternoon, he said, the vendors would pack up their stalls.

We walked until Alastair was tired, determined to enjoy the pleasant weather, then boarded the Métro. It wasn't as busy this time, and we were able to spread out and relax. Alastair happily pressed his face against the glass, enjoying the blur of lights as we sped underground.

When we reached the Jardins des Tuileries, the three of us rode the carousel together. Alastair chose a large cat that went up and down, and Michel and I selected decorative horses side by side. Alastair reprised the high-pitched squeals of delight he had made the last time, and I watched Michel's face light up with pleasure at the sound. Michel then fished out a few coins and tried to teach a half-interested Alastair how to play a hoop-tossing game. When Michel won a stuffed tiger, he handed it to Alastair.

"No, thank you," said Alastair, polite but indifferent.

"Alastair!" I exclaimed. I felt embarrassed, but Michel shook his head at me quickly.

"It's okay," he said, smiling. "Alastair isn't a baby. He doesn't like stuffed toys. Right, *mon ami?*"

"I don't like stuffies," Alastair explained. "I don't like how they feel. Also, I don't understand the point of them."

I thought of the hours of fun I'd had with my dolls and stuffed animals before I'd grown too old to play with them. The tea parties, the dances, the games of school or hospital. I supposed it was different for Alastair, but that didn't mean he shouldn't take the little tiger.

I squatted down so that I was at my brother's level. "I still think you should take it," I said. "You don't have to play with it. But if you put it on your shelf, every time you see it, you will think of me and Michel and the fun time we had. Right?"

Alastair looked thoughtful. "That's true," he said. "I could do that."

"It's a souvenir," I said. "Not just a toy. The point of it is to help you keep your memories."

Alastair nodded slowly. He took the tiger from me and looked at it solemnly. "So when you leave, I won't forget you," he said in a small voice.

"Well, I hope you won't forget me regardless," I said lightly.

"But you might not remember this day. And now you will." I felt sad. Would Alastair forget me when I left? When would I see him again?

"Yes," he said. "Yes, I see now." He stared at the tiger a moment longer, then carefully placed it in his backpack. "Thank you, Michel."

"My pleasure." Michel was watching our exchange with a tender expression. He reached over and squeezed my hand. I squeezed it back and rested my head on his shoulder.

"Can we do the Ferris wheel now?" asked Alastair. He turned to face the large ride, his neck craned upward. "I'm ready."

"Sure," I said, prodding his backpack lightly. "Lead the way."

The line was much shorter than it had been on the previous visit, and soon it was our turn. Bravely Alastair handed over his ticket, and Michel and I helped him on. He was seated snugly between us, so I could hear his breathing quickening, getting louder with each breath. I watched a small bead of sweat trickle down the side of his face, towards his left ear.

"Alastair?" I said in a low voice. "Are you okay?"

The ride started to move. The carriage swayed gently, and Alastair shut his eyes tightly. His body shook, and he began to rock back and forth.

"Vest," I said automatically. I rummaged through his backpack and took it out. Michel and I struggled to help him into it as he continued his rocking. The carriage swayed harder and Alastair made a small mewling sound like an injured kitten.

"I want to get off," he whimpered.

I peered out the side of the carriage. We were approaching the top. Michel gave me a desperate look.

"Keep your eyes closed," I commanded Alastair. "Don't open them or look down."

"Are we at the top?" His voice was small and fearful.

"Nearly," I answered. "It will be over soon."

"I need to get off!" Alastair jumped up suddenly, and stood in the center of the carriage. Michel swore loudly in French and grabbed his arm. Alastair shrieked and batted at Michel's hand, thrashing frantically.

"Alastair," I said, trying to remain calm, though my heart was pounding. "Sit down with me and help me count."

"Count?" he repeated. His voice trembled. His eyes were still squeezed tightly shut.

"Yes." I took a deep breath and reached for my brother, pulling him back to the bench. "I want to count to one thousand, but I don't want to do it alone. Can you help me?"

"One," he said, resuming his rocking. "Two. Three, four, five."

"Good work," I enthused. "Keep going."

We got to six-hundred and twenty-three before the carnival worker unhinged the latch on our carriage and helped us out. Alastair opened his eyes and blinked.

"Alastair," I said, as we descended the ramp from the ride, "you were very brave."

"No, I wasn't," he said. His voice was small. "I didn't like it. I couldn't open my eyes."

"Some people don't like heights," I said matter-of-factly. "You're just one of them. Just because you didn't like it doesn't make you not brave. In fact, it makes you braver, for trying."

Alastair shrugged off the weighted vest and we tucked it into his backpack. His eyes downcast, he shoved his hands into his pockets. "It's because I'm different."

"No," I said firmly. "It's not. Lots of people don't like rides. My friend, Bree? She cried so hard on a roller coaster at Coney Island that she peed in her pants."

Alastair looked up hopefully. "Really? She peed in her pants?"

"She did."

"How old was she?"

"Fourteen," I informed him. He looked aghast.

"Four*teen*? Did people make fun of her?"

I bit my lip. "We did, but in a nice way."

"There's a nice way to make fun of someone?"

"Yes. Teasing, but because you like someone. Not because you want to hurt their feelings."

Alastair pondered this, which I guessed was new information. "I didn't know neurotypical people peed in their pants as teenagers," he said finally.

Michel, who was walking alongside us, laughed. "Everyone does embarrassing things," he said. "And everyone has things they don't like, or are afraid of. I am afraid of wasps."

"Are you?" I asked, interested. I pictured Michel brandishing a fly swatter. "Like, how afraid?"

He looked ashamed. "There was once a nest in the ceiling

of the bakery. When the wasps got in, I ran screaming and left my father there."

I winced. "What happened?"

Michel reddened. "He was stung many times."

"Oh, geez." I shuddered; I was not a fan of wasps myself.

"Clara?" Alastair tugged at my sleeve. "What are you afraid of?"

I paused. What was I afraid of? I was afraid of lots of things. Of silly things, like chocolate, of not-so-silly things like belly flab, and of downright scary things like being unpopular or alone. I didn't say any of this to Alastair, though.

"Bats," I said, lamely. "They freak me out. They're like rats, with wings. They shouldn't even exist."

Michel gave me a look, as if he knew I was being deliberately dishonest about what scares me. Alastair looked thoughtful and informed me that bats eat mosquitoes.

"I still don't like them," I said, shuddering. It wasn't a lie, exactly; I *was* afraid of bats. The fact that, growing up in Manhattan, I had never seen a bat outside of a zoo or natural-history museum, was irrelevant. An animal that looked like an angry flying rodent was worthy of fear.

We walked most of the way home, opting for the Métro only when Alastair looked as if he might buckle under the weight of his backpack.

"Alastair was really brave," I informed Mag and Dad when we returned. "He went on a Ferris wheel today."

"That's wonderful!" Dad beamed, looking thrilled. "Did you like it, Alastair?"

Alastair and I exchanged a knowing look. "No," he said simply. "But I'm glad I tried."

I watched as he removed the small, stuffed tiger from his backpack and carefully placed it on a shelf in his room, so it could be seen from the bed. He stared at it for several seconds before turning away, and I wondered whether he was imprinting it with his memories.

CHAPTER 20

"Is this fancy enough, do you think?" I asked nervously, smoothing the skirt of my dress in front of the hall mirror. Michel had texted me earlier to "dress up" for tonight's date, but he wasn't specific as to whether that meant "your best dress" or "no jeans." In the end, I opted for the one little black dress I'd packed. It wasn't a particularly fancy fabric, but my mother, in her infinite wisdom, had taught me that, whatever the occasion, you can't go wrong with the classic LBD. When it came to etiquette, she was usually correct.

"You look beautiful, Honey," Dad assured me. He was in his typical after-work wear, a pair of faded plaid-flannel pants and a university T-shirt. "Very fancy."

"Thanks." I finished twisting my hair into a neat chignon, which I fastened with a beaded clip. "He won't tell me where we're going."

"That's very romantic," piped up Mag from behind me, sounding wistful. "Your father used to be romantic."

"Ew," I said reflexively. Thinking of a parent as romantic was bad enough; thinking of a parent as romantic with Mag was doubly gross.

"Thanks a lot," said my father dryly.

Alastair was long asleep, tired after today's activities. The two of us had spent the day at the *Centre Pompidou*, immersed in modern art. The museum had a cool kids' zone, where Alastair had spent a full hour carefully designing a foam mobile.

"I have the perfect thing to go with your dress," said Mag suddenly, snapping her fingers. She disappeared into her bedroom and I looked after her warily. How would I politely decline the parrot-feather necklace or dream-catcher earrings she was bound to come back with?

"Here," she announced, reappearing. In her hands was a small, black velvet box. She lifted the latch and it popped open. Apprehensively, I glanced inside.

"Oh!" I exclaimed, looking down at the pink-hued pearls in surprise. "They're beautiful!"

"They were my mother's," she informed me. She unhooked them and held them up to my neck. "What do you think?"

"You—you don't mind?" I asked hesitantly, feeling ashamed of my previous thoughts.

"It's my pleasure," Mag answered firmly. She gently laid the necklace around my collarbone and fastened the clasp. "They look lovely on you."

"They do," I said fervently, running my hand along the strand. "Thank you so much."

"Thank you, Clara," she said quietly. "You've worked wonders for Alastair this summer. It's been such a shock—in a good way, of course—to see him open up like this with you."

"Yes," agreed Dad. He grabbed a dining chair and lugged it over to the hallway, where I was slipping into my shoes and tossing a lipstick into a little pink evening bag I'd picked up in the Marais. "It's worked out really well, I think, having you here. Alastair has really connected with you."

I shrugged, embarrassed. "He's a great kid," I said. "I love spending time with him." As I said it, I realized it was one-hundred-percent true; I loved my brother, and I enjoyed the time I spent with him. Helping and getting to know Alastair satisfied a need in me that I hadn't even known was there.

"He loves you, too," said Mag. She looked teary. "You don't know how unusual it is for him to connect with someone like this."

"It's been remarkable," said my father, nodding. "We've seen such a change in him. Let's hope he'll have a better school year this fall."

I rummaged through the hall closet, where I found the jacket I was looking for. "It's all about being yourself, but, like, not rocking the boat too much. You don't want to be a sheep, but you don't want to get beaten up, either."

Mag cringed. "I see that now," she said softly.

There was a knock at the door. Dad leaped up to answer it. "Go," he said, shooing me away. I stared at him, baffled. "You should make a dramatic entrance," he explained, grinning slyly, and I saw, for the first time, what my mother must have seen all those years ago.

Mag put a hand on my shoulder. "I want to apologize," she said quietly. "I was wrong."

I nodded, feeling uncomfortable. "It's okay," I said.

"I just—I was always the chubby kid. Weird. I would try so hard to be like the other girls—" her voice broke, and to my horror, I saw tears in her eyes. "I would try to wear what they wore, but it was never…quite right. I stopped trying, and then I relished being different. It was just easier. So I thought, with Alastair, that he should just *be* different, from the start. But I was wrong."

"Shoes don't change who you are," I said softly, feeling sorry for Mag. I understood now, why she acted the way she did. "But for someone like Alastair…it can be helpful. Crucial, even."

"I get that now. I do."

My hand went to my neck, where the pearls felt cool against my skin. "Thank you again for lending me your pearls," I said. "They truly are lovely."

Mag brightened. "My pleasure," she said. "Now, go say hello to your date!"

Michel looked handsome and serious in a pair of charcoal slacks, striped shirt, and black sports jacket. He was crouched in our front entryway, scratching at Minou's ears. "Good evening," he said formally, rising. His face spread into a grin when he saw me.

"Clara," he said, holding out a potted orchid. "You look *magnifique*."

"Thanks," I said, blushing. I took the orchid. "This is so nice of you."

"It's a difficult flower," he said gravely, "but worth caring for." His eyes bored deep into mine, and I blushed more deeply.

Michel helped me into my jacket and bid goodnight to Dad and Mag. When we descended the stairs and stepped outside, I was pleased to find the evening weather mild and dry. The sky was clear, and the breeze was gentle. To the west, the sunset was visible as a faint orange glow.

"So," I said, gazing at him sideways, "Are you going to tell me where we're going?"

He beamed at me, and I felt my stomach flutter. "We're going to Le Meurice," he announced, linking his arm through mine. "One of the finest restaurants in Paris. Traditional French."

"Great!" I said, feeling uneasy. What did traditional French mean, exactly? Heavy cream sauces and potatoes au gratin? What would I order?

"It's supposed to be very beautiful inside," Michel enthused. "It was recently redecorated."

"Oh?" I asked absently. My mind was still on the dangerous veloutés bound to be lurking on the menu.

"I didn't see Alastair," he commented, as we crossed a busy street.

"Asleep," I answered. "It's late for a six-year-old."

"Sometimes, I forget he is only six." Michel shook his head. "In many ways, he is much older than his years."

"But in other ways, much younger," I pointed out. "It's tough for Alastair."

Michel nodded. We walked hand in hand, and I felt warm

despite the rapidly cooling air around me. "It must be difficult. In school."

"Yes," I said. "Kids are cruel if you're different."

Michel laughed shortly. "I know all about this." A pained expression crossed his face, and I realized he was referring to his own experience. I squeezed his hand, urging him to continue.

"I was one of only five black students in my year at school," he informed me, looking grim. "The white students didn't like me, because I was black. And the black ones didn't like me, because my mother was white."

I stopped walking and took Michel's other hand in mine. "That's awful, "I said softly.

He shrugged. "I survived," he said, avoiding my gaze. He released my hands, and we resumed walking. "So will Alastair. It is much easier to be an adult. The world is a cruel place for children."

"Do you think it has to be that way?" I asked curiously. "Do you think children can be taught to be more accepting?" I thought of Mag and her class lectures on autism spectrum disorder. Could kids really be lectured into empathy? Could we ever really rid our children and ourselves of the prejudice and insecurity that drives people to behave in cruel or self-destructive ways?

Michel was quiet for nearly a block. "It's hard to say," he answered. "I was teased for being a different color, and Alastair is teased for having a different mind. You have neither of these differences, yet you still long to look like girls who have been photoshopped in a magazine."

"I don't—" I began hotly.

Michel shook his head, interrupting. "I do not mean it as a criticism," he said. "I just don't know. Can we build a world where everyone is accepted, and where no one feels they need to be something they're not? Someone they are not? I hope so, Clara, but I simply do not know."

I didn't know, either. Somberly, we walked on, past street vendors hawking miniature Eiffel Towers and housekeepers walking cherished dogs. The air grew cooler still, and I thought longingly of the scarf I'd left behind in the apartment. I consoled myself with thoughts of the calories I was burning with each step.

"Are you cold?" Michel asked, concerned. "We can call a taxi?"

"No, no," I said hastily. "I'm fine."

"I'm getting a taxi," he said firmly. He spotted one and waved his arms. "Taxi!" he shouted, and I tried to hide a grin. Michel was yelling so loud the entire block had turned to see what the commotion was. I gathered he didn't hail cabs all that often, which made sense: taxis were expensive in Paris, where the Métro was cheap and went everywhere. I fiddled in my pocket for cash.

"Here," I said, trying to press some bills into his hands once we were seated inside the car.

Michel looked affronted. "Never!" he exclaimed. "We are on a date!"

"It's the twenty-first century," I said. "I'm happy to go Dutch."

"Dutch?" he frowned. "What do the Dutch have to do with anything?"

I laughed loudly, and the driver peered at me curiously in the rear-view mirror. I quieted down. "Going Dutch," I explained. "It's when both people split the cost of a date."

Michel sniffed. "That does not sound Dutch. That just sounds silly. I asked you on the date, I pay. I am a gentleman." I raised my palms in defeat. "Okay," I said, grinning. "You win. I surrender to your gentlemanly charm."

He put an arm easily around my shoulders. "You make it too simple, Clara. We have not even had dinner yet. You cannot surrender."

I gave a muffled laugh into his shoulder as we arrived at the restaurant on the Rue de Rivoli, right near the Tuileries and the Louvre. Located within a luxury hotel, it had an impressive, high-ceilinged lobby and smart-looking girls in crisp white shirts, black skirts, and impossibly high heels who took our coats and escorted us to the maitre d'.

Our table was adjacent to a grand window draped with heavy, ivory-damask curtains. The restaurant was breathtaking, reminiscent of a palace set from a period drama. Glittering chandeliers hung every ten feet or so, the wallpaper was soft and velvety, and there was an elaborate fresco above us.

"Michel," I said helplessly. "This is…too much."

"It's beautiful, isn't it?" he said, beaming. "I have never been here, either. I have always wanted to come, though."

I swallowed as a waiter appeared and opened a menu for me. I scanned it anxiously, wincing as I noticed the prices.

"Michel," I hissed when he'd walked away. "We can't afford this!"

He made a face and waved his hand. "It isn't polite to talk about money at the table, Clara," he said severely. "I know that is not just a French custom."

I sighed. "No, but isn't there an exception when the dinner costs more than a pair of shoes?"

He laughed at that. "*Ma chère*, let me worry about it. You just enjoy."

Frustrated, I sat back and scanned the menu. Summer vegetables, thankfully, was an appetizer option. And the main courses seemed to be all fish, which was always a healthy option. I wondered how it was prepared.

"I've been told we should try the lobster," said Michel, leaning towards me. "It is supposed to be excellent."

Which was higher in calories, lobster or turbot, another choice on the menu? Which was fattier, and what sort of fat? Which had more Omega-threes?

"Is it in a sauce?" I asked, trying to sound casual.

He looked at me warily. "I imagine so. This is France."

I flinched, picturing lobster floating in a sea of heavy cream and melted butter. "Maybe I can ask them to prepare it without," I said, thinking aloud.

Michel looked horrified. "You cannot do that."

"Why can't I?" I asked, feeling defensive. "What if I had a food allergy? What if I was lactose intolerant?"

"But you are not lactose intolerant," he pointed out.

"How do you know?" I challenged him, feeling defensive. "Maybe I am."

He sighed, looking frustrated. "Is this what you do in New York? Interfere with the chef and the menu in restaurants?"

I slumped slightly in my chair, thinking of the Italian restaurant debacle, where my mother and I had left without eating. "I don't eat out a lot," I said carefully. "Mainly sushi."

"I see," he said. He looked sad, and I stared hard at my menu, silently reading and reading the word "turbot" until it sounded nonsensical.

The waiter came over to take our order. Michel nodded at me politely. "Clara?" he said. "What would you like?"

"I will have the summer vegetables to start," I said in a small voice. "And—how is the lobster prepared?"

"Medium rare," said the waiter promptly, with a heavy accent.

"No," I said. "I mean—is it in a sauce?"

"*Mais oui,*" he answered, surprised. "Of course."

"Ah," I said. "Well you see, I am lactose intolerant, so—"

"*Pardon?*" he interjected, looking baffled. He turned at Michel for support.

Michel sighed and exchanged words with the waiter in rapid-fire French. I caught the word *Americaine,* and stiffened slightly.

"It's a vinegar sauce," said Michel shortly. "So you need not worry about your…allergy."

Feeling guilty, I muttered a brief "thanks" and stared at my hands.

"Would you like something to drink?" the waiter asked politely.

"Um, a Perrier, *s'il vous plaît,*" I answered uncomfortably.

Michel gave his order, which included a glass of wine. "You don't mind, do you?" he said.

"Of course not," I said, surprised. It seemed so civilized, casually ordering a glass of wine at a restaurant. I thought of my classmates, who would illegally chug bottles of beer or down vodka coolers while their parents were on vacation. This seemed so mature. So…grown up.

"Wait," I said suddenly. "Aren't you only twenty?"

He frowned. "Yes?"

"But then how can you order wine?" I asked. "You have to be twenty-one."

"Oh." He laughed. "I think that is only in America. In France, you can order at eighteen. Of course, here, no one really cares anyway. Most grow up sipping wine with their parents at the dinner table."

"Was it like that for you?" I asked. I tried, and failed, to picture my mom and I enjoying a glass of wine together over sushi.

"No." He laughed. "Papa is Algerian. He's Christian, but Christians are a minority in Algeria. It's a Muslim country, and Muslims forbid all alcohol."

"Right," I said. "So your dad doesn't drink?"

"Not much," he said. "But I grew up French. I'd have sips at friends' houses growing up. I have learned to enjoy wine."

"Hmmm," I said thoughtfully. My experiences with drinking were mostly negative, having ended badly in a bathroom. I wondered if college would change this, or simply worsen it. Maybe I would attend university in France. Michel and I could be together. I would be near Alastair. I felt a surge of adrenaline at the possibility, but didn't say anything out loud. It would sound like I was proposing or something after only a handful of dates.

Our first course arrived, brandished by a different waiter in a white jacket, who placed our plates down in front of us with a flourish and a flurry of rapid French. Michel's pheasant pot pie looked less like a pie and more like a small, domed flying saucer on a bed of arugula. My plate of summer vegetables was artfully arranged by color. I speared a strip of yellow zucchini, drizzled in what appeared to be a sort of oil-and-vinegar dressing, and sniffed at it cautiously.

Michel raised his eyebrows at me. "I am fairly certain that is zucchini," he said mildly.

"Just wondering if the dressing is canola or olive oil," I said, taking a bite. "I think it's olive."

"Olive is healthier, I suppose?" Michel cut into his pheasant spaceship.

"Well, canola can be heart healthy, but overall, olive has more nutrients," I answered matter-of-factly. I took another bite before moving on to some eggplant.

"Would you like to try some of this?" Michel offered, pointing at his plate with his fork. "It's excellent. Very tasty."

"No, thank you," I said quickly, eyeing the heavy, pastry crust. I wondered what had gone into it—butter? Then I recalled that pie crusts are traditionally made with lard. I tried not to shudder as I imagined the belly fat of a pig being sucked out of the poor creature, then funneled into a stand mixer with flour. I concentrated instead on my eggplant.

A waiter appeared with a freshly cut baguette and some butter and placed them between us on the table. I was sure Michel would insist I try it. Why were the French so reluctant to abandon white bread? Did they not know how the refinement of white flour removed any nutrients? That bleaching added toxins?

"Baguette?" asked Michel politely, offering me the basket.

"No, thanks," I said again. "I want to save my appetite for the lobster."

Michel shrugged and took a slice. I watched as he slathered on a thick layer of butter and took a large bite. "Delicious," he said. "Excellent bread. I wonder if they bake in-house." He tipped the basket again in my direction. "Really," he said. "You should try it."

I sighed, feeling slightly irritated. "I've told you I prefer to avoid white bread. Are you not concerned about the bleaching and toxins and—"

"No," he interrupted. He looked annoyed, too. "I am concerned about living in a world devoid of pleasure where everyone throws around terms like toxin, as if eating white bread or rice is chemotherapy."

I didn't answer. Unable to look at him, I focused instead on the assortment of peppers on my plate, dragging them to the side where they were not quite so immersed in dressing. I looked up to see if Michel had noticed, but he was cutting his pie with a certain degree of force. Warily, I watched him stab at it with his knife.

"Would you like to try some veggies?" I asked, breaking the silence between us. "They're lovely."

"Yes, thank you," he said, accepting some squash. "I like to share. It makes the dining experience more pleasurable. You can discuss the flavors." The unspoken words—that my refusal to try his pie or the bread—hung between us.

"The squash is very nice," he said some seconds later. He reached across the table and touched my arm lightly, and I could tell he was feeling badly about the sharing comment. I murmured something in agreement and then placed my knife and fork down delicately on the side of my plate. The vegetables were fresh and tasty and packed with vitamins, but there was no need to devour an entire plateful.

"You're not finishing?" asked Michel, eyeing my cutlery in disbelief. He was only three-quarters finished his pie.

"I told you," I said defensively, pushing the plate away slightly. "I'm saving room for the lobster."

"They're vegetables," he said, shaking his head. "They do not really fill you up."

"Sure they do," I snapped back. "They're full of fiber."

The nature and tone of our interaction was rapidly deteriorating. The mood had changed; I felt it, and I knew Michel did as well. He gave me a sad and lingering stare before shrugging imperceptibly and digging into his pie again. I sat back in my chair, feeling as though I had failed some sort of important test.

Our conversation between courses was strained, with long silences punctuated by meaningless and even awkward chatter. Michel even mentioned the pleasant weather, at which point I realized that the evening was in jeopardy. You didn't discuss the weather on a hot date. You didn't care if it poured. Desperately, I grasped for something to talk about that didn't involve meteorology or nutrition.

"Mag lent me this necklace," I blurted out, grasping at the strand of pearls around my neck. "It was her mother's. She's been so much nicer lately."

Michel, who knew of my ambivalent relationship with my stepmother, looked surprised but pleased, both at the change of subject and the nature of my announcement. "That is wonderful," he said with a genuine smile. "I like Mag. It bothered me that you two batted heads."

It was my turn to grin. "Butted," I corrected him.

"Butted?" He looked baffled.

"Butted," I agreed. "Not batted. You butt heads."

"Interesting," he said, looking genuinely perplexed. "This is not what I think of when I think of butts."

"Do you often think of butts?" I said playfully.

He laughed and reached across the table to tap my hand. "Very funny, Clara."

I bowed my head. "I try."

Yet a third waiter arrived then with two silver-domed platters, carefully placing one before each of us. He whisked away the lids to reveal beautifully presented lobster, tender rose-colored morsels arranged amid rocket leaves and radishes and drizzled in a vinaigrette. There were potatoes piled to one side, chopped and lightly fried and seasoned with large chunks of sea salt. "*Voila*," said the waiter with a flourish. "*Bon appétit.*"

The lobster was superb, moist and tender and fresh tasting. "It's like you can taste the ocean," I said with a sigh of pleasure. Michel brightened visibly.

"I have never heard you speak fondly of food!" He sounded delighted. "I'm so glad you like it."

"It's great," I said, taking another bite. "Thank you for suggesting it."

The mood lightened considerably, I smiled at Michel, then clamped my mouth shut for fear I had green bits stuck between my teeth. I nibbled at the leaves and radishes and happily devoured the lobster. I sat back to take another look around the dining room. I wondered how many individual crystals made up the chandeliers. How much did something like that go for? More or less than, say, a Honda Civic?

"You have not tried your potatoes," commented Michel, gesturing. I glanced down at my plate. Indeed, the potatoes remained untouched. Potatoes were something I generally avoided. Except in conditions of famine, I didn't feel that potatoes were much worth eating. A starchy carb devoid of any real nutritional benefit? No, thanks.

"I'm not a big potato person," I said lightly, taking another bite of lobster. "Feel free to have mine."

"Oh, but Clara!" Michel looked me sadly. "These potatoes are delectable. You will not try even one?"

I grimaced. Could I try one, to avoid derailing the evening? I breathed deeply and jabbed at one with my fork. I felt the fried surface crackle slightly and made a face.

"Go ahead," said Michel encouragingly.

I took a bite of the potato, the outer crispiness giving way to tender innards. I could taste the little bits of salt, felt them crunch pleasantly between my teeth. Then I remembered what I was eating and felt my stomach clench. I grabbed my Perrier to wash it down as if it were Aspirin.

"Wonderful," I said weakly.

"You did not like it," said Michel. It was a statement, not a question.

"It's hard…" I paused, trying to think of how to explain it. "It's hard for me to eat something like that. That's all."

"I apologize," he said, though he didn't look especially sorry. "I did not realize eating a potato was difficult."

Unsure of how to respond, I resumed eating my lobster. It didn't taste quite as good as it had minutes ago.

When the plates were cleared, we were presented with dessert menus. I placed mine face down in front of me. I had no intention of eating dessert.

"You do not want dessert?" Michel looked dismayed.

"I'm full," I said in a small voice. It was true; I was. What did he want from me? I had just eaten two courses in a restaurant. Did he not understand that was significant progress for me? That I was doing the best I could?

"You know," he said, reaching across the table to take my hand again, "there is a special spot in your stomach that remains empty after a meal so you can have dessert."

I forced a small laugh, acknowledging his attempt at light-heartedness. "What did you have in mind?"

"They have house-made chocolates," he said eagerly, pointing at the menu. "Let's try them."

I felt my shoulders sag slightly. I was starting to feel as if this was tantamount to a meeting with Melisa or Call-me-Jane. It felt as if I was being challenged, tested.

"Fine," I said quietly.

When the selection of chocolates came, Michel happily translated the little accompanying key for me, pointing out each one. "Orange crème, coffee, vanilla, seventy percent dark cocoa."

"I'll take that last one," I said quickly. Dark chocolate had antioxidant properties and minimal sugar compared to the others. I allowed Michel to place it on my plate and took a small bite. I so rarely ate any chocolate that it felt strange on my tongue. I tried to embrace it, to recall a childhood full of longing for KitKats.

"It's good," I allowed.

"Excellent," agreed Michel, taking a second. He glanced down at my half-finished chocolate. "Come now, Clara. Just finish it."

"I enjoyed it. Do I have to finish it? Why do I have to finish it?" I definitely felt tested now, not to mention angry. I wanted to leave. I had had quite enough of this endless meal.

Michel sighed. "You don't have to do anything," he said. "I just thought you were doing better with your eating."

I clenched my fists and resisted the impulse to bring them down with force on the white linen tablecloth. "I am doing my best," I said with forced calm. "Small steps. Remember? Do you have any idea how hard this is for me?"

"I didn't—"

"Because it is hard. I don't know when the last time was that I sat down in a restaurant and ate two courses. Possibly never. This is *hard* for me, Michel. I'm sorry, but if you can't accept that, you aren't accepting *me*."

Breathing hard, I released my fists and felt my lower lip tremble. *Do not cry*, I admonished myself. *Keep it together*.

"I'm sorry," said Michel in a low voice. I looked around and noticed other patrons staring at us. I felt my entire body flush warm with shame. Avoiding eye contact, I stood and muttered something about the restroom before fleeing the table.

I skipped the bathroom and headed directly past the maitre d' for the front doors. Relieved at the blast of cool night air, I leaned against an archway and reveled in the chill of the breeze against my hot skin. Still fighting the urge to cry, I glanced out at the twinkling landscape that was Paris after dark. I watched a couple walk by, arm in arm, each holding a cone of gelato. The girl indulged in the frozen treat as if it were no big deal. I felt a wave of intense envy. *Why couldn't I do that?*

"Clara?" Michel appeared at my side, clutching my jacket. "You didn't say you were leaving." He draped it around my shoulders.

"Thanks," I said vaguely. I didn't answer him.

He waited a moment, then exhaled loudly. "I am sorry you're angry."

I sighed. "I'm not angry."

"You are angry." Michel stuffed his hands inside his pockets and shifted from one loafered foot to the other. "But

Clara—you said I don't accept you. And the truth is, maybe I don't."

I stared at him uncomprehendingly. What was he trying to say?

"Food for me—it's important." He spoke slowly, his head lowered, curls rustling slightly in the wind. "It's my profession. And you fear food."

"I do not *fear* food."

"You do," he said calmly. "I watch you. I watch your face as you eat. The food, what is in it, what is not in it—it consumes you, Clara."

"So we're done?" My voice shook, and I felt unsteady on the cobblestones beneath my feet. "That's it?"

"Just until you're ready to truly work on your illness," Michel answered. He looked wretched as he said it, his dark brown eyes full of remorse. "You have learned to say 'I have orthorexia.' But it is not until you believe it—and believe it is wrong—that you can recover."

I thought of how, only an hour or so earlier, I had been contemplating enrolling at a French university. I felt a mixture of shame and stupidity. "I would like to go home now," I said abruptly. I turned away so he couldn't see my face. I felt the first tears prick at my eyes, heard the tell-tale warbling when I spoke.

"I understand. We can call a taxi—"

"Alone," I said harshly. "I want to go home alone."

As I stormed away, I let the tears flow at will.

CHAPTER 21

I unlocked the front door and pushed it open carefully, making a valiant effort to suppress any noisy creaking that would wake Dad, Mag, or Alastair. I was surprised to find the lights on and Dad and Mag at the dining table. Both were clutching mugs of steaming tea and looking worried. Dad looked as if he might have been crying.

"What's wrong?" I asked immediately. I dropped my purse and felt my heart rate pick up as they exchanged a wary look. "Where's Alastair? What's happened to him?"

Dad cleared his throat. "Alastair is fine," he said. "It's not Alastair. Come and sit down."

"Just tell me." I heard my voice tremble for the second time that evening. "What's happened?"

"It's your mother," said Dad carefully. He put down his mug. "She—"

"She's dead, isn't she," I whispered. I sank to the floor. "I kept avoiding her texts and calls and now she's gone. It's all my fault. It's—"

"Clara," interjected Mag. She came over and knelt down before me and grabbed my arms. "Your mother is not dead."

"Oh," I whispered. I allowed myself to be helped back up and led to the table by Mag. "Then—what?"

"She's had an accident," Dad said quietly. "She fell during a performance. Her hip is broken."

"Her hip is broken?" I repeated. "That…that sucks."

Dad and Mag exchanged a worried glance.

"I mean, she'll be in, what, a body cast? For how long?" I paused briefly, then resumed speaking. "And the rehab—I guess it'll be months before she gets back on the stage. She must be livid." I recalled my mother after last year's debacle during *Les Sylphides* and felt sorry for whatever team of medical professionals were responsible for her care.

"Clara," said Mag gently. "Your mother needs a hip replacement. And she—she won't ever dance again, Sweetheart."

I blinked at her. "What?" I said stupidly.

"She had osteoporosis in her hip. It had all but disintegrated. It needs replacing, and…well, there's always teaching, or choreography, or…."

Something in my face must have made her stop talking. Her voice trailed off and she simply reached over and squeezed my hand.

"Can I talk to her?" I asked.

"She's in surgery now," Dad said. He sounded tired. "Get some sleep and you'll talk to her first thing tomorrow."

"She's all alone," I said in a small voice. "I should go home. She needs me."

Dad shook his head. "She wants you to stay here. She was pretty firm on that."

Mag nodded. "The director is with her," she said. "That Jack fellow."

"Jacques," I muttered guiltily. I'd nearly ruined his career, yet when my mother needed someone, it was Jacques who was there and not me.

"Yes, him. We spoke with him, and he seems well in control of the situation. He was shouting at people and ordering them about."

I grinned in spite of myself, imagining Jacques imperiously shaking his fists at cowering residents. "Yeah, that's definitely him."

"It's a fairly long surgery and recovery period, so you really should get some sleep," said Mag. "You won't be able to speak with her until the anesthetic has worn off."

I stared at my father, who seemed unusually quiet, staring fixedly at his mug of tea. Mag looked from him to me and stood up. "Why don't you two take a moment together," she said. She put a hand on my shoulder. "I'm sorry, Clara, but it will be okay. I promise."

I nodded mutely and stared at my dad, waiting. "Dad?" I asked, tentative.

He put down his mug and released his breath as if he had

been holding it for hours. "I feel so guilty, Clara," he said, shaking his head. "It wasn't a hard fall, apparently. Her hip just… crumbled."

He looked older in the faint light of the kitchen lamp overhead, the gray streaks in his hair more visible and the lines around his eyes more pronounced. I waited for him to continue.

"She was so beautiful," he said, his voice cracking. "So beautiful, and so alive, when I met her. I fell in love with her, everyone did. I knew she was sick, even then, but I didn't do anything about it. The food scales, the obsessive calorie counting. And I was a doctor—I knew what could happen. What kind of person am I? And when it got too much to bear, I just left. I left you. And now you're sick, too." He began to sob, his head in his hands. "I failed you both. I've tried to redeem myself by doing better this time, with Mag and Alastair, but I see now there's no such thing. I'm a failure."

I didn't know what to say. "Dad?" I said. His head was buried in his arms, face down, on the table. "Dad. It's not your fault."

With effort, he straightened, his forehead marked with indentations from the woven placemat he'd slumped down on. "Of course it is."

"No," I said firmly. "It isn't. It's the ballet's fault, society's. I don't know. But there wasn't anything you could have done, not about the eating. She didn't want to change." As I finish the thought, I realize that it's true. There was nothing anyone could have done, because Mom didn't want to fix things. Was it the same for me? Was I headed in that direction? Would I be brittle-boned by my thirties, my skeleton prematurely aged beyond repair?

"Listen to me," said Dad, grabbing my hands firmly. I stifled my surprise and turned to face him. "You don't want to end up like this. Your mother's career is over. The thing she loved most, which drove her illness—it's been taken from her. You have to stop before it's too late for you."

I felt myself wilt, my shoulders sagging. I pictured Michel's sad expression as I abandoned him outside Le Meurice. I imagined my mother watching from the sidelines, as another woman danced her role. *She didn't want to change*, I told myself again. *But there's still time for you.*

"I'm sick," I announced, then, suddenly. For the first time, I meant it. I really, truly believed what I was saying. Until now, I had played along, made my effort to try cheese and nibble at chocolate, never actually buying that the healthy and so-called "clean" lifestyle I embraced was slowly draining me. "I have an eating disorder." It felt good to admit it, but it also felt, ultimately, daunting and unwinnable. Now that I'd admitted I had a problem, I had to fix it. And I had no idea how that was done.

Dad began sobbing again, and this time I joined in, tasting a mix of salt and mascara as the tears ran black down my cheeks. When he reached out to gather me in his arms, I didn't pull away.

CHAPTER 22

"Mom?" I hit the speaker button on my phone. "Mom, can you hear me?"

I had suggested a FaceTime call via text to Jacques, but to my relief he wrote back that Mom had vetoed that request. I felt a pang of guilt, knowing she was doing it to protect me. She knew from her previous injury how difficult I found hospitals; once, I had nearly fainted watching her have an IV inserted. As presumably she was now hooked up to a host of tubes, needles, and other assorted devices, I couldn't help but feel relief on reading Jacques' text.

"Clara?" her voice was weaker than normal, softer, with a slight hoarseness to it. "Clara, I'm so sorry."

"You're sorry?" I had an urge to both laugh and cry at the same time. "I'm sorry. I should be there. I wanted to book the next flight home, but—"

"No," she interjected firmly, and her voice was suddenly much stronger. "No. That's the worst thing you could do right now."

"But you're alone. What will happen to you?" I felt desperate. I rose from my bed and began pacing the small room. "Who is going to help you get dressed, or get food, or…" My voice trailed off.

"I have to go to a rehab center," she answered calmly. "I'll be out in two weeks."

"Two weeks?" I said, stunned. I froze on the spot and leaned against Alastair's wardrobe for support. "You have to live there for two weeks?"

"I don't have to," my mother said. "I want to. I'm going to get rehab for my hip, and I'm going to have a psychologist and nutritionist help me with my eating disorder."

My eating disorder. So she had owned it, like I had last night. Ownership is a powerful thing.

"That's…that's good," I said, my voice quavering. I walked back to the bed and sat down hard on the duvet. "Are you in pain?"

"Nope," she said, sounding more cheerful now. "They've got me loaded up on painkillers. Can't feel a thing. I guess it will be a different story once they start to wear off, but in the meantime I feel great."

"Ha," I said weakly. "Well, at least you're comfortable."

There was an awkward silence. The dead air hung between us, as if you could hear the waves of the Atlantic Ocean that separated her hospital room from Dad's apartment.

"Mom—" I began.

"Clara—" she said at the same time.

We both laughed nervously. "You go first," said Mom.

"I'm just...so sorry," I said. I stood again and resumed my pacing. "I...Mag and Dad said...your dancing—"

"It's okay, Clara." She sighed. "I'm old for a ballerina, anyway."

"You're not old," I said automatically, and she laughed.

"I am so, and you know it." There was a sound, and a pause. I heard Mom say something to someone, and there was a rustling sound.

"Sorry," said Mom, returning. "I had to take a pill of some kind. They've got me drugged up here."

"Anyway," she continued. "I'm going to help with choreography, and the New England school is always looking for teachers. There will be plenty for me to do."

Her tone was light, but I could sense the pain behind it. My mother had loved the stage, and the stage had loved her back. How would she cope with life out of the spotlight? Could she ever truly be happy behind the scenes?

"Your turn now," she said. "How are you doing there? I know you've been avoiding me."

I felt the guilt hit me again. "I haven't," I said feebly.

She snorted. "Come on. It's okay, Clara. I understand. You need to keep away from me, really. I made you sick."

"You didn't," I protested, stung.

"I did. I didn't do it on purpose, but I did it. All that fussing over nutrition. I told myself I just wanted you to be healthy, but you know what? I also wanted you to be thin. I did. I wanted us both to be thin. This is my punishment, and I accept it."

I sighed. "The universe is not so neat and tidy, Mom. It's much messier than that."

"Still." She sounded stubborn now. "I don't care about myself anymore. I care about you. How is your eating disorder? Is it at all better?"

"I…" I paused, unsure of how to proceed. "I thought so," I said finally. "I thought I was doing better. But I don't think I really admitted to myself that I actually have an…illness until yesterday." *Illness*. It was still difficult to say.

"Good," she said, and I could hear the fatigue in her voice. Talking to me like this couldn't be easy on her; she had been in surgery the evening before and in various states of recovery since. "Good. We're going to fix this, Clara. I promise."

"Don't worry about me," I said. I dug my toes into Alastair's rug, feeling frustrated. "Just concentrate on getting better. Please."

"I'm a bit tired," she admitted, yawning. "I think that might have been a sedative."

"Go," I said quickly. "Go to sleep."

"Clara?"

"Yes?"

"Will you call me again tomorrow?" Her voice sounded small. "Please?"

I felt the tears prick at the corners of my eyes. "Of course," I said. "We'll talk every day from now on. Though, it would be easier if I just came home and—"

"No!" Her voice was anxious now, louder. "Your father is better for you right now. Please. No."

"Okay, okay," I said, feeling hurt. Why did she really not want me there? Was it for my sake, or hers? Was she too proud? Did she prefer Jacques?

"I love you," she said faintly. "I'll talk to you tomorrow."

"I love you, too," I said.

I tapped my phone screen, ending the call, and sat back down on the bed, unmoving. My mother had broken her hip. She would never perform again, but she was worried about me. A year ago, I might have reveled in her attention, basked in the glow of her sudden interest in good parenting. Everything was different now, though. I had changed, and so had she. For months, we had been moving unknowingly towards a moment like this, an event that would force us to reconsider ourselves and the ideas we had always believed to be unshakable. If it had not been this, I realized, it would have been something else.

I glanced at the time. Dad needed me to watch Alastair later on, but until then I had some free time. The sun was out again, making an encore appearance, and I longed for a walk and perhaps an hour alone at a café to clear my head. I recalled my first day here, when I'd caught a glimpse of a girl sipping a warm drink outdoors. I'd been here well over a month, but had barely enjoyed a moment on my own. I grabbed my denim jacket and carefully knotted a silk scarf around my neck the way the girls did it here.

"Clara?" Alastair walked into the room and eyed me questioningly.

I sighed. No matter how many times I explained the notion of knocking to Alastair, the concept of privacy continued to baffle him. "Hey, Alastair."

"I heard your Mom got hurt. Do you feel sad?"

"I do," I agreed. "I feel very sad."

"Dad said to tell you I'm sorry, but I'm not sorry, because I didn't do it." He came over and stood opposite me, his eyes wide.

"It's more that you say you're sorry that the person is feeling sad," I explained. I made a face at my hair in the mirror, which was being decidedly uncooperative. Annoyed, I grabbed a clip and piled the entire mess on top of my head and fastened it there.

"I don't like that you're sad," said Alastair. "But I'm not really *sorry*."

I sighed. I felt badly, but I simply was not in the mood.

"Do you want to come build with me? I'm making a carousel out of K'NEX." Alastair shifted anxiously from foot to foot. "Like from the Tuileries."

"Cool," I said. I buttoned my jacket. "How about we do it later? I was just going to go for a walk right now. I need to think about some stuff."

"Oh." His voice was small. "Are you going back to New York?"

I pictured my mother, small and crumpled in a hospital bed. She was insisting I stay, but was it her decision to make?

"I don't know," I said honestly. "She said I should stay, but she's alone in the hospital. I feel like I should be there with her."

Alastair's eyes went wide and round with panic. "You're leaving?"

I sighed again. I didn't have the patience for Alastair at that moment. "I really don't know. Can we talk about it later?"

I gently sidestepped my brother and made for the doorway, him trailing slowly behind me.

"Dad?" I called out. "I'm going for a walk."

He appeared, scruffy and unshaven, a stack of term papers in his arms. "No problem," he said, yawning. "Did you talk to your mom?"

"Yeah," I answered. I waited for him to ask me more, but he didn't press.

"I spoke to Jacques," he admitted.

"Right," I said, irritated. I felt much younger than my sixteen years, then, like a child in a roomful of adults who were whispering directly over her head. Could I not be trusted with so-called "grown-up" information? Frustrated, I yanked on my shoes.

"I'll see you later," I said shortly. I looked around for Alastair, but he had disappeared. I snatched my purse and resisted the temptation to let the door slam behind me on the way out.

Outside, the fresh air was a welcome change. I breathed deeply, enjoying the sensation of cool air inflating and deflating my lungs. I glanced in the direction of the bakery, wondering if Michel was inside baking croissants or madeleines. *Who cares*, I told myself firmly. I ignored the little pull I felt on my heartstrings as I pictured his smile. *Mom is more important.*

Mom. I pictured her onstage, a vision in lavender sparkles and tulle. The Sugar Plum Fairy role, my favorite. When I was very small, I'd assumed I'd one day follow in her footsteps and at least dance the part of my namesake, the little girl whose dreams form the landscape of the famed Christmas ballet. When it became quickly apparent that a career in dance was not in my future, I stopped fantasizing about playing Clara, but never stopped loving the ballet. My mother had danced the Sugar Plum role every year since I could remember. What would she do now? Could she be satisfied teaching the little Claras of tomorrow?

I kicked a small pebble as I turned down what was now a familiar street. All around me, people carried on with their lives as normal. Couples held hands, mothers pushed baby carriages, toddlers tried to escape their parents' firm grasps. Businessmen and businesswomen hurried past, checking their phones. It was comforting, in a way, to know that, even in spite of my own personal misery, Paris went on.

I stopped at a small café and took a seat outside at one of the little tables. I ordered a café au lait, and didn't bother, as I did usually, to try and convey, in my improved, but still rudimentary, French that I would like skim milk. *It will not kill you to drink whole milk*, I told myself firmly. *It will not clog your arteries. It will not make you fat. It is full of calcium to protect your bones.* I looked to my left, where a girl my age was digging into a bowl of French onion soup. She was slim and petite, with long, curly dark hair tumbling partway down her back. A spoon in one hand and a novel in the other, she took absent bites of cheese as she turned the pages of her book, absorbed in its contents. I wondered what book it was. I wondered if the soup was tasty. And I wondered if she had ordered it simply because she wanted it, because she felt like eating melted cheese and toasted bread and piping hot soup, without thinking about calories and trans fats and basal metabolic rate and atherosclerosis.

"*Merci*," I said politely, as the waiter placed my drink before me. He smiled and winked as he whipped out a tiny saucer holding two *macarons* in delicate pastel colors. One pink, and one green, light and fluffy-looking.

"Oh," I said, flustered. "I didn't order these."

"*Non*," agreed the waiter. "On zee house." He beamed, winking again as he walked away.

I tried and failed to remember what was inside a macaron. Icing? Meringue? Coconut? All of the above? My hand went automatically for the phone in my jacket pocket, but I resisted pulling it out. Cautiously, I picked one up and eyed it up close, holding it gently between my thumb and forefinger. I felt the top crack slightly, giving way to the spongy center.

Do it, I told myself firmly. *Prove you can. Do it so you can tell Mom you did it.*

I took a bite of the small pink treat. It had a wonderful texture, not quite like marshmallow, but something approaching it. The taste was sweet and light, like strawberries dusted with icing sugar. I washed it down with a sip of my drink, then talked myself into taking a second, bigger, bite.

It tastes good, I thought to myself, valiantly working to

block the other, less pleasant, thoughts that came unbidden into my mind. *I can do this.*

When I was done, I exhaled loudly, releasing a breath I hadn't even realized I was holding. I looked over at the girl next to me. She was nearly finished her soup, still sipping at it and twirling the melted cheese around her spoon with the same absentminded expression. On the side plate next to her was a slice of bread, and I watched her reach over and take a large bite without turning her head.

One day, I told myself, *I will be like her.* I wondered what it would take to get there. When I got home, though, I planned to try. Maybe Melisa could help me. And if not her, then perhaps someone else.

I extended the daydream and pictured my mother across from me, also indulging in cheese and carbohydrates. I felt a stab of pity, imagining a cane, sinister and insidious, leaning against the back of her chair, but also, unexpectedly, resentment. If not for her, would I be able to have a cookie like a normal person? Or would I have found my way to disordered eating regardless? It was easy to blame my ballerina mother, but how many girls didn't have their mother to blame?

The waiter came by with some water, and I politely inquired about the time in French.

"Eleven-thirty," he responded in English.

It was time to go; Dad would need me back soon. I dug around in my purse for the appropriate change and dropped it on the table. I was about to rise when I noticed the second macaron, looking lonely on the little saucer. Carefully, I took my napkin and wrapped it up, placing it in my purse. I would give it to Alastair; I'd been impatient with him earlier.

Should I go home to New York? I thought it over as I started to walk back. I was happy here in Paris, but could I continue to be happy knowing my mother was suffering alone? Did she mean it about staying? Was it, in fact, better for me—maybe for both of us? Was my influence on her eating as bad as her influence on mine? I pictured the two of us, alternately, as Miss Muffet and the spider. Each time one of us meant to eat, the other frightened her away.

When I reached the apartment building, Dad and Alastair were waiting outside, sitting on the front steps. Alastair looked slight and anxious, huddled into a small, ball-like shape as he hugged his knees, his knapsack rounding out his back like a turtle shell.

"There she is," I heard Dad say, sounding relieved. "I told you she was coming back."

"What's up?" I asked, rounding the corner. "Everything okay?"

"Alastair wasn't sure you were coming back," explained Dad. He put his hand on Alastair's shoulder. "He was worried."

I squatted down in front of my brother. "I would never leave without saying goodbye," I told him. "I promise."

"You said you might go to New York." It came out high-pitched and wobbly.

I grinned in spite of myself. "I would have to pack, wouldn't I?"

He considered this. "I suppose," he said reluctantly.

"I'm off," said Dad, interrupting. He looked apologetic. "I'm going to be late. I'll be back later." He kissed the tops of my and Alastair's heads, despite both of us ducking, embarrassed. "I'll text you."

We watched him disappear around the corner and presumably down the steps to the Métro. I sat down on the step next to Alastair and put an arm around him.

"What would you like to do?" I asked him. "I'm all yours this afternoon."

He eyed the bakery. "I'm hungry," he said. "Can we see if Michel and his dad have any pain au chocolat?"

I thought of having to face Michel, and cringed slightly. "Michel's probably busy," I said brusquely. Then I remembered the macaron in my purse, and brightened.

"Here," I said, reaching for it. I opened the napkin and placed the treat in Alastair's hand. "Have this cookie. I think it's mint."

"Thanks," he said, brightening. He brought it to his lips and took a bite, chewing thoughtfully.

"It doesn't taste like mint," he informed me.

"No?" I zipped my purse and dusted the crumbs from my hands. "What does it taste like?"

But Alastair didn't answer. His face had turned bright red, and he made a small, whistling sound.

"Alastair?" I said, alarmed, searching his face. "What's wrong?"

My eyes landed on the macaron. *Not mint. Pistachio. And almond. Nuts.*

"Alastair!" I cried out.

I yanked open his backpack and started tossing out the carefully organized contents. Finally, I found the little pouch containing the EpiPen.

"What do I do?" I wailed. Frantically, I skimmed the directions on the side. Push against outer thigh. Designed to work through clothing. Hold for ten seconds.

"Okay," I said, sweating. "Okay." I held the orange tip near his thigh, then swung and pushed against it until I heard a clicking sound. Alastair's lips were swollen like two halves of a hot dog bun and shaded an unearthly blue. His breathing was raspy and shallow.

"Help!" I cried out. "Someone, please, help me! *Aidez-moi!*"

Had ten seconds passed? Could I move the needle? Where was my phone? I fumbled for it with my other shaking hand, then realized I had no idea what the number for emergency services was in France. How could I not have had this vital piece of information? What was wrong with me?

"Clara!" I heard a voice call out anxiously from behind me, and the sound of boots pounding hard against the pavement. Michel.

"Nut reaction," I blathered, hysterical. "What is nine-one-one here? Hurry!"

Michel whipped out his phone and with an urgent calm barked out instructions in French to the operator. Meanwhile, Alastair's breathing seemed improved. His lips had reduced to the approximate size and shape of edamame, and were distinctly pinker. I clutched at him, tears rolling down my face.

"It's okay, Alastair," I whispered. "You're going to be okay."

Michel's eyes traveled to the EpiPen, which had dropped from my hand and rolled to the ground. "You gave him the adrenaline?"

"Yes," I said anxiously. "I hope I did it right. Michel, I'm so scared."

Michel squeezed my arm. "The ambulance will be here very soon. He will be fine." Michel cocked his head towards Alastair, who still could not speak but was definitely breathing with greater ease. "Right, *mon petit copain?* You will be—"

Interrupted by the wail of blaring sirens followed by flashing lights, Michel abruptly stopped speaking and stood, running towards the vehicle. The paramedics moved swiftly, hoisting Alastair onto a stretcher and ushering us all inside.

"Nut allergy," I said frantically, throwing a desperate look at Michel.

"*Allergie aux noix,*" he translated. "*Analphylaxie.*"

The paramedics set to work on Alastair while I pressed myself against the ambulance wall, trying unsuccessfully not to cry. I ducked as an IV pole nearly took out my left arm. Michel handed the used EpiPen to one of the paramedics, who examined it, nodding. He said something to Michel, who turned to me.

"He says you probably saved his life," said Michel softly, placing a hand on my shoulder. He motioned for me to sit down on the little bench, but I shook my head, my eyes focused on Alastair.

"I also almost killed him," I said, hiccupping. "I gave him

a pistachio macaron. A macaron, Michel. How could I have done that?"

Michel winced. "It was a mistake."

"It was stupid." I covered my face with my hands. "He trusted me. Didn't even ask about ingredients."

"It happens, Clara. Alastair has an allergy. It isn't your fault."

The paramedics were monitoring Alastair's vitals. I hugged my knees as I watched them take his blood pressure and examine his throat.

"More adrenaline," explained one as he gave Alastair a second shot. Alastair whimpered slightly and I cringed, shrinking back into Michel. Was he in pain? Poor Alastair. What had I done?

"You should call your papa," said Michel. "Tell him to meet us at the hospital."

I dialed Dad's number—no answer. I left him an incoherent message before taking a deep breath and calling Mag. What could I even say to her? Sorry that I almost killed your only child?

"Clara?" Mag sounded surprised to hear my voice. "Is everything okay with your mother?"

"It's Alastair," I said in a rush. "I had to give him the EpiPen, we're on our way to—" I paused, and looked up. "Where are we going? What hospital?"

"Necker," called out the driver. "*Enfants Malades.*"

"Necker," I informed Mag, my voice breaking. "I'm so sorry, I gave him a macaron, I'm so stupid—"

"Calm down," said Mag, sounding frightened but composed. "You gave him the EpiPen?"

"Yes, and they're giving him more adrenaline now, in the ambulance," I said. I willed myself to look at Alastair's face, which was nearly restored to its normal shape and color. "He looks better."

Mag exhaled shakily. "He'll be fine," she said resolutely. "I'm coming right over."

"Alastair, Mum is on her way," I told him. He looked improved, but clearly he still couldn't speak. I tried not to imagine what it must feel like to have a swollen throat. I recalled from grade school a boy with peanut allergies who had matter-of-factly described the feeling of anaphylaxis as trying to breathe with a baseball stuck in your windpipe. Shuddering, I reached towards my little brother, glancing questioningly at the closest paramedic. He nodded his approval and I gripped Alastair's hand tightly, half-expecting him to pull away. He did not, though. I don't know if it was the reaction, the medication, or just Alastair himself, but even when I went to release him from my grasp, he would not let me go.

CHAPTER 23

"He's going to be fine." Mag put her hand on my shoulder and I broke into fresh sobs, this time from relief. In the Emergency waiting room, I had, despite all evidence to the contrary, convinced myself that Alastair was not going to make it. Michel had tried to point out that he had been doing better even in the ambulance, but all I could picture were the blue, hot-dog-bun lips. Michel, eventually aware that nothing he could say would placate me, sat silently at my side, his hand over my own.

"I'm so sorry," I said again, collapsing against Mag.

"I've done it too," she said calmly. "And I'm his mother. It was Thai food. Much stupider than a macaron."

"It was a *pistachio* macaron," I said, anguished. I wrung my hands. "I thought it was mint. If I had just stopped to think—"

"Stop," she said firmly. "Going over and over it is not going to undo what happened. And Alastair is fine. His swelling is nearly gone. They want to keep him here a few hours to make sure, but he is going to be just fine. He wants to see you."

I stood, heart hammering. What would I say? How could I begin to apologize for nearly killing him with baked goods?

Mag squeezed my hand. "Clara," she said. "I know this is going to sound strange, but for Alastair to have taken the biscuit from you without demanding to know the ingredients—well, he must really care for you. He doesn't trust anyone like that."

It felt like being stabbed in the gut. "So he trusted me, and I blew it," I said. My shoulders sagged.

"No, no." Mag shook her head. "I didn't mean it like that. I just—well, it's very hard for Alastair to form bonds. Other than with his Dad and me, he has never shown any real inclination. But he loves you." Her eyes sparkled with tears. "To us it feels a bit…miraculous."

I didn't know how to respond. I still felt like a criminal.

"Go on, then," she said, nudging me. "He's waiting for you."

I walked down the hallway, trying not to make eye contact with the parents of a small red-headed girl in a wheelchair. Around me, nurses in cheerful printed scrubs bustled about as if working with sick children was no big deal. I breathed through my mouth, trying not to smell the pungent scent of antiseptic and floor cleaner that pervaded the entire department.

I stepped hesitantly into Alastair's room. He was in a room with another little boy, but a cartoon-covered curtain was drawn between them.

"Hey, Buddy," I said, my voice wobbling as he looked up

at me. Propped up with a pillow, he had an IV in his arm and was fiddling with a cotton blanket.

"Hi, Clara." His voice was solemn. "Mum says you think I'll be upset because you gave me the biscuit."

"Well," I said, trying to keep my composure. "I should have known better. I should have remembered, and realized—"

"I am not upset." He shook his head. "It wasn't on purpose."

"No, but—"

"I forgot to ask about ingredients," he said. "I forgot, because I was very afraid you had gone to New York and I was glad that you were still here."

I stared at him, overwhelmed with emotion. "Alastair," I said softly, "I promise you I will never leave without saying goodbye."

"That's what Dad said." He frowned, his eyebrows furrowing. "But I felt scared."

Tentatively, I went over and sat down gingerly beside him on the hospital bed. He reached his hand out to me, and I took it, surprised.

"I thought you didn't like holding hands," I said, feeling his small fingers intertwine with my own.

"It's okay if I know it's coming," he informed me. He paused. "I also know that you like it and I want you to feel happy."

I felt the tear factory behind my eyes rev up again. "You're amazing, Alastair," I said, choking with emotion. "Never let anyone tell you that being different is bad."

He shrugged. "Okay."

"And I'm sorry about the macaron. I really am."

He shrugged again, like any normal kid. I half expected him to say "no biggie" the way a typical American kid would, but this was Alastair. Instead he said, "I don't blame you, so you shouldn't apologize. But if I did blame you, I would forgive you."

I grinned in spite of myself. "I think I can live with that."

"Is Michel here?" He looked around me, at the doorway.

"Outside in the waiting room," I said quickly. I wondered if he was still there. Would he stick around? "Family visitors only right now."

"Maybe you will get married and you'll move to Paris," said Alastair hopefully.

I thought of Michel in the waiting room versus Michel last night. Where did I stand? What, exactly, was going between the two of us?

"I don't know about that," I said lightly. "I'm a bit young to get married."

Alastair looked disappointed, and I laughed. "Concentrate on getting better," I said. "We'll stay in tonight and do K'NEX, or Lego."

He brightened. "The carousel."

"Yes," I agreed. "I want to help you finish it. Can I?"

"Yes," he said, nodding. "I need help with the horses. I'm not good at making animals."

"I'll do my best," I promised.

From behind me, I felt a hand on my shoulder, and jumped.

"Sorry," said a familiar voice. "I got here as fast as I could."

"Hey, Dad." I stood and hugged him. "I'll leave you two. I'll see you later, Alastair?"

"Yes," he said. "Clara?"

"Yeah?" I was halfway to the door, but turned back. He looked so small in the oversized hospital bed, like a doll or a prop of some kind.

"I love you."

It was the first time he'd ever said it to me; the first time I'd ever heard him say it at all.

"I love you too, Alastair," I said, my voice breaking.

The waterworks erupted as soon as I was out of the room.

CHAPTER 24

Michel offered to escort me home from the hospital while Dad and Mag remained with Alastair for a period of observation. Now that the crisis had passed, I began reliving the night before and feeling distinctly awkward in his presence. He clearly felt it too, because both of us were being excessively formal towards each other.

We walked in silence down the street, away from the hospital. All around us, people were out enjoying the good weather. My mother, in hospital with a broken hip, would never dance again. Alastair had nearly died from nibbling on a cookie. Still, life went on. I stole a sidelong glance at Michel. I needed to fix things.

"About last night—" I began.

"Clara—" he said simultaneously.

We both laughed nervously, stopping in our tracks. We

stood facing each other, and Michel motioned towards an unoccupied bench.

"I'll go first," he said. He reached for my hand and pulled me down next to him. "Clara, I'm sorry for what happened yesterday. I was too hard on you."

"No," I shook my head. "I'm sorry. I need to admit I have a problem, and get help. But it's okay. I get it now. After what happened to my mom last night—"

"Your mom?" Michel looked puzzled.

"Oh. Right." I exhaled loudly. "You don't know."

"Is everything all right?" He looked anxious.

"No. Well, not exactly." Brushing my hair from my eyes, I filled Michel in on my mother's condition. He looked stricken.

"Clara." He put an arm around me. "I am so sorry to hear this. It must be such a shock."

"Well, yes and no." I leaned into him slightly. I wasn't sure where we stood, but it felt good to lean on him, literally and figuratively. "I knew she had osteoporosis, from her eating disorder. I just didn't expect this to happen so soon."

We were both quiet a moment, and then Michel spoke up softly. "Do you blame her, Clara? For your own problems?" His tone was delicate. It was a bold question.

"I don't know," I said honestly. "Who's to say it wouldn't have happened anyway? Everywhere you go, models are airbrushed and girls my age are posting pictures of themselves all over Instagram with hashtags promoting 'clean living' or 'goals,' which basically means 'don't eat.' This might just be me. I think that scares me more, actually." As I admitted it out loud for the first time, I realized it was true.

"But then, I think of being little, and having to throw out my Halloween candy, or not having cake at my birthday party." My tone is resentful now, and it feels strange to speak so candidly. "And I think, how could I have ended up any other way?"

"Perhaps it doesn't matter," said Michel thoughtfully. "Your mother is sick, too. Blaming isn't going to help."

"I know," I said, sighing. "I don't want to play the blame game, either. My mom was a single mother and a dancer. She raised me the only way she knew how. But now we both need help."

When I didn't continue, Michel spoke up hesitantly. "I wanted to help you."

"Oh, you have!" I assured him. It was true, too. Being with Michel—and with Alastair—had made me, for the first time, want to get better.

"I think, though," I said slowly, "that I need help. Professional, I mean. I had this counselor in New York, Melisa—I never gave her a chance. But I want to, now."

Michel looked sad. "I wish I could have done more."

I smiled gently. "There's only so much you can do to help someone. After that, they need to help themselves. And of course, there are limits." I thought of Alastair, and the shoes. They would help him avoid being targeted, but at the end of the day he was still Alastair, still on the spectrum. And that was okay, too. I said as much to Michel, and he nodded.

"It is the same for me, in a way," he said. "I was always running away from my Algerian roots. I wanted to be French. I tried so hard to fit in, but I cannot change my skin color, and I wouldn't want to. I can be both."

We sat quietly, watching an elderly woman tear chunks off a stale baguette and toss them to the birds. Flocks of pigeons emerged as though from thin air, desperately chasing the free meal. It would never occur to the pigeons to starve themselves—they took what they could get, and eagerly. I noticed that among the sea of gray, there was a lone white pigeon. I nodded at it.

"Do you think the other pigeons are mean to it?" I asked Michel.

"It's a good question," he mused. "I'd have to say no. I think racism is a uniquely human condition."

"I was just thinking that about eating," I admitted, pulling my jacket closed. "You wouldn't see a bird turn down dessert."

"Come on," said Michel, standing. He held out his hand to me, and I took it readily. "I have an idea."

"An idea about what?"

"For Alastair." He checked his watch. "He should be home by supper time. We can make him his favorite meal. A little party."

I smiled, both at Michel's enthusiasm as well as his firm belief that a properly prepared dish was a universal cure-all. "Okay. Pizza?"

"No, no." Michel pulled me along impatiently. "He likes to make pizza. But his favorite thing to eat is—"

"Croque monsieur," we both said at the same time. I thought of how many of those decadent sandwiches I'd watched him eat over the past weeks.

"Yeah, he'd love that."

"Not to brag," added Michel, "but I happen to make an excellent croque monsieur."

"How hard is it?" I asked, teasing. "Isn't it just a ham sandwich with melted cheese or whatever?"

Michel stopped walking and, steadying himself against a lamppost, melodramatically placed a hand over his heart. "Just a sandwich with melted cheese!"

"Okay, okay," I said, laughing. "It requires culinary skill and finesse I could only ever dream of possessing."

"Absolutely," he answered seriously. "Making the perfect croque monsieur is an art. Lucky for you, I am willing to share my secrets."

"I consider myself very fortunate," I said gravely, smirking.

"First stop, the Marais," said Michel. "There's an excellent little charcuterie there where I get my ham. Best in Paris."

"We're going all the way to the Marais for deli meat?" I stared at him in disbelief. "Isn't there, like, a grocery store or something on the way home?"

He shot me look that was both horrified and offended. "We do not buy ham at the grocery store."

"*Excusez-moi*," I said, exaggerating my American accent. "Lead on, then, my Paris chef."

Laughing, Michel turned me so that we were facing each other directly. His eyes bore into my own and his lips were slightly parted. He took my chin in his hand, a questioning expression on his face. The unspoken words—*can I kiss you?*—hung between us.

I nodded slightly, and closed my eyes. The kiss was brief and sweet and tender, the sort of kiss that conveys both passion and intimacy.

"And now, sandwiches," he said gravely.

CHAPTER 25

It turned out that Michel didn't just have a favorite spot for ham; he also, when the markets have closed for the day, has a favorite spot for cheese. By the time we made it home, I was exhausted.

"I didn't realize this was going to be a private food tour of the city," I said, dumping the bag of Gruyère and Parmesan on the counter. "I can barely stand."

"I'm sorry," he said, abashed. "But it is important to have good ingredients. Who wants to eat subpar Gruyère?"

"I'm not sure most people would notice," I replied, collapsing onto a dining chair and kicking off my ballet flats.

"That's just sad," said Michel, shaking his head gravely. "No one should have to eat bad Gruyère."

I grinned as he unloaded his shopping bags: an assortment of fresh ham, butter, milk, and—of course—some just-out-of-the-oven bread from his father.

"This is the perfect bread," he assured me, fishing around the kitchen drawers for a bread knife. "Nice and crusty on the outside, soft on the inside."

I watched Michel slice the bread carefully, neat slices falling thickly on their sides like dominoes. Next, he rummaged through Mag's pot drawer and pulled out a small saucepan and skillet.

"At least she has a proper pan," he said approvingly, brandishing the skillet. "The right pan can make all the difference when you're cooking."

"I'll take your word for it," I said.

Michel poked his head deep into the cutlery drawer and emerged with butter knives, measuring spoons, a spatula, and a whisk.

"Flour," he said, frowning. "We need flour, I forgot. Please, tell me there is flour here somewhere in this kitchen."

"I'll check." Sliding off my chair, I opened the pantry and peered inside. It was, I realized, the first time I'd done so, despite living here for nearly two months. Not once during that time had it occurred to me to fetch a snack or prep a meal. Scanning each shelf, I began to fear another trip to the shops before I found an appropriately labeled canister.

"Here," I said triumphantly, brandishing the container. "Flour."

"Wonderful." He set it down next to the stove, then pointed to the two blocks of cheese. "You're in charge of the cheese."

"I am?" Warily, I stared at the two misshapen rectangles. "What do I do with it?"

Michel handed me a cheese knife and grater. "Cut ten slices of Gruyère, then shred the rest," he instructed. "You can shred all of the Parmesan."

"Okay," I said, shrugging. I got to work, enjoying the sensation of the cheeses as they scraped against the metal teeth of the grater. Michel peered over at my progress as he whisked together the butter, milk, and flour mixture over the stove.

"Try some," he suggested casually. "It's delicious."

"Okay," I said, taking a deep breath. I nibbled at a bit, then made a face. "I don't know," I said. "It's...weird."

"Weird?" He looked offended. "How is it weird?"

"I don't know." I frowned, trying to put it into words. "It's like a salty version of tart or something. Or a savory version of sour?"

Michel raised his eyebrows. "You know you're not making any sense, correct?"

I started to laugh. "I know. I'm having trouble explaining it."

"You'll like it melted," he assured me.

Michel lifted the saucepan and removed it from the heat.

"Now we add the cheese to the roux," he announced, motioning for the plate I'd prepared.

"Roo?" I said, baffled. I pictured the tiny kangaroo from *Winnie the Pooh*.

"Roux," he repeated. "R-o-u-x. When you mix together butter, flour, and milk, that's what it's called."

"Ohhh," I said. I handed him the plate of cheese. "I was thinking—well, never mind."

Michel scraped the last of the cheese into the pot, whisking until smooth.

"Can you butter the bread?" he asked, nodding at the thickly cut slices. "I'll get a baking sheet ready."

"Okay," I said.

Like assembly-line workers, we moved in harmony, me buttering bread and handing it to him, Michel adding the sliced cheese and ham and slathering on Dijon mustard we'd found in the fridge. Once the sandwiches were properly assembled, Michel heated up the skillet and tossed each in the pan, browning the bread on the outside and ensuring the cheesy insides were rendered into a melted ooze.

"Next, we add the roux and bake them," he said, cranking the oven dial. I nodded, handing him the appropriate-sized spoon.

He ladled the sauce carefully over the sandwiches, slowly drizzling the mixture as if each combination of bread, ham, and cheese were a carefully constructed work of art.

"Now we bake them?" I guessed.

"Yes." Michel nodded, then glanced worriedly at the clock. "I hope they're back soon. A croque monsieur is best straight from the oven."

"We can set the table," I suggested. "The plates are in that cupboard, there. By your head. I'll do the silverware."

Quietly, we set out placemats and napkins, cutlery and plates. My thoughts wandered to my mother, immobile against the cold metal of a hospital bed.

"Are you okay, Clara?" My face must have betrayed my thoughts. I set down the last of the forks and shook my head.

"Just thinking about my mother," I mumbled, looking away. "I should be there."

"But she wants you to stay here?"

"Yes. She says it's better for me."

"Maybe it's better for her, too," he said quietly.

I frowned, feeling defensive. I turned to face him, leaning against the hard wood of the table. "What do you mean?"

"Well," he said carefully, placing a glass at Alastair's seat. "You've said you both have…problems. With food."

"And?" I said.

"And…maybe it is easier for you to recover without her. And maybe for her to recover without you."

I opened my mouth to retort, then abruptly closed it. Was Michel right? Did my mother and I feed off of each other—an unhealthy, obsessive pas de deux around the kitchen? I pictured my mother measuring out slices of cucumber. I thought of my mother's voice on the phone, weak but insistent that I remain here. Did she realize this, too? That not only was she bad for me, but me for her?

I blinked at Michel as he handed me a glass of Perrier.

"Thanks," I said, taking a sip. "Maybe you're right."

"I don't know your mother," he added hastily. "And I am not a psychologist."

"No," I agreed solemnly. "But you might be right."

He put a hand on my arm and, for the first time, I saw

in his face comprehension that I wasn't just being an irritating teenaged girl, avoiding dessert to get into a pair of new jeans. I moved towards him.

"Clara?"

Michel and I pulled apart abruptly as Dad, Mag, and Alastair noisily entered the apartment, Alastair clutching a foil Lego-man balloon firmly by a bright blue ribbon.

"I got a balloon," he announced triumphantly, brandishing it before us. "There was a clown at the hospital. He was horrid and scary, but he gave me this balloon."

"It's very cool," I said, grinning. Alastair seemed fine—I stared at him, searching, but could see no sign of what had transpired earlier. He looked the picture of health.

"It's a Lego man," he informed me, jumping from foot to foot. "There is a Lego movie, did you know? Mum is going to let me watch it. You'll watch it too, right Clara?"

"Of course," I assured him, amused. He was much more animated than usual.

Dad finished hanging his coat and, grinning, placed a hand on Alastair's shoulder. "It's the adrenaline," he said to me and Michel quietly. "Makes him a bit jumpy. It'll wear off in an hour or two."

"Ohhhh," I said. I watched my brother twirl around the living room, still tightly grasping his prize.

"It smells delicious in here," said Mag, sniffing. "What is that?"

Michel beamed, gesturing towards the oven. "Clara and I made croque monsieurs," he said. "Your timing is perfect."

"Croque monsieur is my favorite!" shouted Alastair. He let go of the balloon, which floated aimlessly to the ceiling and remained there. "I'm hungry!"

I couldn't help but laugh at this caricature of Alastair, who rushed over and plopped down at the table, loudly clinking his fork against the rim of his plate in a demand for food.

Michel retrieved the sandwiches from the oven, and served them to each of us. Mag was right—they smelled heavenly. I felt my entire body brace against the pleasant odor. *Enjoy it*, I told myself firmly. *Embrace the smell, don't push it away.* I took deep, mindful breaths and focused on the meal before me, the roux bubbling with heat, the cheese seeping through the sides of the bread and melding to the plate.

Everyone dug in. Forks and knives scratched against ceramic plates in a sort of sandwich-celebrating symphony, and I watched the expressions of pleasure on their faces as they savored their first bites.

You don't have to eat the whole thing, I told myself. *But you have to try to enjoy it.*

Determinedly, I picked up knife and fork.

CHAPTER 26

"Are you sure you want to do this?" I stared up at the vast iron structure, its famous lattices glittering in the sun. "We don't have to."

Alastair didn't answer for a moment, absorbed by the view of the Eiffel Tower from our vantage point in the grassy gardens below. Finally, he cleared his throat and turned to face me.

"Yes," he said, sounding determined. "I'm sure."

It was my final day in Paris; my flight was booked for the following morning. While Alastair and I had spent weeks dutifully taking in the sights, sounds, and museums of Paris, we had thus far avoided the most recognizable landmark of all. It wasn't just Alastair's fear of heights. Growing up in New York, I tended to avoid the so-called "tourist traps" when I traveled. But Mag and Dad had both insisted the Eiffel Tower was worth it.

"It's a beautiful view," said Mag. "You should see it before you go."

"It's interesting architecturally as well," added Dad. "I can go with you, if you want."

But Alastair surprised us all.

"No," he said firmly. "I want to go with Clara."

Dad, Mag, and I exchanged glances.

"Are you sure, Buddy?" said Dad cautiously. "Because you don't have to, if you don't want to."

"But I do want to." He looked very serious. "I think I can do it."

I remembered the Ferris wheel and felt immediately wary. "Alastair," I said, "remember what we talked about? You don't have to like everything, do everything. It's okay sometimes to say no and be different."

"I know that," he said calmly, "but the Eiffel Tower doesn't seem as scary as the Ferris wheel. The Ferris wheel was open and shaky. It felt like we could fall out."

I considered his words. "That's true," I said, nodding.

We decided to go early, to avoid the crowds. Brave or not, I still vividly recalled our first outing with Dad to the Louvre and the effect on Alastair of the throngs of people. The earlier the better, even if it did mean dragging myself from the warm comfort of bed at an ungodly hour. It was, after all, my final day in Paris.

"Last day," said Dad, looking sad as he handed me my mug of coffee. "Last breakfast."

"Nope," I said. "There's still tomorrow, before the airport. Michel said he would come by with croissants."

Dad brightened. "I'm glad to hear that, for everyone's sake."

"Everyone's sake?" I asked, puzzled.

He grinned. "I love those croissants."

I grinned back and returned to my coffee. It was a beautiful day. In the living room, Minou chased a sunbeam as it danced slowly across the hardwood floor.

"Alastair is going to miss you," said Dad quietly. He offered me an apple, which I accepted. Sitting down, I also took some cheese and a boiled egg. I took a deep breath and stared at my plate.

"I'm going to miss him, too," I said. I swallowed hard, and felt the hot coffee travel all the way down my throat, deep into my belly.

"We'll come visit this winter," said Dad. He paused. "Are you really thinking of applying to school here? Because we would love that, but I don't want to pressure you."

"I don't know," I said honestly. I'd thought a lot about it—even visited the Sorbonne with Michel. The prospect of attending university in France was exciting, but daunting, too. Even with the option of classes in English, I'd need to improve my French. And what about Mom? She was doing well in rehab, but I'd need to think about it. Anyway, I had nearly a whole year to make that decision.

"Well," said Dad. "As I said, you're always welcome here. So give it some thought."

"That I will definitely do," I agreed. For the umpteenth time, I pictured myself in Paris as a student, hand in hand with Michel and with Alastair and Dad and Mag nearby. Mom would visit at Christmas, and I would go home during summers to New York. It was a pleasant daydream, to be sure.

I'd spoken with Mom again the night before, this time on FaceTime. Leaning against a barre on the screen, she didn't look that different than when she was in the studio. It was only the scrub-clad professionals in the background that called attention to the fact that she wasn't practicing for the *Nutcracker* but instead relearning how to walk unaided. I caught sight of Jacques, too, shouting into his own phone, pacing angrily back and forth next to what appeared to be the nurses' station.

"Some things never change," said Mom, moving her eyes in Jacques' direction. "The understudy isn't hacking it, apparently."

"He's been good to you, though," I said, and it was true. The fearful, tempestuous Jacques, my perennial scapegoat, had proven himself a staunch supporter of my mother, even now that her dancing career was over. The past couple of weeks with him as both her champion and caretaker had forced me to re-examine my own feelings about him. How much had been real, and how much had simply been jealousy over his easy command of my mother's time and affection? I promised myself to be kinder in the future. My mother and I had ended our conversation with excited smiles and "see you tomorrows."

Now, Alastair and I purchased our tickets and boarded the first of a series of elevators, Alastair had dressed in his weighted vest as a preventative measure. The elevator was crowded, but not packed; clearly, arriving early had been a prudent move. All around us, people chatted excitedly in a variety of languages. I caught snatches of not only French and English, but also Spanish, Chinese, Japanese, and what I thought might be Dutch.

We exited at the first level, Alastair keeping close to my side. We wandered around, examining the educational exhibits. I read aloud to Alastair, explaining the historical significance of the structure in which we stood.

"When Gustave Eiffel built the tower for the 1889 World's Fair, it was criticized by many of France's leading artists and intellectuals," I informed him.

"Really?" He looked surprised. "I didn't know that."

"Yes," I said, nodding. "At first people didn't like it. They thought it was strange and ugly. But now, it's one of the most famous structures in the world."

"How does that happen?" asked Alastair, puzzled.

I searched for the right words. "Things change," I said. "What people think is nice, or good, or appropriate—it changes with time."

Alastair considered this. "So, something that people think is weird today could end up being normal in a hundred years?"

"Sure," I said, nodding. "Absolutely."

For a moment, neither of us spoke, absorbed by our surroundings and the significance of my words. Finally, I gestured to a sign.

"Do we want to try the glass floor, or skip it?"

Alastair didn't have to think too long. "Skip it," he said firmly. "It sounds scary."

"I agree with you on that one," I said, grinning. "Shall we go check out the view?"

We took another elevator and got out on the second level. We still hadn't reached the top, but the views on this floor were impressive nonetheless. The beautiful buildings had shrunk to miniatures, a doll's-house version of Paris. Below, the cars looked like Hot Wheels toys. Alastair fished out his camera.

"Stand over there," he commanded, gesturing.

I followed his gaze and stood, smiling brightly.

He shook his head. "More this way," he said, pointing to the left. "Where the clouds are."

"You want the clouds in your picture?"

"Yes," he said, as if it were obvious. "What is the point of a photo of the sky without the clouds?"

I couldn't refute this, so I obediently shifted left. Alastair nodded, but waved his hand. "Don't smile."

"What?" I asked, startled. "Why?"

"Because people look nice when they don't smile, too," he said seriously. "In real life, you aren't always happy."

"But I'm happy now," I protested. "I'm happy here, with you."

He was quiet for a minute. "Okay," he said finally. "But not a fake smile. A normal one, like you make when you're happy."

I faltered. What did he mean? I smiled, but without teeth this time.

"No," said Alastair firmly. "With your eyes."

I took a deep breath. I thought of Alastair when he was absorbed by his cooking or Lego. I thought of Dad, getting up early to make me coffee. Of my mom, who was making a remarkable recovery back home, surpassing all her doctors' expectations in rehab. And of Michel, and how he tugged at his curls when he thought no one was watching.

"Perfect," said Alastair, snapping the button. Instantly, the photo popped out of the camera, still dark and blurry.

We waited, watching the initial photo fog slowly clear, giving way to a view of Paris and of me, my face, my hair gently blowing in the wind.

"You look nice," said Alastair, holding it up. "See? Smiling with your eyes."

I studied the photograph. My eyes shone, and my mouth turned upward ever so slightly at the corners. "Nice work, Alastair," I said sincerely. "You're very talented."

He nodded, accepting the compliment as his due, and I considered how refreshing that was. No fake protestations, no blushing, no stammering of thanks. Just a nod, and a comfortable silence.

"Let's go to the top," he said then, and I caught a quaver in his voice.

"We don't have to," I told him. "The view here is beautiful. We can stop here, if you want."

"No," he said, sounding determined this time. "To the top."

We boarded the glass elevators that would transport us to the very top. There were fewer people packed in this time, and there was space for us to press our faces against the glass. We watched the city blocks shrink to tiny specs on the landscape below, the trees reduced to miniatures.

"It looks like Lego," said Alastair. He pulled away from the glass, looking a bit queasy. "We're very high up."

"We are," I agreed. "Are you okay?"

"Yes," he said, breathing deeply.

The doors opened and we looked around. Completely enclosed, the platform wasn't nearly as scary as I'd thought it would be.

"Look, Alastair," I said, motioning at the bubble surrounding us. "You don't have to be afraid. It's closed in and safe."

Alastair walked around, looking critically at the view below. "It is safer," he agreed thoughtfully, "but not as beautiful."

I looked out in the distance and had to agree. The Plexiglas that shielded us dulled the view and made the experience less alive, somehow, than on the second level. The safety had come at a price.

"Come on," I said to him. "Let's go back to the floor below. I want a picture of you."

We descended, and I fished out my phone from my bag, snapping a near-candid photo of Alastair.

"I wasn't ready," he protested.

"I like you like this," I said. I showed him the photo. "This is how I want to remember this moment. Real, not fake. Just like you said."

Alastair nodded. He moved closer to me, and for a long time, neither of us said anything. I watched his hair dance in the wind, reddish curls blowing back and forth, his small shoulders squared and bold.

"I'm ready to go now," he said finally. "Can we go back down?"

"Definitely," I said. "Alastair, you were very brave today."

He nodded, accepting it as his due. "I know."

I laughed and shook my head. "Okay," I said. "Who's ready for a pain au chocolat?"

His face brightened. "Me!" he said, then paused. "Clara?"

"Yes?" I gestured for him to follow me towards the exit.

"Are you going to have one too?" His voice was small.

I stopped and turned around. I studied my brother's questioning face, and smiled at the raw honesty in his expression.

Yes," I said. "I am."

Alastair reached forward, and took my hand.

ACKNOWLEDGMENTS

I was inspired to write *On the Spectrum* by two things: an increasing awareness that eating disorders are being passed off as "healthy" or "clean" living, and the notion that being on the autism spectrum is not the same as Dustin Hoffman's character in *Rain Man*. I wanted to convey to readers that girls with eating disorders aren't all anorexic or bulimic—that disordered eating and body image disorders exist on spectrum—and to show that being on the autism spectrum is not a curse of some kind. The autism community uses the terms "neurotypical" and "atypical" and I think this is a brilliant way of looking at things. There is much to be learned by those who are different and from how they see the world.

Thank you to Margie Wolfe, Kathryn Cole, Carolyn Jackson, Emma Rodgers, Allie Chenoweth, Melissa Kaita, and all the other hardworking women at Second Story Press who believed in the book and brought it to publication. Thank you, too, to all the great book bloggers, small bookstore owners, and librarians out there who help get books like *On the Spectrum* into the hands of readers. For me as an author, the most frustrating challenge is getting the book out there, and you folks all work tirelessly to bring books like mine to the attention of teens and other interested readers.

Thanks to all my friends and to my coworkers at the Ontario Medical Association for their encouragement and day-to-day friendship and support: I couldn't do it without you. I love you all. A special shout-out to Dara Laxer, who beta reads for me and is always first in line as my personal cheerleader, and Cheryl Ellison, whom I've known forever and whose thirty years of friendship I often draw upon in my writing.

Finally, thank you to my amazing family who supports me in everything I do: Paul, Jess, and Myles Gold; Michael, Deborah, and Sydney Goodman; my wonderful parents, Howard and Karen Gold; and of course Adam and Teddy and Violet, who are a constant source of love and inspiration.

ABOUT THE AUTHOR

JENNIFER GOLD won her first creative writing award at nine years old for a short story about Bigfoot sponsored by Lipton Soup. A lawyer and mom of two, she is now the author of several novels for teens, including *Soldier Doll*, a Bank Street Best Book (2015) and White Pine Award finalist (2016), and *Undiscovered Country*. Jennifer's writing has appeared in *The Globe and Mail*, and she has twice been CBC Radio's expert on Canadians who hate camping. She lives in Toronto with her family.